WARRIOR
CATS

Watch out for more books

in the WARRIOR CATS series

ERIN HUNTER

WARRIOR CATS

Fire and Ice

HarperCollins *Children's Books*

First published in the USA by HarperCollins Children's Books
First published in Great Britain in paperback by HarperCollins *Children's Books* 2005
HarperCollins *Children's Books* is an imprint of HarperCollins*Publishers*
Ltd, 77-85 Fulham Palace Road, Hammersmith London W6 8JB

The HarperCollins *Children's Books* website address is
www.harpercollins.co.uk

10

Series concept © Working Partners Limited 2001
Text © Working Partners Limited 2003

ISBN 10: 0-00-721788-9
ISBN 13: 978-0-00-721788-5

*For my son, Joshua, whose smiles kept me happy as
I wrote, and Vicky, my editor, without whom
Fireheart would never have become a warrior*

Special thanks to Kate Cary

ALLEGIANCES

 thunderclan

LEADER	**BLUESTAR** – blue-grey she-cat, tinged with silver around her muzzle.
DEPUTY	**TIGERCLAW** – big, dark brown tabby tom with unusually long front claws
MEDICINE CAT	**YELLOWFANG** – old, dark-grey she-cat with abroad, flattened face, formerly of the ShadowClan
WARRIORS	(toms, and she-cats without kits)

WHITESTORM—big white tom.
APPRENTICE, SANDPAW

DARKSTRIPE – sleek black-and-grey tabby tom.
APPRENTICE, DUSTPAW

LONGTAIL – pale tabby tom with dark black stripes.
APPRENTICE, SWIFTPAW

RUNNINGWIND – swift tabby tom.

WILLOWPELT – very pale grey she-cat with unusual blue eyes.

MOUSEFUR – small dusky brown she-cat.

FIREHEART – handsome ginger tom.
APPRENTICE, CINDERPAW

GREYSTRIPE – long-haired, solid, grey tom.
APPRENTICE, BRACKENPAW

APPRENTICES (more than six moons old, in training to become warriors)

SANDPAW – pale ginger she-cat.

DUSTPAW – dark brown tabby tom.

SWIFTPAW – black and white tom.

CINDERPAW – dark-grey she-cat.

BRACKENPAW – golden brown tabby tom.

QUEENS (she-cats expecting or nursing kits)

FROSTFUR – beautiful white coat and blue eyes.

BRINDLEFACE – pretty tabby.

GOLDENFLOWER – pale ginger coat.

SPECKLETAIL – pale tabby, and the oldest nursery queen.

ELDERS (former warriors and queens, now retired)

HALFTAIL – big dark brown tabby tom with part of his tail missing.

SMALLEAR – grey tom with very small ears. The oldest tom in ThunderClan.

PATCHPELT – small black-and-white tom.

ONE-EYE – pale grey she-cat, the oldest cat in ThunderClan. Virtually blind and deaf.

DAPPLETAIL – once-pretty tortoiseshell she-cat with a lovely dappled coat.

shadowclan

LEADER   **NIGHTPELT** – old black tom.

DEPUTY   **CINDERFUR** – thin grey tom.

MEDICINE CAT   **RUNNINGNOSE** – small grey-and-white tom.

WARRIORS   **STUMPYTAIL** – brown tabby tom.
APPRENTICE, BROWNPAW

WETFOOT – grey tabby tom.
APPRENTICE, OAKPAW

LITTLECLOUD – very small tabby tom

QUEENS   **DAWNCLOUD** – small tabby.

DARKFLOWER – black she-cat.

TALLPOPPY – long legged light brown tabby she-cat

ELDERS   **ASHFUR** – thin grey tom.

windclan

LEADER	**TALLSTAR** – a black-and-white tom with a very long tail.
DEPUTY	**DEADFOOT** – a black tom with a twisted paw.
MEDICINE CAT	**BARKFACE** – a short-tailed brown tom.
WARRIORS	**MUDCLAW** – a mottled dark brown tom.
	APPRENTICE, WEBPAW
	TORNEAR – a tabby tom.
	APPRENTICE, RUNNINGPAW
	ONEWHISKER – a young brown tabby tom.
	APPRENTICE, WHITEPAW
QUEENS	**ASHFOOT** – a grey queen.
	MORNINGFLOWER – a tortoiseshell queen.

riverclan

LEADER   **CROOKEDSTAR** – a huge light-colored tabby with a twisted jaw.

DEPUTY   **LEOPARDFUR** – unusually spotted golden tabby she-cat.

MEDICINE CAT **MUDFUR** – long-haired light brown tom.

WARRIORS   **BLACKCLAW** – smoky black tom.
APPRENTICE, HEAVYPAW

STONEFUR – a grey tom with battle-scarred ears.
APPRENTICE, SHADEPAW

LOUDBELLY – a dark brown tom.
APPRENTICE, SILVERPAW

SILVERSTREAM – a pretty slender silver tabby.

WHITECLAW – a dark warrior.

cats outside clans

SMUDGE – plump, friendly black-and-white kitten who lives in a house at the edge of the forest.

BARLEY – black-and-white tom who lives on a farm close to the forest.

BROKENSTAR – long-haired dark brown tabby, formerly ShadowClan leader.

BLACKFOOT – large white tom with huge jet-black paws, formerly ShadowClan deputy.

CLAWFACE – battle-scarred brown tom.

BOULDER – silver tabby tom.

RAVENPAW – sleek black cat with a white-tipped tail.

PRINCESS – a light brown tabby with a distinctive white chest and paws: a kittypet.

CLOUDKIT – Princess's firstborn kit: a long-haired white tom.

PROLOGUE

ORANGE FLAMES LAPPED at the cold air, throwing sparks up into the night sky. The firelight flickered across a wasteland of ragged grass, making silhouettes of the Twolegs huddled there.

A pair of white lights appeared in the distance, heralding the approach of a monster. It roared past on a Thunderpath that rose high into the sky, filling the air with sour fumes.

At the edge of the wasteland, a cat moved, its eyes glinting in the shadows. Pointed ears twitched, then flattened against the noise. More cats followed one by one, on to the filthy grass. They carried their tails low and sniffed the bitter air with their lips curled.

"What if the Twolegs see us?" hissed one of the cats.

A large tom answered, his eyes like amber disks reflecting the firelight. "They won't. Their night sight is weak." As he padded forwards the flames lit up the black and white fur on his powerful shoulders. He held his long tail straight up, sending a message of courage to his Clan.

But the other cats crouched low against the grass, trembling. This was a strange place. The noise of the monsters battered their sensitive ear fur, and the acrid stench stung their nostrils.

"Tallstar?" A grey queen flicked her tail uneasily. "Why have we come *here?*"

The black and white tom turned to the she-cat. "We've been driven from every place we've tried to settle, Ashfoot. Perhaps we can find some peace here," he meowed.

"Peace? Here?" Ashfoot echoed in disbelief. She pulled her kit towards her and sheltered it beneath her belly. "With fire and monsters? My kits won't be safe!"

"But we weren't safe at home," meowed another voice. A black tom pushed his way forwards, limping heavily on a twisted paw. He held Tallstar's amber gaze. "We couldn't protect them from ShadowClan," he spat. "Not even in our own camp!"

Anxious yowls rose from some of the cats as they remembered the terrible battle that had driven them from their home in the uplands, at the edge of the forest. A young apprentice wailed: "Brokenstar and his warriors may still be hunting us!"

The cry alerted one of the Twolegs around the fire. It stood unsteadily and stared towards the shadows. At once the cats fell silent, crouching lower; even Tallstar lowered his tail. The Twoleg shouted into the darkness and flung something towards them. The missile flew over their heads and exploded in a burst of thorn-sharp pieces on the Thunderpath behind.

Ashfoot flinched as a shard grazed her shoulder, but she stayed silent, curling her body around her terrified kit.

"Keep down," hissed Tallstar.

The Twoleg at the fire spat on the ground, then sat back down.

The cats waited for a few moments before Tallstar stood once more.

Ashfoot stood too, wincing at the new pain in her shoulder. "Tallstar, I fear for our safety here. And what shall we eat? I can't smell any prey."

Tallstar stretched his neck and rested his muzzle gently on the queen's head. "I know you're hungry," he meowed. "But we'll be safer here than back in our old territory, or in the Twoleg fields and woods. Look at this place! Even ShadowClan wouldn't follow us here. There's no scent of dogs and these Twolegs can hardly stand." He turned to the black tom with the twisted paw. "Deadfoot," he ordered, "take Onewhisker and see if you can find anything to eat. If there are Twolegs, there must be rats."

"Rats?" spat Ashfoot, as Deadfoot and a smaller brown tabby bounded away. "That's no better than crowfood!"

"Hush!" hissed a tortoiseshell beside her. "Rat meat is better than starving to death!"

Ashfoot scowled and dipped her head to lick her kit behind its matted ears.

"We must find a new place to settle, Ashfoot." The tortoiseshell went on more gently: "Morningflower needs to rest and eat. Her kits will be born soon. She needs to be strong."

The lean shapes of Deadfoot and Onewhisker emerged from the shadows.

"You were right, Tallstar," called Deadfoot. "There are rat scents everywhere, and I think I've found somewhere we can shelter."

"Show us," Tallstar ordered, gathering the rest of his Clan with a flick of his tail.

Cautiously, the cats padded across the wasteland after Deadfoot. He led them towards the raised Thunderpath, the firelight making their shadows loom against its huge stone legs. A monster roared overhead and the ground shook. But even the tiniest kit sensed the need for silence and trembled without crying out.

"Here," meowed Deadfoot, stopping beside a round hole, two cats high. A black tunnel sloped down into the ground. A constant stream of water trickled into it.

"The water's fresh," Deadfoot added. "We'll be able to drink it."

"We'll have wet paws day and night!" Ashfoot complained.

"I've been inside," the black tom told her. "There's some space away from the stream. At least we'll be safe from Twolegs and monsters."

Tallstar stepped forwards and lifted his chin. "WindClan has travelled for long enough," he declared. "It's nearly a moon since ShadowClan drove us from our home. The weather is turning colder and leaf-bare will be here soon. We have no choice but to stay."

Ashfoot narrowed her eyes but said nothing. Silently she joined her Clan as, one by one, they filed into the shadowy tunnel.

CHAPTER 1

FIREHEART SHIVERED. HIS flame-coloured fur was still greenleaf-light; it would be a few moons before it was thick enough to keep out cold like this. He shuffled his forepaws on the hard earth. The sky was finally growing light as dawn crept slowly in. But even though his paws were cold, Fireheart could not suppress a glow of pride. After many moons as an apprentice, he was a warrior at last.

In his mind, he replayed yesterday's victory at the ShadowClan camp: Brokenstar's glittering eyes as the ShadowClan leader backed away, hissing threats, before fleeing into the trees after his traitorous companions. The remaining ShadowClan cats had been grateful to ThunderClan for helping them to get rid of their cruel leader and for the peace ThunderClan had promised them while they recovered. Brokenstar had not just brought chaos to his own Clan – he had driven the whole of WindClan from their camp, right out of Clan territory. He had been a dark shadow in the forest since before Fireheart had left his kittypet life to join ThunderClan.

But for Fireheart, there was another shadow troubling his mind: Tigerclaw, ThunderClan's deputy. Fireheart shivered as he thought of the great ThunderClan warrior who had terrorised his apprentice, Ravenpaw. In the end, Fireheart and his best friend, Greystripe, had helped the frightened apprentice to escape into the Twoleg territory beyond the uplands. Afterwards, Fireheart had told ThunderClan that Ravenpaw had been killed by ShadowClan.

If what Ravenpaw said about Tigerclaw was true, it was best if the ThunderClan deputy believed his apprentice had died, for he knew a secret that Tigerclaw would do anything to conceal. Ravenpaw had told Fireheart that the mighty tabby warrior had murdered Redtail, the old ThunderClan deputy, in the hope that he would become the new deputy, which, eventually, he had.

Fireheart shook his head to clear it of these dark thoughts and turned to glance at Greystripe sitting beside him. Greystripe's thick grey fur was ruffled up against the cold. Fireheart guessed he was looking forwards to the first rays of sunshine too, but he didn't say this out loud. Clan tradition demanded silence on this night. This was their vigil – the night when a new warrior guarded the Clan and reflected on his new name and status. Until last night, Fireheart had been known by his apprentice name of Firepaw.

Halftail was one of the first cats to wake. Fireheart could see the old cat moving among the shadows in the elders' den. He glanced towards the warriors' den at the other side of the clearing. Through the branches, he recognised the broad shoulders of Tigerclaw as he slept.

At the foot of Highrock, the lichen that draped the entrance to Bluestar's den twitched, and Fireheart saw his Clan leader push her way out. She stopped and lifted her head to sniff the air. Then she padded silently out of Highrock's shadow, her long fur glowing blue-grey in the dawn light. *I must warn her about Tigerclaw*, thought Fireheart. Bluestar had mourned Redtail's death with the rest of the Clan, believing him to have been killed in battle by Oakheart, the deputy of RiverClan. Fireheart had hesitated before, knowing how important Tigerclaw was to her, but the danger was too great. Bluestar needed to know that her Clan was harbouring a cold-blooded murderer.

Tigerclaw emerged from the warriors' den and met Bluestar at the edge of the clearing. He murmured something to her, his tail flicking urgently.

Fireheart stifled his instinctive meow of greeting. The sky was growing light, but until he knew for sure that the sun was above the horizon, he dared not break his silence. Impatience fluttered in his chest like a trapped bird. He must speak with Bluestar as soon as he could. But for now, all he could do was nod respectfully at the two cats as they passed him.

Beside him, Greystripe nudged Fireheart and pointed upwards with his nose. An orange glow was just visible on the horizon.

"Glad to see the dawn, you two?" Whitestorm's deep meow took Fireheart by surprise. He had not noticed the white warrior approaching. Fireheart and Greystripe nodded together.

"It's all right; you may speak now. Your vigil is over." Whitestorm's voice was kind. Yesterday he had fought side by side with Fireheart and Greystripe in the battle with ShadowClan. There was a new respect in his eyes as he looked at them.

"Thank you, Whitestorm," Fireheart meowed gratefully. He stood and stretched his stiff legs one at a time.

Greystripe pushed himself up too. "Brrrr!" he meowed, shaking the chill from his fur. "I thought the sun would never come up!"

A scornful voice mewed from outside the apprentices' den. "The great warrior speaks!"

It was Sandpaw, her pale orange coat fluffed up with hostility. Dustpaw was sitting beside her. With his dark tabby pelt, he looked like Sandpaw's shadow. He puffed out his chest importantly and mocked, "I'm surprised such heroes even feel the cold!" Sandpaw purred with amusement.

Whitestorm shot them a stern look. "Go and find something to eat; then rest," he ordered Fireheart and Greystripe. The older warrior turned away and padded towards the apprentices' den. "Come on, you two," he meowed to Sandpaw and Dustpaw. "It's time for your training."

"I hope he has them chasing blue squirrels all day!" Greystripe hissed to Fireheart as they headed towards the corner where a few pieces of fresh-kill remained from last night.

"But there aren't any blue squirrels," Fireheart mewed in confusion.

"Precisely!" Greystripe's amber eyes gleamed.

"You can't exactly blame them. They did begin their training before us," Fireheart pointed out mildly. "If they'd fought in the battle yesterday, they'd probably have been made warriors too."

"I suppose." Greystripe shrugged. "Hey, look!" They'd reached the fresh-kill pile. "One mouse each and a chaffinch to share!"

The two friends picked up their meal and looked at each other. Greystripe's eyes suddenly sparkled with delight. "I suppose we take it to the *warriors'* side of the camp now," he meowed.

"I suppose we do," Fireheart purred, padding after his friend to the patch of nettles where they had often watched Whitestorm, Tigerclaw and the other warriors share fresh-kill.

"Now what?" asked Greystripe, gulping down his last mouthful. "I don't know about you, but I think I could sleep for half a moon."

"Me too," Fireheart agreed.

The two friends got to their paws and made their way towards the warriors' den. Fireheart stuck his head through the low-hanging branches. Mousefur and Longtail were still asleep on the other side of the den.

He pushed his way inside and found a patch of moss at the edge. The smell told him it wasn't a sleeping place already used by another warrior. Greystripe settled down beside him.

Fireheart listened as Greystripe's steady breaths relaxed into long, muffled snores. Fireheart felt equally exhausted, but he was still desperate to talk to Bluestar. From where he lay, his head flat to the earth, he could just see the camp entrance. He stared at it, waiting for his leader's return, but gradually his eyes began to close, and he gave in to his longing for sleep.

Fireheart could hear a roaring around him, like wind in tall trees. The acrid stench of the Thunderpath stung his nostrils, together with a new smell, sharper and more terrifying. Fire! Flames lapped at the black sky, throwing glowing cinders up into a starless night. To Fireheart's amazement, silhouettes of cats flitted in front of the fire. Why hadn't they run away?

One of them stopped and looked straight at him. The tom's night-eyes glinted in the darkness and he lifted his long, straight tail, as if in greeting.

Fireheart trembled as a memory burst into his mind of the words that Spottedleaf, the former ThunderClan medicine cat, had said to him before her untimely death: "Fire will save the Clan!" Could it be something to do with the strange cats that showed no fear of fire?

"Wake up, Fireheart!"

Fireheart flicked up his head, startled out of his dream by Tigerclaw's growl.

"You were mewing in your sleep!"

Still dazed, Fireheart sat up and shook his head. "Y-yes, Tigerclaw!" With a pang of alarm, he wondered if he had repeated Spottedleaf's words out loud. He had dreamed like this before – dreams so vivid that he could taste them, and which had later come true. Fireheart certainly did not want Tigerclaw to suspect him of having powers that usually StarClan gave only to a medicine cat.

Moonlight shone through the leafy den wall. Fireheart realised he must have slept through the whole day.

"You and Greystripe will join the evening patrol," Tigerclaw told him. "Hurry up!" The dark tabby turned and stalked out of the den.

Fireheart let the fur relax on his shoulders. Clearly Tigerclaw didn't suspect anything unusual about his dream. But while Fireheart's secret was safe, he was equally determined to expose the murderous truth about Tigerclaw's role in Redtail's death.

Fireheart licked his lips. Greystripe lay beside him washing his flank. They had just finished sharing a meal beside the camp clearing. The sun had set and Fireheart could see the moon, almost full now, gleaming in a cold, clear sky.

The past few days had been busy. It seemed that every time they lay down for a rest, Tigerclaw sent them out on patrol or a hunting mission. Fireheart had stayed alert, looking for a chance to talk with Bluestar alone, but when he wasn't on one of Tigerclaw's missions, the ThunderClan leader always seemed to have her deputy at her side.

Fireheart began to wash his paw, his eyes flicking around the camp, searching hopefully for Bluestar.

"What are you looking for?" meowed Greystripe through a tongueful of fur.

"Bluestar," Fireheart answered, lowering his paw.

"Why?" Greystripe stopped washing and looked up at his friend. "You've had one eye on her ever since our vigil. What are you planning to do?"

"I have to tell her where Ravenpaw is, and warn her about Tigerclaw," Fireheart meowed.

"You promised Ravenpaw you'd tell them he was dead!" Greystripe sounded amazed.

"I only promised to tell *Tigerclaw* he was dead. Bluestar should know the whole story. She needs to know what her deputy is capable of."

Greystripe lowered his voice to an urgent hiss. "But we only have Ravenpaw's word that Tigerclaw killed Redtail."

"Don't you believe him?" Fireheart couldn't help feeling shocked by his friend's doubts.

"Look, if Tigerclaw lied about killing Oakheart in revenge

for Redtail's death, that means Redtail must have killed Oakheart himself. And I can't believe that Redtail would have deliberately killed another Clan deputy in battle. It goes against the warrior code – we fight to prove our strength and defend our territory, not to kill each other."

"But I'm not trying to make accusations against Redtail!" Fireheart protested. "It's Tigerclaw who is the problem." Redtail had been the ThunderClan deputy before Tigerclaw. Fireheart had never met him, but he knew Redtail had been deeply respected by all the Clan.

Greystripe didn't meet Fireheart's gaze. "What you are saying has implications for Redtail's honour. And none of the other cats have a problem with Tigerclaw. It was only Ravenpaw who was scared of him."

An uneasy shiver ran down Fireheart's spine. "So you think Ravenpaw made the story up because he didn't get along with his mentor?" he meowed scornfully.

"No," mumbled Greystripe. "I just think we should be careful."

Fireheart looked into his friend's worried eyes and began to wonder. He supposed Greystripe did have a point – they had been warriors for only a few days, so they were in no position to start hurling accusations at the Clan's most senior warrior.

"It's OK," Fireheart meowed at last. "You can stay out of it." A twinge of regret flickered in his belly as Greystripe nodded and returned to washing. Fireheart believed that

Greystripe was wrong to think it was only Ravenpaw who had a problem with Tigerclaw. Fireheart's own instincts told him that the ThunderClan deputy should not be trusted. He had to share his suspicions with Bluestar, for her safety and the safety of the Clan.

A glimpse of grey fur on the other side of the clearing told Fireheart that Bluestar had emerged from her den – alone. He scrambled to his paws, but the ThunderClan leader leaped straight up on to the Highrock and called to the Clan. Fireheart lashed his tail impatiently.

Greystripe's ears flicked excitedly as he heard Bluestar's call. "A naming ceremony?" he meowed. "It must be Longtail getting his first apprentice. He's been dropping hints for days." He bounded over to join the cats gathering at the edge of the clearing and, still itching with frustration, Fireheart followed.

A small black and white kit padded into the clearing. His soft paws made no sound on the hard earth. He walked towards the Highrock with his pale eyes lowered and Fireheart almost expected to see him tremble – there was something in the slope of this kit's shoulders that made him seem too young and timid to be an apprentice. *Longtail won't be impressed!* Fireheart thought, remembering Longtail's scorn when Fireheart had arrived at the camp for the first time. The warrior had taunted him viciously on his first day with the Clan, mocking his kittypet origins. Fireheart had disliked him ever since.

"From this day forward," Bluestar meowed, staring down at the kit, "until he has earned his warrior name, this apprentice will be called Swiftpaw."

There was no flash of determination in the eyes of the black and white kit as he looked up at his leader. Instead his amber eyes were wide with anxiety.

Fireheart turned his head as Longtail padded towards his new apprentice.

Bluestar spoke again. "Longtail, you were Darkstripe's apprentice. He taught you well, and you have become a fierce and loyal warrior. I hope you will pass some of these qualities on to Swiftpaw."

Fireheart searched Longtail's face for an expression of disdain as he looked down at Swiftpaw. But the warrior's eyes softened as he met his new apprentice's gaze, and gently the two Clan cats touched noses. "It's OK, you're doing fine," Longtail murmured encouragingly. *Yeah, right,* Fireheart thought bitterly. *Just because he's Clanborn. Longtail certainly didn't welcome me like that.* He glanced around the rest of the Clan and felt a pang of resentment as they began to murmur congratulations to the new apprentice.

"What's up with you?" whispered Greystripe. "That'll be us one day."

Fireheart nodded, suddenly cheered by the thought of getting his own apprentice, and pushed away his resentment. He was a part of ThunderClan now, and surely that was all that mattered?

*

The next night brought the full moon. Fireheart knew he should be looking forward to his first Gathering as a warrior, but he was still determined to find a chance to tell Bluestar everything he knew about Tigerclaw, and the thought of it lay like a cold stone in his stomach.

"Have you got maggot-gut or something?" meowed Greystripe beside him. "You're pulling some very weird faces!"

Fireheart looked at his friend, wishing he could confide in him, but he'd promised to leave Greystripe out of it. "I'm fine," he meowed. "Come on. I hear Bluestar calling."

The two cats trotted over to the group assembling in the clearing. Bluestar dipped her head to acknowledge their arrival. Then she turned and led the cats out of the camp.

Fireheart paused while the other cats scrambled past him up the steep trail that led to the forest above. This journey might give him just enough time to speak to Bluestar, and he wanted to gather his thoughts.

"Are you coming?" Greystripe's voice called down.

"Yep!" Fireheart flexed his powerful hind legs and began to leap from boulder to boulder, leaving the camp behind.

At the top, he paused to catch his breath, his sides heaving. The forest stretched away before him. Beneath his paws he could feel the crisp crackle of newly fallen leaves. Silverpelt glittered in the sky like morning dew scattered on black fur.

Fireheart thought of his first journey to Fourtrees with Tigerclaw and Lionheart. He felt a pang of sadness as he remembered Lionheart, Greystripe's mentor, and ThunderClan's deputy between Redtail and Tigerclaw. He had been a warmhearted, golden warrior, but he'd been killed in battle, and Tigerclaw had taken his place. On Fireheart's first visit to Fourtrees, Lionheart had taken the apprentices on a roundabout route, through Tallpines, past Sunningrocks, and along the RiverClan border. Tonight Bluestar would lead them straight through the heart of ThunderClan territory. Fireheart could see her already disappearing into the undergrowth, and he charged after the other cats.

Bluestar was at the front, next to Tigerclaw. Fireheart ignored Greystripe's surprised meow and caught up with the Clan leader. "Bluestar," he called, panting, as he drew up beside her. "May I talk to you?"

Bluestar glanced at him and nodded. "Take the lead, Tigerclaw," she meowed. She let her pace slow, and Tigerclaw bounded past her. The other cats followed the dark tabby without question as he raced on through the undergrowth.

Bluestar and Fireheart dropped into a steady trot. Within a moment they were alone.

The path emerged from the thick ferns into a small clearing. Bluestar leaped on to a fallen tree and sat down, curling her tail over her front paws. "What is it, Fireheart?" she asked.

Fireheart hesitated, suddenly struck by doubt. Bluestar was the cat who had encouraged him to leave his kittypet life and join the Clan. Since then she had trusted him time and time again when other cats had questioned his loyalty to a

Clan whose blood he didn't share. What would she say when Fireheart told her that he had lied about Ravenpaw?

"Speak," Bluestar ordered as the pawsteps of the other ThunderClan cats faded into the distance.

Fireheart took a deep breath. "Ravenpaw's not dead." Bluestar's tail twitched in surprise, but she listened silently as Fireheart continued. "Greystripe and I took him to WindClan's hunting grounds. I... I think he may have joined Barley." Barley was a loner, not a forest cat but not a kittypet either. He lived on a Twoleg farm that lay on the route to Highstones, a sacred place for all the cats in the forest.

The ThunderClan leader stared past Fireheart into the depths of the forest. Fireheart searched her face anxiously, trying to read her expression. Was she angry? But he could see no anger in her wide, blue eyes.

After several long moments, Bluestar spoke. "I am glad to hear that Ravenpaw is still alive. I hope he is happier living with Barley than he was in the forest."

"B-but he was born into ThunderClan!" Fireheart stammered, taken aback by his leader's calm acceptance of Ravenpaw's departure.

"That doesn't necessarily mean he was suited to Clan life," Bluestar pointed out. "After all, you aren't Clanborn, yet you've become a fine warrior. Ravenpaw may find his true path elsewhere."

"But he didn't leave ThunderClan because he wanted to," Fireheart protested. "It was impossible for him to stay!"

"Impossible?" Bluestar rested her blue gaze on him. "What do you mean?"

Fireheart looked down at the ground.

"Well?" Bluestar prompted.

Fireheart's mouth was dry. "Ravenpaw knew a secret about Tigerclaw," he croaked. "I... I think Tigerclaw was planning to kill him. Or else turn the Clan against him."

Bluestar's tail flicked from side to side, and Fireheart saw her shoulders stiffen. "Why would you think that? What was this secret that Ravenpaw knew?"

Fireheart answered reluctantly, meeting her stern expression as boldly as he dared. "That Tigerclaw killed Redtail in the battle with RiverClan."

Bluestar's eyes narrowed. "A warrior would never kill another of his Clan! Even you should know that – you've lived with us long enough." Fireheart recoiled at her words, flattening his ears. It was the second time tonight she'd referred to his kittypet roots.

Bluestar went on. "Tigerclaw reported that it was RiverClan's deputy, Oakheart, who killed Redtail," she meowed. "Ravenpaw must be mistaken. Did he actually *see* Tigerclaw kill Redtail?"

Fireheart nervously flicked his tail, stirring the leaves behind him. "He said he did."

"And you know that by saying this you are questioning Redtail's honour, because he must have been the cat that was responsible for Oakheart's death? One deputy would never kill another in battle, not if it could possibly be avoided. And Redtail was the most honourable warrior I have ever known." Bluestar's eyes clouded with pain and Fireheart felt a pang of dismay that he should have hurt her memory of her former deputy, even if unintentionally.

"I cannot account for Redtail's actions," he murmured. "I only know that Ravenpaw truly believes Tigerclaw was responsible for Redtail's death."

Bluestar sighed and relaxed her shoulders. "We all know that Ravenpaw has a vivid imagination," she meowed gently, her eyes sympathetic. "He was badly injured in the battle and he left before the fighting was over. Can you be sure he didn't fill in the parts he'd missed?"

Before Fireheart could reply, a yowl echoed through the forest and Tigerclaw bounded out of the undergrowth. His eyes flickered suspiciously over Fireheart for a moment before he addressed Bluestar. "We're waiting for you at the border."

Bluestar nodded. "Tell them we'll be there in a moment." Tigerclaw dipped his head, turned, and raced back through the ferns.

As Fireheart watched him disappear, Bluestar's words echoed in his mind. She was right; Ravenpaw did have a strong imagination. Fireheart remembered his first Gathering, when apprentices from every Clan had hung on Ravenpaw's words as he described the battle with RiverClan. And he hadn't mentioned Tigerclaw then.

Fireheart jumped up as Bluestar stood. "Are you going to

bring Ravenpaw back to the Clan?" he asked, suddenly afraid he had caused even more trouble for his friend.

Bluestar gazed deep into Fireheart's eyes. "He is probably happier where he is," she meowed quietly. "For now, we will let the Clan carry on believing he is dead."

Fireheart stared back at her, his eyes wide with shock. Bluestar was going to lie to the Clan!

"Tigerclaw is a great warrior, but he is very proud," Bluestar went on. "It'll be easier for him to accept that his apprentice died in battle rather than ran away. And it would be better for Ravenpaw, too."

"Because Tigerclaw might go looking for him?" Fireheart dared to ask. Was it possible that Bluestar believed him, even just a little bit?

Bluestar shook her head with a flash of impatience. "No. Tigerclaw might be ambitious but he is not a murderer. Ravenpaw will be better remembered as a dead hero than a live coward."

Tigerclaw's call sounded again and Bluestar jumped down from the log and disappeared into the ferns. Fireheart cleared the tree trunk in one leap and raced after his leader.

He caught up with her at the edge of a stream. He watched while she crossed, jumping from stone to stone to the other side. Fireheart followed carefully, his mind whirling. The knowledge about Redtail's death had been resting heavily on his shoulders for days. Now he had finally told Bluestar, but nothing had changed. The Clan leader clearly didn't think

Tigerclaw was capable of cold-blooded murder. And worst of all, Fireheart himself had begun to doubt whether Ravenpaw had been telling the truth. He leaped on to the far bank and charged on through the undergrowth.

Fireheart skidded to a halt behind Bluestar as they reached the other ThunderClan cats. The group had paused at the top of the slope that led down to Fourtrees, the giant oaks where cats from the four Clans of the forest met in peace at each full moon.

Fireheart's fur prickled as he felt Tigerclaw watching him. Did the dark warrior suspect what had passed between him and Bluestar? Fireheart shook his head to clear his mind and tried to think like Bluestar. Of course Tigerclaw would be interested in what Fireheart had said to Bluestar; he was the Clan deputy, so he would want to know anything that might affect the Clan. Fireheart looked again at Tigerclaw; the dark tabby was staring down the slope, his ears pricked and alert. The cats around him shuffled their paws in anticipation. Tigerclaw glanced at each of them, silently rallying them with his steady amber gaze.

Bluestar lifted her nose and sniffed the air. Fireheart sensed a tightening of muscles and prickling of fur around him. Then Bluestar signalled with a flick of her tail and the ThunderClan cats plunged down the slope towards the Gathering.

CHAPTER 2

BLUESTAR HALTED ON the edge of the clearing with her Clan lined up beside her. Some of the cats from RiverClan and ShadowClan turned and acknowledged their arrival.

"Where'd you disappear to?" Greystripe appeared at Fireheart's shoulder.

Fireheart shook his head. "Doesn't matter." He was still troubled and confused by his conversation with Bluestar and felt glad when Greystripe didn't press him, turning his head instead to peer around the clearing.

"Hey, look," he meowed. "The ShadowClan cats are looking stronger than I thought they would. After all, Brokenstar left them half-starved."

Fireheart followed his gaze to a sleek ShadowClan warrior. "You're right," he agreed, surprised.

"Mind you, we did do most of their fighting for them!" scoffed Greystripe.

Fireheart's amused purr was interrupted by Whitestorm. "The ShadowClan cats fought as hard as we did to chase out Brokenstar. We should honour their determination to recover," he meowed sternly, before padding over to a group of warriors gathered beneath one of the great oaks.

"Oops!" mewed Greystripe with a guilty glance at Fireheart.

The young warriors stayed on the edge of the clearing. Fireheart could easily pick out the apprentices from the other Clans – their fur looked kit-soft, their faces round, and their paws plump and clumsy.

Two warriors approached Greystripe and Fireheart. A small brown apprentice tagged after them. Fireheart recognised the grey tabby tom from ShadowClan, but not the smoky black tom who walked with him.

"Hi!" meowed the grey tom.

"Hello, Wetfoot," replied Fireheart. He glanced at the dark brown cat.

Wetfoot meowed, "This is Blackclaw of RiverClan."

Greystripe and Fireheart nodded their greeting. The apprentice stepped timidly forward.

"And this is my apprentice, Oakpaw," added Wetfoot.

Oakpaw looked up at Fireheart with wide, anxious eyes. "H-hi, Fireheart," he mewed. Fireheart nodded his head in greeting.

"I hear Bluestar made you warriors after the battle," meowed Wetfoot. "Congratulations! It must've been a cold vigil."

"It was!" Greystripe agreed.

"Who's that?" Fireheart broke in. A sleek she-cat with a mottled brown pelt had caught his attention. She was sharing words with Tigerclaw beside the Great Rock that stood in the centre of the clearing.

"That's Leopardfur, our deputy," growled the RiverClan warrior.

Fireheart's fur stiffened as he thought about the previous RiverClan deputy, Oakheart, and how he had died in battle with ThunderClan. He was saved from having to say anything by Bluestar bounding on to the top of the rock to start the meeting. Two other cats joined her, and one of them, an elderly black tom, sounded the call for all cats to gather beneath the rock. Fireheart recognised the black tom and couldn't help feeling surprised. Had old Nightpelt become ShadowClan's leader since Brokenstar had fled?

When the cats had settled in front of the Great Rock, Bluestar spoke. "ThunderClan bring to this Gathering their new medicine cat, Yellowfang," she announced formally. She paused while all eyes turned to the old she-cat with the thick fur and flattened muzzle. Fireheart noticed her shuffle her haunches on the hard ground. Early in his apprenticeship he had spent almost a whole moon nursing the she-cat back to health after she had come to the ThunderClan camp. Now he could tell by the way her right ear twisted slightly that she was uncomfortable under the gaze of the other Clans. Yellowfang had been medicine cat to ShadowClan, and cats hardly ever left one Clan to join another. She looked around the crowd slowly until she met the gaze of Runningnose, ShadowClan's new medicine cat. There was a brief pause; then they exchanged a respectful nod. Yellowfang's ear straightened and Fireheart relaxed.

Bluestar spoke again. "We also bring two newly named warriors – Fireheart and Greystripe."

Fireheart held his head high, but as he felt all eyes turn to look at him, a surge of self-consciousness made his tail flick nervously.

Nightpelt stepped forwards, brushing past Bluestar to stand on the highest part of the rock. "I, Nightpelt, have taken over the leadership of ShadowClan," he announced. "Our former leader, Brokenstar, broke the warrior code and we were forced to chase him out."

"No mention of the fact we helped them to do it," Greystripe whispered to Fireheart.

Nightpelt continued, "The spirits of our ancestors have spoken to Runningnose and chosen me as leader. I have not yet travelled to Mothermouth to receive StarClan's gift of nine lives, but I will make this journey tomorrow night while the moon is still full. After my vigil at the Moonstone, I shall be known as Nightstar."

"Where is Brokenstar now?" called a voice from the crowd. It was Frostfur, the white ThunderClan queen.

"I think we can assume that he has left the forest with

the other banished warriors. He knows it would be dangerous for him to try to return," answered Nightpelt.

"I hope so," Fireheart heard Frostfur murmur to her neighbour, a plump brown queen.

RiverClan's leader, Crookedstar, stepped forwards. "Let's hope Brokenstar has had the sense to leave the forest for good. His greed for territory threatened us all."

Crookedstar waited for the yowls of agreement to die down before he went on. "While Brokenstar was ShadowClan's leader, I allowed him to hunt in our river. But now ShadowClan has a new leader and this agreement can no longer stand. The prey in our river belongs to RiverClan alone."

Mews of triumph rose from the other RiverClan cats, but Fireheart saw with a feeling of alarm that Nightpelt was bristling.

Nightpelt raised his voice. "ShadowClan has the same needs as it did under Brokenstar. We have many mouths to feed, Crookedstar. You made an agreement with the whole of ShadowClan!"

Crookedstar leaped to his paws and turned on Nightpelt. He flattened his ears and hissed, and the cats below fell silent.

Quickly Bluestar stepped between the two leaders. "ShadowClan has suffered many losses recently," she mewed softly. "With fewer mouths to feed, Nightpelt, do you really need RiverClan's fish?"

Crookedstar hissed again, but Nightpelt held his gaze without flinching.

Bluestar spoke again, this time more forcefully. "You have just driven out your leader and several of your strongest warriors! And Brokenstar went against the warrior code when he forced Crookedstar to agree to share the river."

Fireheart swallowed uneasily as he noticed Nightpelt unsheathe his claws, but Bluestar didn't blink. Her icy blue gaze glinted in the moonlight as she growled: "Remember you have not even received your nine lives from StarClan. Are you so confident you can make these demands?" Fireheart tensed as he felt the bristling of fur around him. The whole crowd was waiting for Nightpelt's response.

Nightpelt looked away angrily. His tail flicked from side to side but he said nothing.

Bluestar had won. Her voice softened. "We all know ShadowClan has suffered much these past few moons," she meowed. "ThunderClan has agreed to leave you in peace until you have had time to recover." She turned her gaze on Crookedstar. "I'm sure that Crookedstar will agree to show you the same respect."

Crookedstar narrowed his eyes and nodded. "But only as long as ShadowClan is not scented in our territory," he growled.

Fireheart relaxed, letting the fur lie flat on his shoulders. Now that he knew what it was like to fight in a real battle, he admired his leader's courage even more in challenging these two great warriors. Muffled mews of relief and agreement sounded in the crowd as the tension on the Great Rock suddenly eased.

"You won't scent us, Crookedstar," meowed Nightpelt. "Bluestar was right – we don't need your fish. After all, we have the uplands to hunt in, now that WindClan have left their territory."

Crookedstar looked at Nightpelt, his eyes brightening. "That's true," he agreed. "This will mean extra prey for all of us."

Bluestar drew up her head sharply. "No! WindClan must return!"

Crookedstar and Nightpelt looked at the ThunderClan leader. "Why?" asked Crookedstar.

"If we share WindClan's hunting grounds, it will mean more food for all our kits!" Nightpelt pointed out.

"The forest needs four Clans," Bluestar insisted. "Just as we have Fourtrees and four seasons, StarClan has given us four Clans. We must find WindClan as soon as possible and bring them home."

The ThunderClan cats raised their voices in support of their leader, but Crookedstar's impatient yowl rose above them. "Your argument is weak, Bluestar. Do we really need four seasons? Wouldn't you rather go without leaf-bare, and the cold and hunger it brings?"

Bluestar looked calmly at the warriors beside her.

"StarClan gave us leaf-bare to let the earth recover and prepare for newleaf. This forest and the uplands have supported four Clans for generations. It is not up to us to challenge StarClan."

Leopardfur, the RiverClan deputy, spoke up. "Why should we go hungry for the sake of a Clan that cannot even defend its territory?" she yowled.

"Bluestar is right! WindClan must return!" Tigerclaw spat back, drawing himself up so that he towered above the cats around him.

Bluestar spoke again. "Crookedstar," she meowed, turning to the RiverClan leader, "RiverClan's hunting grounds are known for their richness. You have the river and all the fish it contains. Why do you need extra prey?" Crookedstar looked away and didn't answer. Fireheart noticed how RiverClan murmured anxiously among themselves. He wondered why Bluestar's question had ruffled their fur.

"And Nightpelt," Bluestar went on, "it was Brokenstar who drove WindClan from their home." The broad-shouldered she-cat paused. "That is why ThunderClan helped you to chase him out."

Fireheart narrowed his eyes. He knew that Bluestar was gently reminding Nightpelt of the debt he owed to ThunderClan.

The ShadowClan leader half-closed his eyes. After a silence that felt like an age, Nightpelt opened his eyes wide and meowed, "Very well, Bluestar. We will allow WindClan to return." Fireheart saw Crookedstar turn his head away in anger, his eyes black slits.

Bluestar nodded. "Two of us have agreed, Crookedstar," she meowed. "WindClan must be found and brought home. Until then, no Clan should hunt in their territory."

The Gathering began to break up as the cats prepared to travel back to their camps. Fireheart stayed where he was for a moment, watching the leaders on the Great Rock. Bluestar touched noses with Crookedstar and jumped down to the forest floor. On the rock, Crookedstar turned to Nightpelt. There was something about the look that passed between them that made Fireheart's fur prickle. Could it be that Bluestar did not really have Nightpelt's support after all? Fireheart looked quickly around. He could tell from the anger in Tigerclaw's eyes that ThunderClan's deputy had not missed this exchange either.

For once, Fireheart shared Tigerclaw's concern. This was a shift in Clan alliances he had not expected. After the risk ThunderClan had taken by helping ShadowClan to drive out Brokenstar, how could they side with RiverClan now?

CHAPTER 3

BLUESTAR LED THE way swiftly back to camp. The noise of their return awoke the cats who had remained behind. As the group streamed through the gorse entrance, sleepy figures began emerging from the dens.

"What's the news?" called Halftail.

"Was ShadowClan there?" asked Willowpelt.

"Yes, they were," Bluestar replied gravely. She strode past Willowpelt and leaped up on to Highrock. There was no need for her customary call for a Clan meeting – the cats were already gathering below the rock. Tigerclaw jumped up beside her.

"There was much tension between the Clans tonight," Bluestar began. "And I became aware of a possible new allegiance between Crookedstar and Nightpelt."

Greystripe squeezed into the small space next to Fireheart.

"What are they talking about?" he asked. "I thought Nightpelt agreed with Bluestar."

"Nightpelt?" croaked One-eye's ancient voice from the back of the crowd.

"He has been named as ShadowClan's new leader," Bluestar explained.

"But his name – hasn't he been accepted by StarClan yet?" asked One-eye.

"He plans to travel to the Moonstone tomorrow night," Tigerclaw told him.

"No leader can speak for their Clan at a Gathering without receiving StarClan's approval first," muttered One-eye, loudly enough for all the cats to hear.

"He has the support of ShadowClan, One-eye," answered Bluestar, nodding at the old she-cat. "We cannot ignore what he said tonight." One-eye gave a disgruntled sniff, and Bluestar lifted her head to address the whole Clan. "At the Gathering, I suggested we find WindClan and bring them home. But Crookedstar and Nightpelt don't want them to return."

"They're hardly likely to join forces, though, are they?" called Greystripe. "They almost had a scrap over hunting rights in the river."

Fireheart turned to his friend. "Didn't you see the looks they were swapping by the end of the meeting? They're both desperate to get their paws on WindClan's territory."

"But why?" asked Sandpaw, who was sitting beside her mentor, Whitestorm.

Whitestorm answered her. "I suspect ShadowClan are not as weak as we thought they would be. And Nightpelt seems to have more ambition than any cat expected."

"But why does *RiverClan* want to hunt WindClan's grounds? They have always grown fat on the fish from their precious river!" yowled Willowpelt. "The uplands are a long way to go for a few windblown rabbits!"

The once-beautiful queen, Dappletail, spoke up in a voice cracked with age. "At the Gathering, some of the RiverClan elders spoke of Twolegs taking over part of their river."

"That's right," added Frostfur. "They say Twolegs have been living in shelters beside the river, disturbing the fish. The RiverClan cats have had to hide in the bushes and watch them with empty stomachs!"

Bluestar looked thoughtful. "For now, we must be careful to do nothing that may bring ShadowClan and RiverClan closer together. Go and rest now. Runningwind and Dustpaw, you will take the dawn patrol."

A cold breeze rattled the dying leaves in the trees overhead. The cats, still murmuring among themselves, went to their dens.

For the second night in a row, Fireheart dreamed. He was standing in the dark. The roar and the stench of a Thunderpath was very close by. Fireheart felt himself buffeted and blinded by the monsters that roared up and down with glaring eyes. Suddenly, through the din, Fireheart heard the pitiful cry of a young cat. The desperate wail sliced through the thundering of the monsters.

Fireheart awoke with a start. For a moment he thought that the cry had woken him. But the only noise was the muffled snores of warriors sleeping beside him. A growl came from somewhere near the middle of the den. It sounded like Tigerclaw. Fireheart felt too unsettled to go back to sleep, so he crept silently out of the den.

It was dark outside, and the stars dotting the black sky told him dawn was still far off. With the wail of the young cat echoing in his mind, Fireheart padded over to the nursery, his ears pricked. He could hear pawsteps beyond the camp wall. He sniffed the air. It was just Darkstripe and Longtail. Fireheart picked up their scents as they guarded ThunderClan's territory.

The calm of the sleeping camp soothed Fireheart. *Every cat must have nightmares about the Thunderpath*, he told himself. He crept back into the den and circled comfortably back into his nest. Greystripe purred briefly in his sleep as Fireheart settled beside him and closed his eyes.

Greystripe's nose woke him, prodding his side. "Leave me alone," Fireheart grumbled.

"Wake up!" Greystripe hissed.

"Why? We're not on patrol!" Fireheart complained.

"Bluestar wants to see us in her den, now."

Fuzzy-headed, Fireheart scrambled to his paws and

followed Greystripe out of the den. The sun was beginning to turn the sky pink, and there was frost on the trees around the camp.

The two cats bounded across the clearing to Bluestar's den and announced their arrival with hushed mews.

"Enter!" It was Tigerclaw's voice that answered from behind the draped lichen. Alarm swept through Fireheart as he remembered his conversation with Bluestar on the way to the Gathering. Had she told Tigerclaw about his accusations? Greystripe pushed his way into Bluestar's den. Fireheart followed him uneasily.

Bluestar was sitting in her nest, her head up and her eyes bright. Tigerclaw stood in the middle of the smooth sandstone floor. Fireheart tried to read his expression, but the great tabby's eyes were as cold and steady as always.

Bluestar began at once. "Fireheart, Greystripe, I have an important mission for you."

"A mission?" Fireheart echoed. Relief and excitement swept away his anxiety.

"I want you to find WindClan and bring them back to their territory," announced Bluestar.

"Before you get too excited, bear in mind this could be very dangerous," Tigerclaw growled. "We don't know where WindClan has gone, so you will have to follow what is left of their scent – probably into hostile territory."

"But you've been through WindClan territory when you travelled with me to the Moonstone," Bluestar pointed out.

"Their scent will be familiar, as will the Twoleg territory beyond the uplands."

"Will it just be us?" asked Fireheart.

"Our other warriors are needed here," meowed Tigerclaw. "Leaf-bare is coming and we need to gather as much fresh-kill as possible. Many prey-poor moons lie ahead."

Bluestar nodded. "Tigerclaw will help you prepare for the journey." Fireheart's paws prickled with unease. Bluestar had as much faith in her deputy as ever. Why was Fireheart the only cat in ThunderClan who didn't trust him?

"You must leave as soon as possible," Bluestar continued. "Good luck."

"We'll find them," Greystripe promised.

Dragging his thoughts back to the journey ahead, Fireheart nodded.

Tigerclaw followed them out of Bluestar's den. "Do you remember how to get to WindClan territory?"

"Oh, yes, Tigerclaw, we were there only—"

Fireheart interrupted Greystripe's eager reply, "Only a few *moons* ago," he meowed quickly. He flashed a warning glare at his friend. Greystripe had almost given away their journey several nights earlier with Ravenpaw.

Tigerclaw hesitated. Fireheart held his breath. Had he noticed Greystripe's mistake?

"And can you recall WindClan's scent?" the deputy meowed. Fireheart sent silent thanks to StarClan.

The young warriors nodded, and Fireheart began to

picture himself charging through the prickly gorse of the uplands in search of the lost Clan.

"You will need herbs for strength and to keep your hunger away. Fetch them from Yellowfang before you leave." Tigerclaw paused. "And don't forget that Nightpelt is planning to travel to the Moonstone tonight. Keep well out of his way."

"Yes, Tigerclaw," replied Fireheart.

"He'll never know we're out there," Greystripe assured him.

"As I would expect," meowed Tigerclaw. "Now, go!" Without another word, he turned and bounded away.

"He might have wished us good luck," Greystripe complained.

"He probably thinks we don't need it," joked Fireheart as they crossed the clearing towards Yellowfang's den. But at the same time, he reflected, Tigerclaw seemed to be treating them with as much respect as he would any warrior – was it possible that he wasn't the traitor that Ravenpaw thought? It was still cold, despite the rising sun, but neither cat shivered – Fireheart could feel his fur beginning to thicken as the days grew shorter.

Yellowfang's den lay at the end of a tunnel under ferns. A large split rock stood in a corner of a small shaded glade. Spottedleaf had lived here before Yellowfang. The memory of the gentle tortoiseshell medicine cat tugged at Fireheart's heart. Spottedleaf had been killed by a ShadowClan warrior. He missed her desperately.

"Yellowfang!" Greystripe called. "We've come for traveling herbs!"

The two cats heard a hoarse mew from the shadow in the centre of the rock, and Yellowfang squeezed out of the crack. "Where are you going?" she asked.

"We've got to find WindClan and bring them home," Fireheart told her, unable to hide the pride in his voice.

"Your first warrior mission!" rasped Yellowfang. "Congratulations! I'll fetch the herbs you will need." She returned a few moments later carrying a small bundle of dried leaves in her mouth. "Enjoy!" she purred, laying them on the ground.

Fireheart and Greystripe chewed obediently on the unappetizing leaves. "Yuck!" spat Greystripe. "Just as bad as last time." Fireheart nodded, screwing up his face. Spottedleaf had given them the same herbs when they'd journeyed with Bluestar to the Moonstone.

Greystripe swallowed the last mouthful and nudged Fireheart's shoulder with his nose. "Come on, slow slug! Let's get going! Bye," he called to Yellowfang over his shoulder, as he sprinted out of the glade.

"Wait for me," meowed Fireheart, chasing after his friend.

"Goodbye! Good luck, youngsters!" Yellowfang meowed after them.

As he raced through the tunnel, Fireheart heard the ferns rustling in the morning breeze. They seemed to be whispering, "Good luck! Travel safely!"

CHAPTER 4

As THEY HEADED out of the camp, the two young warriors nearly crashed into Whitestorm, who was leading Sandpaw and Runningwind into the forest for the dawn patrol.

"Sorry!" panted Fireheart. He stopped and Greystripe skidded to a halt beside him.

Whitestorm dipped his head. "I hear you two are going on a mission," he meowed.

"Yes," Fireheart replied.

"Then may you have StarClan's protection," meowed Whitestorm gravely.

"What you going for?" Sandpaw sneered. "Off to catch voles?"

Runningwind, a lean tabby, turned and whispered something into Sandpaw's ear. Her expression changed and the contempt in her green eyes switched to guarded curiosity.

The patrol stepped aside to let Fireheart and Greystripe pass. The pair raced on and scrambled up the side of the ravine.

The two friends shared few words as they followed the route through the forest to Fourtrees, saving their breath for the long journey ahead. They paused at the top of the steep slope on the far side of the oak-shaded clearing, their sides heaving from the climb.

"Is it *always* windy up here?" grumbled Greystripe, fluffing out his thick fur against the blast of cold air that swept across the uplands.

"I suppose there aren't any trees to block it," Fireheart pointed out, screwing up his eyes. This was WindClan's territory. As Fireheart sniffed the air, he detected a scent that all of his senses told him should not be there. "Do you smell RiverClan warriors?" he murmured uneasily.

Greystripe lifted his nose. "No. Do you think there might be some here?"

"Maybe. They might want to make the most of WindClan's absence, especially since they know WindClan will be back soon," Fireheart warned.

"Well, I can't smell anything now," whispered Greystripe.

They continued along a frozen turf trail sheltered by heather. A fresh scent stopped Fireheart in his tracks. "Can you smell that?" he hissed to Greystripe.

"Yes," whispered Greystripe, flattening himself against the ground. "RiverClan!"

Fireheart dropped into a crouch, keeping his ears below the heather. Beside him, Greystripe lifted his dark grey head to peer over the bushes. "I can see them," he murmured. "They're hunting."

Fireheart stretched up cautiously to look.

Four RiverClan warriors were chasing a rabbit through a patch of gorse. Fireheart recognised Blackclaw from the Gathering. The smoky-black warrior pounced, his claws unsheathed, but sat up again with nothing to show for the chase. The rabbit must have made it to the safety of her warren.

Fireheart and Greystripe dropped down again and pressed their bellies against the cold turf.

"They're not good rabbit hunters," Greystripe hissed scornfully.

"I guess they are more used to catching fish," Fireheart whispered back. His nose twitched as he smelled the scent of a terrified rabbit coming nearer. With a pang of dread, Fireheart heard the pawsteps of the RiverClan warriors fast approaching after it. "They're coming this way! We'll have to hide!"

"Follow me," whispered Greystripe. "I smell badgers this way."

"Badgers?" Fireheart echoed. "Is that safe?" He'd heard the story of how Halftail had lost his tail in a fight with a bad-tempered old brock.

"Don't worry. The scent is strong but stale," Greystripe

reassured him. "There must be an old set near here."

Fireheart sniffed. His scent glands picked up a strong, almost foxlike scent. "Are you sure it's abandoned?"

"We'll know soon enough. Come on; we've got to get out of here," replied Greystripe. He led the way quickly through the low bushes. The rustle of heather behind them told Fireheart the RiverClan warriors were closing in.

"Here!" Greystripe shouldered aside a tuft of heather to reveal a sandy hole in the ground. "Get inside! The badger's scent will disguise ours. We can wait till they're gone."

Fireheart slipped speedily into the dark hole, and Greystripe followed him. The stench of badger was overwhelming.

Paws thudded on the ground overhead. Both cats held their breath as the steps halted and one of the RiverClan warriors yowled, "Badger set!" From the rasping mew, Fireheart knew it was Blackclaw.

A second voice answered: "Is it abandoned? The rabbit may be hiding inside."

Fireheart felt Greystripe's fur bristling beside him in the dark. He unsheathed his claws and stared at the entrance to the hole, ready to fight if the warriors came inside.

"Wait! The scent leads this way," meowed Blackclaw. There was a scrabble of paws overhead as the RiverClan warriors charged away.

Greystripe slowly let out his breath. "D'you think they've gone?"

"Perhaps we should wait a bit longer, make sure none of them stayed behind," Fireheart suggested.

No more noises came from outside. Greystripe nudged Fireheart. "Come on," he meowed.

Fireheart followed Greystripe cautiously out into the daylight. There was no sign of the RiverClan patrol. The fresh breeze cleared Fireheart's scent glands of the badger stench. "We should look for the WindClan camp," he meowed to Greystripe. "It'll be the best place to pick up their scent."

"OK," answered Greystripe.

They moved slowly through the heather, keeping their mouths slightly open to pick up the scent of RiverClan warriors. They stopped at the foot of a large flat rock that sloped up steeply, past the tops of the gorse bushes.

"I'll climb up and have a look around," offered Greystripe. "My pelt will blend better with the stone."

"OK," Fireheart agreed. "But keep your head down."

He watched his friend creep up the rock. Greystripe crouched at the top and gazed around the plateau, then skidded back down to Fireheart. "There's a hollow over there, I think," Greystripe puffed, signalling with his tail. "I can see a gap in the heather."

"Let's check it out," meowed Fireheart. "It could be the camp."

"That's what I thought." Greystripe nodded. "It's probably the only place up here that's sheltered from the wind."

As they neared the hollow, Fireheart raced past Greystripe

and gazed over the edge. It looked as if a StarClan warrior had reached down from the sky, scooped a pawful of peat from the plateau, and replaced it with a thick tangle of gorse that grew almost to the level of the ground on either side.

Fireheart sniffed. He could smell many scents, all WindClan, old and young, male and female, and, in the background, the faint odour of fresh-kill that had long since become crowfood. This had to be the abandoned camp.

Fireheart bounded down the slope and plunged into the bushes. The gorse tugged at his fur and scratched his nose, making his eyes water. He could hear Greystripe behind him, cursing as thorns snagged his ears. They pushed through into a sheltered clearing. The sandy ground had been trodden hard by generations of paws. At one end of the clearing stood a rock, worn smooth by the wind.

"This is their camp, all right," Fireheart murmured.

"I can't believe Brokenstar managed to drive WindClan out of such a well-protected place!" meowed Greystripe, rubbing his sore nose with one paw.

"It looks like they put up a good fight," Fireheart pointed out, realising with a jolt how badly ravaged the camp was. Clumps of fur littered the ground and dried blood stained the sand. Mossy nests had been dragged out of dens and torn apart. And everywhere, stale ShadowClan scents mingled with the smell of terrified WindClan cats.

Fireheart shuddered. "Let's find the scent trail out of here," he meowed. He began to sniff the air carefully and moved forwards, following the strongest scent. Greystripe padded after him to a narrow gap in the gorse.

"WindClan cats must be even smaller than I remember!" grumbled Greystripe as he squeezed through after Fireheart.

Fireheart glanced at his friend, amused for a moment. The scent trail was quite clear now – definitely WindClan, but mixed and pungent, as if made by many frightened cats. Fireheart looked down. Drops of dried blood dotted the ground. "We're heading the right way," he meowed darkly. Two moons of rain and wind had failed to wash away the signs of suffering. Fireheart could clearly picture the defeated and injured Clan fleeing from their home. With a surge of anger he bounded after his friend.

The trail led them to the far edge of the uplands, where they stopped to catch their breath. In front of them the ground sloped away to the Twoleg farmland. Far in the distance, where the sun was beginning to set, loomed the towering shapes of Highstones.

"I wonder if Nightpelt is there yet," Fireheart murmured. In a tunnel below Highstones lay the sacred Moonstone, where the leaders of each Clan shared dreams with StarClan.

"Well, we don't want to find him down there!" Greystripe flicked his tail at the wide expanse of Twoleg land. "It'll be hard enough dodging Twolegs, rats and dogs, without meeting the new ShadowClan leader as well!"

Fireheart nodded. He thought back to their last journey across this land, with Bluestar and Tigerclaw. They had almost been killed by an attack of rats and only the arrival of Barley, the loner, had saved them. Even so, Bluestar had lost one of her lives; the memory of it stung Fireheart like a wood ant.

"Do you think we'll find any trace of Ravenpaw down there?" Greystripe meowed, turning his broad face towards Fireheart.

"I hope so," Fireheart replied solemnly. The last he had seen of Ravenpaw had been the white tip of his tail disappearing into the storm on the uplands. Had the ThunderClan apprentice made it safely to Barley's territory?

The two warriors started down the slope, carefully sniffing each clump of grass to make sure they stayed on the WindClan trail.

"It doesn't look as if they were heading for Highstones," Greystripe remarked. The trail took them sideways into a wide grassy field. They skirted the edge, staying near the hedgerow as WindClan had done. The scent led them out of the field and on to a Twoleg path through a small copse of trees.

"Look!" Greystripe meowed. Sun-bleached piles of prey bones lay scattered in the undergrowth. Mossy bedding had been gathered beneath the thickest patches of brambles.

"WindClan must have tried to settle here," Fireheart meowed in surprise.

"I wonder what made them leave?" asked Greystripe, sniffing the air. "The scent is old."

Fireheart shrugged and the two cats followed the trail onwards to a thick hedge. With a bit of a struggle, they wriggled through on to a grass verge. Beyond a narrow ditch lay a wide earth track.

Greystripe leaped nimbly over the ditch and on to the hard red track. Fireheart looked around, stiffening as he recognised a hard-edged silhouette in the distance. "Greystripe! Stop!" he hissed.

"What's up?"

Fireheart pointed with his nose. "Look at that Twoleg-place over there! We must be near Barley's territory."

Greystripe's ears twitched nervously. "That's where those dogs live! But WindClan definitely came this way. We'll have to hurry. We need to get past the Twoleg nest before sunset."

Fireheart remembered Barley telling them that the Twolegs let the dogs loose at night, and the sun was already sinking towards the craggy tops of Highstones. He nodded. "Perhaps the dogs chased WindClan out of the woods." With an anxious twinge, he thought of Ravenpaw. "Do you think he found Barley?" he asked.

"Who? Ravenpaw? Why not? We made it this far!" meowed Greystripe. "Don't underestimate him. Remember the time Tigerclaw sent him to Snakerocks? He came back with an adder!"

Fireheart purred at the memory as Greystripe leaped across the track and through the hedge on the far side.

Fireheart chased after him, quickening his pace to match his friend step for step.

A dog barked furiously from the Twoleg nest, but its vicious snarling soon faded into the distance. The temperature plunged as the sun set and frost began to form on the grass.

"Should we keep going?" asked Greystripe. "What if the trail takes us to Highstones after all? Nightpelt will definitely be there by now."

Fireheart lifted his nose and sniffed the browning fronds of some ferns. The smell of WindClan, sour with fear, pricked at him. "We'd better keep going," he meowed. "We'll stop when we have to."

The cold breeze carried another odour to Fireheart's nose – there was a Thunderpath nearby. Greystripe screwed up his face. He'd smelled it too. The warriors exchanged a look of dismay, but pushed on. The stench grew stronger and stronger until they could hear the roar of Thunderpath monsters in the distance. By the time they reached the hedge that ran alongside the wide grey path, it was hard to make out the WindClan trail at all.

Greystripe stopped and looked around, uncertainty showing in his eyes. But Fireheart could just make out the fear-scent. He crept through the shadows beside the hedge until he reached a place where the hedge was less thick. "They sheltered here," Fireheart meowed, imagining the terrified WindClan cats staring through the hedge at the Thunderpath.

"This was probably the first time most of them had seen the Thunderpath," Greystripe remarked as he joined Fireheart by the hedge.

Fireheart looked at his friend in surprise. He had never met a WindClan cat – they had been driven out of their territory almost as soon as he had become an apprentice. "Didn't they patrol their borders?" he asked, puzzled.

"You've seen their territory – it's pretty wild and barren, and the prey's not easy to catch. I guess they never thought any of the other Clans would bother hunting there. After all, RiverClan has their river and, in a good year, our forests are filled with prey, so no cat needs their skinny rabbits."

A monster roared past on the other side of the hedge, its night eyes glaring. Fireheart and Greystripe flinched as the wind buffeted their fur even through the wall of leaves. When the noise had faded away, they sat up cautiously and sniffed around the roots of the hedge.

"The trail seems to lead under here." Fireheart squeezed on to the grass verge that lay along the Thunderpath. Greystripe scrabbled through behind him.

But on the other side of the hedge the scent trail stopped abruptly.

"They must have either doubled back or crossed the Thunderpath," Fireheart meowed. "You look around here and I'll check out the other side." He fought to keep his voice calm, but exhaustion was making him desperate. Surely they couldn't have lost the trail now, not after coming so far?

CHAPTER 5

FIREHEART WAITED UNTIL the only sound he could hear was the pounding of blood in his ears. Then he padded to the edge of the Thunderpath. It stretched ahead of him, wide and foul-smelling, but silent. Fireheart darted out. The ground beneath his paws felt cold and smooth. He didn't stop until he reached the grass on the other side.

The air here was tainted by the acrid smell of the Thunderpath and its monsters, so Fireheart headed towards the hedge. Still there was no trace of the WindClan cats. His heart sank.

Suddenly a monster tore past, making Fireheart leap into the air with terror. He scrambled underneath the hedge and crouched, trembling, frantically wondering what to do next.

Then he smelled it: the faintest trace carried on the wind that the monster had stirred up. WindClan had been here!

Fireheart called as loudly as he could to Greystripe. There was a pause, then the sound of Greystripe pounding across the Thunderpath to join him.

"Have you found it?" puffed his friend.

"Not sure. I got a whiff, but I can't pinpoint it." Fireheart pushed his way through the hedge, Greystripe right behind him. He lifted his nose towards the open field ahead of them. "Have you any idea what's over there?"

"No," replied Greystripe. "I shouldn't think any Clan cat has ever been this far before."

"Except WindClan," muttered Fireheart darkly. Away from the confusing fumes of the Thunderpath, the trail was suddenly clear. WindClan had definitely come this way. The two cats struck out through the long grass, straight across the field.

"Fireheart!" Greystripe sounded alarmed.

"What is it?"

"Look!"

Fireheart stopped and lifted his head. He saw a Thunderpath ahead of them arching high into the air on massive stone legs, illuminated by the eyes of the monsters that moved along it. Another Thunderpath ran below, veering off into the darkness.

Greystripe nodded towards a tall thistle. "And smell this!"

Fireheart inhaled the scent. It was a fresh WindClan marker!

"They must have settled somewhere near here!" Greystripe murmured in disbelief.

A pang of excitement twisted Fireheart's stomach. Both cats looked silently at each other for a moment. Then, without a word, they moved on towards the stinking Thunderpaths.

Greystripe spoke at last. "Why would WindClan come to a place like this?"

"I guess not even Brokenstar would want to follow them here," Fireheart answered grimly. He stopped. A thought was nagging at him.

Greystripe paused beside him. "What is it?"

"If WindClan is hiding so near the Thunderpaths," Fireheart meowed slowly, "they must be fairly desperate not to be found. They're more likely to trust us if we arrive in daylight than if we creep up on them in darkness."

"Does that mean we can rest?" asked Greystripe, sitting down heavily.

"Just until it's light," meowed Fireheart. "We'll find somewhere to hide and see if we can get some sleep. Are you hungry?" Greystripe shook his head. "Me neither," Fireheart agreed. "I don't know if it's those herbs or because the stench from the Thunderpath is making me feel sick."

"Where shall we sleep?" Greystripe looked around.

Fireheart had already noticed a dark shadow in the ground up ahead. "What's that?"

"A burrow?" Greystripe sounded puzzled. "It's too big for a rabbit. Surely there can't be a badger set here!"

"Let's take a look," Fireheart suggested.

The hole was larger than a badger set, smooth and lined

with stone. Fireheart sniffed it, then put his front paws on its rim and peered cautiously inside. A stone tunnel sloped away, down into the ground. "I can feel air flowing through it," he meowed, his voice echoing away into the shadows. "It must come up somewhere over there." He ducked back out and pointed his nose towards the tangle of Thunderpaths.

"Is it empty?" Greystripe asked.

"Smells like it."

"Come on then." Greystripe led the way into the tunnel. After a few fox lengths, the slope levelled out.

Fireheart halted and sniffed the damp air. He could smell nothing but the fumes of the Thunderpath. A roaring noise rumbled overhead. Fireheart's paws trembled as the stone floor vibrated. Was the Thunderpath *above* them? He fluffed out his coat against the relentless draft and felt Greystripe's fur brush against him – his friend was circling, preparing to settle down to sleep. Fireheart crouched down and huddled beside his friend. He closed his stinging eyes and thought of the gentle forest breezes and the rustling of the leaves. Exhaustion fought briefly with a pang of longing to be at home in his den, before he gave in to the blackness that swam into his mind.

When Fireheart opened his eyes again, grey light was glowing at the end of the tunnel. Dawn must be near. Fireheart's bones ached from the cold hard ground. He nudged Greystripe, who grunted. "Morning already?"

"Almost," Fireheart answered, getting to his paws. Greystripe stretched and stood up too.

"I think we should head that way," Fireheart meowed, craning his neck away from the light. "I think this tunnel leads right under a Thunderpath. It might take us nearer to the…" His voice trailed off; he had no words to describe the tangle of Thunderpaths they had seen last night. Beside him Greystripe nodded, and together they began to pad wordlessly into the darkness.

Before long Fireheart spotted light ahead of them. They quickened their pace until they were racing up a short, steep slope that led them into a world filled with grey dawn light.

They had come up near the edge of a patch of barren, dirty grass. Thunderpaths enclosed it on two sides, and another arched overhead. A fire burned in the middle of the grass. A few Twolegs lay around it. One of them stretched and rolled over and another grunted angrily in its sleep, but the noise and stench from the Thunderpaths didn't seem to wake them.

Fireheart watched them warily, then froze as something else caught his eye: dark outlines that flitted back and forth in front of the flames. Cats! Could it be WindClan? Fireheart looked at the fire and the cats, and his mind flooded with the memory of his dream – the noise of the Thunderpath, the sight of the flames and the cats, and Spottedleaf's voice murmuring, "Fire will save the Clan".

A surge of emotion made Fireheart's legs feel weak. Did

this mean that ThunderClan's fate was bound up with the fate of WindClan?

"Fireheart? Fireheart!"

Greystripe's voice jolted Fireheart back to reality. He breathed deeply to calm himself.

"We must find Tallstar and speak with him," he meowed.

"Then you think it *is* WindClan?" asked Greystripe.

"You smelled their marker – who else could it be?" Fireheart replied.

Greystripe looked at him, his eyes shining with triumph. "We found them!"

Fireheart nodded. He didn't point out that finding WindClan was only half their mission. They still had to convince them that it was safe to return home.

Greystripe braced himself, ready to leap forwards. "Let's go!"

"Hang on," Fireheart warned. "We don't want to startle them."

Just then, one of the Twolegs sat up with a jolt and began shouting at the ragged cats around the fire. The noise roused the other Twolegs, who joined in with rough, angry voices.

The WindClan cats scattered. All caution forgotten, Fireheart and Greystripe raced after them. Fireheart could feel his fur prickle with fear as he and Greystripe ran straight towards the fire and the Twolegs. Every instinct told him to keep away, but he dared not lose sight of the fleeing WindClan cats.

One of the Twolegs staggered to its feet, looming up in front of him. Fireheart skidded, sending up a spray of dust. Something exploded beside him, pelting him with hard-edged splinters, but nothing pierced his thick coat. He glanced backwards, checking for Greystripe. He was relieved to see his friend right behind him, his eyes wide with alarm and his fur standing on end.

They charged into the safety of the shadows beneath the soaring Thunderpath. Ahead, Fireheart watched the WindClan cats stop close to one of the Thunderpath's great stone legs. And then, one by one, the cats disappeared into the ground.

"Where did they go?" meowed Greystripe in amazement.

"Another tunnel?" Fireheart suggested. "Come on, let's find out."

Cautiously, the two friends approached the spot where the WindClan cats had vanished. As they neared, they saw a hole in the earth. Like their resting place on the previous night, the entrance was round and lined with stone, sloping away into utter blackness.

Fireheart led the way, all his senses alert for a WindClan patrol. The floor beneath his paws felt wet and slimy, and the sound of trickling water echoed around them. As the tunnel levelled out, Fireheart pricked his ears and opened his mouth. The damp air smelled rank and bitter – worse than the tunnel they had slept in. Here the Thunderpath fumes mingled with the fear-scent of WindClan cats.

It was too dark to see anything, but after a few paces Fireheart's whiskers sensed a turning in the tunnel. Fireheart flicked his tail, touching Greystripe lightly with its tip. He couldn't see his friend in the blackness, but Greystripe must have felt the signal, because he stopped beside Fireheart and together they peered around the corner.

Ahead of them, the tunnel was lit by a narrow hole in the ceiling that led to the wasteland above. Fireheart could see many cats huddled together in the grey light – warriors and elders, queens and kits, all pitifully thin. A cold breeze blew relentlessly through the hole in the roof, stirring the thin fur on the skinny bodies. Fireheart shuddered, for the breeze carried to him the stench of sickness and crowfood.

Suddenly the tunnel shook as a monster roared overhead. Greystripe and Fireheart, already tense, jumped, but the WindClan cats didn't react. They simply huddled with half-closed eyes, numb to their surroundings.

The noise died away. Fireheart took a deep breath and stepped around the corner, out into the thin light.

A grey WindClan tom spun around, his fur standing on end as he yowled an alarm to the rest of the Clan. In one smooth movement the WindClan warriors formed a line across the tunnel in front of the queens and elders, their backs arched, hissing fiercely.

With a feeling of dread, Fireheart saw the glint of unsheathed claws and thorn-sharp fangs. These half-starved cats were about to attack.

CHAPTER 6

Fireheart pressed his body against Greystripe, who had padded out to join him. They had to show no threat if they were to survive.

The WindClan warriors stood their ground without moving a muscle. *They're waiting for a signal from their leader!* Fireheart realised. *They still follow the warrior code, even though they have to live like this.*

From behind the line of warriors, a black and white tom weaved his way to the front. With a jolt, Fireheart recognised the long-tailed cat from his dream. This must be Tallstar, leader of WindClan.

Tallstar sniffed the air, but Fireheart and Greystripe were downwind, their scents carried away by the steady breeze. As the black and white cat walked towards them, Fireheart breathed in the rank odour of crowfood that hung on his coat. Like Greystripe, he remained perfectly still, his eyes down, as Tallstar circled them, sniffing their fur closely.

Finally Tallstar returned to his warriors. Fireheart heard him murmur, "ThunderClan." The warriors flattened their fur but remained in a defensive line, shielding the rest of the cats.

Tallstar turned to face his visitors and sat down, curling his tail carefully around his paws. "I was expecting ShadowClan," he growled. His eyes burned with hostility. "Why are you here?"

"We came to find you," Fireheart meowed, feeling his voice crack with tension. "Bluestar and the other Clan leaders want you to return to your home."

The WindClan leader's voice was still wary. "That land is not safe for my Clan ," he meowed. There was a hunted look in Tallstar's eye that sent a pang of sorrow through Fireheart.

"ShadowClan has driven out Brokenstar," he meowed. "He is no longer a threat."

The warriors behind Tallstar turned and looked at one another. Murmurs of surprise rippled back through the Clan.

"You must return as soon as possible," Fireheart urged. "ShadowClan and RiverClan are starting to hunt in the uplands. We saw a RiverClan hunting patrol near the old badger set while we were on our way here."

Tallstar bristled angrily.

"But they are poor rabbit hunters," Greystripe added. "I think they went home with empty bellies."

Tallstar and his warriors purred with satisfaction. Their good spirits encouraged Fireheart, but he could see how weak they were. This Clan would find the journey back to the uplands long and hard. "May we travel with you?" he suggested respectfully.

Tallstar's eyes flashed. He knew the question was a tactful offer of help. He looked steadily at Fireheart. "Yes," he replied at last. "Thank you."

Fireheart realised he hadn't introduced himself. "This is Greystripe," he meowed, dipping his head. "And I am Fireheart. We are warriors of ThunderClan."

"Fireheart," repeated Tallstar thoughtfully. Sunlight was flooding through the gap in the roof now, making Fireheart's orange pelt glow in the dim tunnel. "The name suits you."

Another monster roared overhead. Fireheart and Greystripe flinched. Tallstar watched them with amusement and flicked his tail. It must have been a signal, for the line of warriors behind him split up. "We shall leave at once," he announced, standing up.

"Are we all fit for the journey?" Tallstar asked as the warriors began to move among the queens and elders.

"All except Morningflower's kit," replied a mottled brown warrior. "He is too young."

"Then we must take turns carrying him," answered Tallstar.

The WindClan cats shuffled forwards, their eyes dull with pain and exhaustion. A tortoiseshell queen was holding a tiny kit gently by the scruff of its neck. The little creature's eyes were hardly open.

"Ready?" called Tallstar.

A black tom with a misshapen paw looked around the Clan and answered for them. "Ready," he meowed.

Fireheart and Greystripe turned and made their way back to the tunnel entrance and waited while the WindClan cats emerged blinking into the daylight. Some of the elders blinked so long, their faces screwed up against the weak sun, that Fireheart guessed they had not been outside the tunnel for some time. Tallstar padded out of the tunnel last of all and walked to the head of his Clan.

"Shall we take you back the way we came?" Fireheart asked him. "I believe it's a shortcut."

"Is it safe?" asked Tallstar. Fireheart saw the hunted look once more in the leader's eyes.

"We met no trouble coming here," Greystripe meowed.

Tallstar flicked his tail decisively, as though he were brushing away any doubt. "Good," he declared. "You come with me, Greystripe. Show me the way. Fireheart, travel beside the Clan. Tell my deputy if you see trouble."

"Which one is he?" asked Fireheart.

Tallstar nodded towards the black tom. "Deadfoot," he meowed. The warrior turned at the sound of his name and pricked his ears.

Fireheart dipped his head in greeting. He left Greystripe with Tallstar and joined the other cats.

As the Clan made their way under the Thunderpath arch, Fireheart could still smell the fire, but when they padded out on to the patch of wasteland, the Twolegs were nowhere to be seen. Greystripe headed straight for the tunnel where he and Fireheart had spent the night. Tallstar entered first, while Fireheart waited at the back until all the Clan had disappeared inside. Only Deadfoot remained.

"Are you sure it leads to daylight?" the black tom meowed warily.

"It just leads under the Thunderpath. Have you never used this tunnel?" Fireheart asked, surprised.

"When our warriors cross the Thunderpath, they prefer to see where they're heading," growled Deadfoot. Fireheart nodded, and the deputy added, "You go first."

Fireheart padded down into the dark hole.

He emerged to find the WindClan cats staring across the field that led to the final Thunderpath. Fireheart saw Tallstar consult briefly with Greystripe before they set off into the long, frost-crisp grass. Fireheart walked with the rest of the Clan, flanking one side while Deadfoot limped steadily on the other.

Before they were halfway across the field, it was clear that many of the cats were having trouble keeping up the pace. "Tallstar!" yowled Deadfoot. "We need to travel more slowly!"

Fireheart looked over his shoulder and saw some of the cats falling further and further behind. Morningflower was among them, the kit swinging from her mouth. Fireheart bounded over to her. She was panting heavily. It couldn't have been long since her kitting.

"Let me carry him," Fireheart offered. "Just until you have caught your breath."

Morningflower glanced warily at Fireheart, but her eyes softened when they met his. She put her kit down and Fireheart took it gently, walking next to her so that she didn't lose sight of her precious bundle.

Tallstar slowed the pace, but only a little. In spite of his obvious exhaustion, and the fact that every rib showed under his fur, he burned with a fierce energy that lent swiftness to his paws.

Fireheart could understand part of the reason for his urgency. The sun was steadily climbing above the horizon. Some of the WindClan cats were sick, some old, and all of them were weak from hunger. If they were going to cross the Thunderpath without losing any of their number, they would have to do it quickly, before the monsters came in their swarms.

By the time Fireheart and Morningflower arrived at the hedge, WindClan was gathered around its leader.

"We cross the Thunderpath here," Tallstar announced above the noise of a monster racing past. The WindClan leader squeezed under the hedge. Deadfoot, Greystripe and a younger warrior followed him.

Morningflower leaned towards Fireheart and took hold of her kit. She had stopped panting now and as she took the kit from Fireheart she brushed her cheek gratefully against his. He dipped his head to the tortoiseshell queen and followed Greystripe under the hedge.

Tallstar and Deadfoot sat staring wordlessly at the wide grey path. Greystripe stood beside them. He flicked his tail towards the younger warrior. "This is Onewhisker," he told Fireheart.

A monster sped past, almost drowning out Greystripe's words and whipping up stinging dust.

Through streaming eyes, Fireheart mewed a greeting to Onewhisker and turned his attention to the Thunderpath. "We should try to get the Clan over in small groups," he meowed. "Greystripe and I will stay with any that need help." He looked at the Clan leader. "If you agree, Tallstar," he added.

Tallstar nodded. "The strongest group will go first," he meowed.

The other WindClan cats began to appear through the hedge. Before long the whole Clan was clustered beside them, pressed against the sharp twigs, as far back from the Thunderpath as possible.

Fireheart and Greystripe moved to the edge, watching for a break in the line of monsters. The Thunderpath was much busier than it had been when they'd crossed last night.

Onewhisker led the first group forwards.

"Do you want us to cross with you?" Fireheart offered. He could smell the young tom's fear. The mottled brown tabby shook his head. The cats beside him peered along the Thunderpath first one way, then the other. All was quiet, and the group dashed safely over to the other side.

Two warriors came next, accompanied by a pair of skinny elders. "Now!" Fireheart ordered as a monster flashed safely past.

The four WindClan cats stepped out on to the empty Thunderpath. The elders winced as they padded across on paws raw from the damp tunnel. Fireheart willed them on breathlessly as they neared the other side. A monster was zooming towards them.

"Look out!" Greystripe yowled. Even the two elders bounded forwards, fur bristling, and hurled themselves on to the other side, a heartbeat before the monster raced past.

Two larger groups crossed, leaving just one more. Only once they were safely over would Tallstar and Deadfoot cross. Morningflower and her kit stepped up to Fireheart's side. Behind her trembled three very elderly cats.

"We'll cross with you," Fireheart meowed. He looked at Greystripe, who nodded. "Tell us when it's safe to go, Greystripe." Fireheart leaned forwards to take Morningflower's kit, but she pulled back, her ears flat. Fireheart looked deep into her frightened amber eyes and understood. She and her kit would live or die together.

"Now!" At Greystripe's yowl, Fireheart and Morningflower stepped out on to the Thunderpath. The elders crept out behind them with Greystripe beside them.

Time seemed to stand still as the elders hobbled slowly forwards on stiff, battle-scarred legs. *If a monster comes now, we're all fresh-kill,* Fireheart thought. The other side was still several rabbit leaps away.

"Come on," urged Greystripe. The elders tried to hurry, but one stumbled and Greystripe had to nose him back on to his paws.

Fireheart heard the distant roar of a monster. "Go on ahead!" he hissed to Morningflower. "We'll bring the elders."

Morningflower stumbled forwards. Her kit squealed as it bumped against the hard ground. Fireheart and Greystripe pressed themselves against the elders' scrawny bodies, nudging them forwards. The noise of the approaching monster grew louder and louder.

Fireheart grabbed the nearest elder by the scruff of the neck and dragged him forwards, before turning to haul the second closer to the verge. The monster raced closer. Fireheart closed his eyes and braced himself.

There was a screech and an acrid smell that stung his throat, then a fading roar as the monster sped away. Fireheart opened his eyes and looked around. Greystripe was crouching in the middle of the Thunderpath, unscathed, but staring with eyes as wide as full moons. One elder cowered between them; the other two trembled near the verge. The monster was hurtling away from them, swerving across the Thunderpath.

Thank StarClan! It had missed them all.

Fireheart took a shuddering breath. "Come on," he meowed to the last elder. "Almost there."

Tallstar bounded across with Deadfoot and gathered his trembling Clan around him on the verge.

Onewhisker touched Fireheart's nose with his own. "You would have died for us," he murmured. "WindClan will never forget that."

Tallstar's voice sounded behind them. "Onewhisker is right; we shall honour you both in our stories. We must keep going," he continued. "We have a long journey ahead of us."

As the cats prepared to move off, Fireheart padded over to Morningflower. She was busy licking her kit.

"Is he all right?" Fireheart asked.

"Oh, yes," answered Morningflower.

"What about you?" asked Fireheart.

Morningflower didn't answer.

Fireheart turned to a grey queen, who answered his unspoken question. "Don't worry," she meowed. "I'll take the kit next."

The Clan followed the hedgerow along the Thunderpath before turning away to join the track through the woods. The scents here seemed to soothe the WindClan cats, but the journey had taken its toll; they were traveling slower than ever. And when they reached the fence at the far side, it took all Fireheart's strength to help the weakest cats over.

The sun had passed its highest point by the time Fireheart spotted the Twolegplace in the distance. He sniffed the air hopefully but there was still no scent of Ravenpaw. Fireheart felt a stab of grief and tried to ignore the nagging thought that he should never have sent his friend here alone.

Clouds billowed up over Highstones, growing blacker as they covered the sinking sun. A cold wind ruffled the cats' fur, bringing the first drops of rain.

Fireheart looked at the WindClan cats. There was no way they could travel through a long, wet night. He was tired too and, for the first time since he'd eaten Yellowfang's herbs, he was feeling the effects of hunger. A glance at Greystripe told him that his friend felt the same way. The big grey warrior's tail drooped and his ears were flattened against the spattering rain.

"Tallstar," Fireheart called. "Perhaps we should stop soon and shelter for the night."

The WindClan leader stopped and waited while Fireheart caught up with him. "I agree," he meowed. "There's a ditch here; we can shelter in that until sunrise."

Greystripe and Fireheart exchanged glances. "We might be better sheltering in the hedgerow," Fireheart suggested. "There are rats in these ditches."

Tallstar nodded. "Very well." He turned to his Clan and announced that they would be spending the night here. The queens and elders flopped down at once, despite the rain, while the warriors and apprentices gathered to discuss hunting patrols.

Fireheart and Greystripe joined them. "I don't know how

good the hunting will be here," Fireheart meowed. "There are too many Twolegs."

Greystripe's stomach growled as if in agreement. The other warriors turned to him with amused but sympathetic eyes. Then they froze as the grass behind them rustled. The WindClan warriors bristled and arched their backs, unsheathing sharp claws, but Fireheart and Greystripe turned their heads joyfully. The wind carried a scent as familiar as their own den.

"Ravenpaw!" Fireheart gasped as a sleek black cat emerged from the long grass.

Fireheart raced over to his old friend and nuzzled him. "Thank StarClan you're safe!" he purred. He stepped back and studied Ravenpaw in surprise. What had happened to the skinny, scared black apprentice? This cat was plump and sleek, and his fur, usually so dull before, now shed the rain like a holly leaf.

"Firepaw!" Ravenpaw meowed in delight.

"Fire*heart*," Greystripe corrected him. He stepped forwards and touched noses with the black cat. "We're warriors now! I'm Greystripe."

"Do you know this cat?" snarled Deadfoot.

The hostility in his voice made Fireheart flinch. He looked at the bristling WindClan cats and silently cursed himself for calling Ravenpaw's name out loud. He just hoped Tallstar's warriors had been too distracted to hear it. If WindClan mentioned it at a Gathering, it would spread through the Clans like a forest fire. Ravenpaw was supposed to be dead!

"Is he a loner?" asked Onewhisker.

"He can help us find food," Fireheart meowed quickly, glancing at Ravenpaw.

The black cat nodded. "I know all the best places to hunt around here!" he meowed. His fur didn't even bristle beneath so many hostile gazes. *How much he has changed!* Fireheart thought.

"Why would a loner help us?" demanded Deadfoot.

"Loners have helped us before," Greystripe told him. "Another loner once saved us from a rat attack near here."

Ravenpaw stepped forwards and bent his head respectfully as he addressed the WindClan warriors. "Let me help you! I owe my life to Fireheart and Greystripe and if they're traveling with you then you must be friends." He lifted his eyes and let his gaze rest on the WindClan cats. They returned his stare, more weary now than hostile. The rain was falling harder and, with their fur bedraggled, they looked skinnier than ever.

"I'll go and find Barley," Ravenpaw meowed. "He will help, too." He turned and disappeared through the long grass.

Tallstar's eyes burned with curiosity, but all he asked Fireheart was, "Can we trust him?"

Fireheart met Tallstar's gaze. "Completely."

Tallstar nodded to his warriors. They let the fur lie flat on their shoulders and settled down to wait.

Fireheart was almost wet through to his skin when Ravenpaw appeared again. This time Barley was with him. Fireheart greeted the black and white loner with a friendly mew. It was good to see him again.

Barley took one look at the dripping cats and meowed, "We need to find you some proper shelter. Follow me!"

Fireheart leaped forwards at once, glad to move his stiffening legs. Greystripe was right behind him, but the WindClan cats hung back, fear and suspicion showing in their eyes.

Tallstar blinked at his Clan. "We have to trust him," he growled, before turning to follow the loner. One by one, the WindClan cats fell in step behind their leader.

Barley and Ravenpaw led them through the hedge into another field. In an overgrown corner, among the brambles and nettles, stood an abandoned Twoleg nest. The walls were full of holes where stones had fallen out and only half the roof was left.

The WindClan cats stared fearfully at it. "You won't get me in there!" muttered one of the elders.

"Twolegs never come here now," Barley reassured them.

"It'll give us some shelter from the rain," urged Fireheart.

One of the apprentices whispered loudly, "I'm not surprised he wants to hide in a Twoleg nest – once a kittypet, always a kittypet."

Fireheart bristled. He hadn't heard that insult for several moons. But the story that a kittypet had joined a Clan must have made rich gossip at any Gathering. Of course WindClan would know. He whipped around and glared at the apprentice. "You've spent two moons living in a Twoleg tunnel. Does that make you a rat?"

The WindClan apprentice drew himself up, ruffling out his fur, but Greystripe stepped between them. "Come on; we're just getting wetter the longer we stand out here."

Tallstar meowed: "We've faced worse than a Twoleg shelter these past moons. One night here will do us no harm."

The WindClan cats murmured nervously among themselves. They were clearly reluctant, but with a glance at Fireheart, Morningflower picked up her kit and padded into the Twoleg shelter. The grey queen followed after her, nudging her own kit forwards out of the rain. The other cats gradually followed until every cat was inside.

Fireheart looked around the gloomy shelter. The ground was bare except for patches where weeds had burrowed their way under the stone walls. The wind and rain found their way through the gaps in the walls and roof, but it was drier and more sheltered than anywhere outside. He watched the WindClan cats sniffing cautiously around. As they began to settle themselves away from the dripping holes and drafty cracks, he glanced at Greystripe, relieved. Only Tallstar and Deadfoot remained on their paws.

"What about food?" asked Deadfoot.

Barley spoke. "You should all be resting," he meowed. "Raven—"

Fireheart interrupted him before Barley could finish saying Ravenpaw's name out loud. "Why don't you two show me and Greystripe the best places to hunt around here?"

"Deadfoot and Onewhisker will go with you," meowed Tallstar. Fireheart couldn't decide if the WindClan leader still didn't trust these two strangers or if he was determined to show that his Clan could look after itself.

The six cats ventured back out into the rain. Hunting would be hard, but Fireheart was starving. Hunger always made him a better hunter. Tonight the voles and mice wouldn't stand a chance. "Just show me where they are!" he meowed to Barley and Ravenpaw.

The two cats led them into a small patch of woodland. Fireheart breathed in a lungful of the familiar scent. Then he dropped into a hunting crouch and began to stalk into the ferns.

When the hunting party returned, each cat carried a mouthful of fresh-kill. The WindClan cats shared a feast with their new allies that night. Every cat from the eldest to the youngest ate their fill, then curled up together to share tongues in mutual grooming, while outside the wind and rain lashed at the walls of the shelter.

As darkness settled in, Barley got to his paws. "I'm off. Rats to catch!" he meowed.

Fireheart stood and touched the loner's nose with his

own. "Thank you again," he purred. "This is the second time you've helped us."

"Thanks for sending Ravenpaw to me," replied Barley. "He's turning into a fine ratter. And it's good to share a meal with a fellow cat from time to time."

"Is he happy here?" asked Fireheart.

"Ask him yourself," meowed Barley, and with that he turned and disappeared into the night.

Fireheart padded over to Tallstar, who was washing his paws. Fireheart couldn't help noticing how swollen and painful they looked. "We'll take it in turns to keep watch tonight, if you like," he offered, flicking his head towards Greystripe and Ravenpaw.

Tallstar looked up at him gratefully, exhaustion clouding his eyes. "Thank you," he meowed. Fireheart blinked respectfully at the WindClan leader and went to tell Ravenpaw and Greystripe.

His offer to Tallstar had been genuine, but it also meant he could be alone with his two friends. He was desperate to get Ravenpaw out of earshot of the WindClan cats and ask him what he had been up to. Greystripe and Ravenpaw bounded over to his side as soon as he called them.

Fireheart led them to a corner of the Twoleg nest, close enough to the entrance for them to keep watch, but far enough away from the other cats that they could talk in private. "So what happened after we left you?" he asked Ravenpaw as soon as the three friends had settled down.

"I headed straight across the WindClan territory, like you suggested."

"What about the Twolegs' dogs?" Greystripe put in. "Were they loose?"

"Yes, but it was easy to avoid them," Ravenpaw told him.

Fireheart was surprised by how casually his friend dismissed the dogs. "Easy?" he echoed.

"I could smell them from a long way off. I just waited until dawn and once the dogs were tied up again, I tracked down Barley. He's been great. I think he likes having me around." Ravenpaw's expression suddenly clouded. "Which is more than Tigerclaw ever did," he meowed bitterly. "What did you tell him?"

Fireheart recognised the hunted look in Ravenpaw's eyes as he spoke about his old mentor. "We said you'd been killed by a ShadowClan patrol," he answered quietly. Two WindClan apprentices were wandering towards them. Fireheart twitched his ears to warn his friends they had an audience.

"Oh, yes," meowed Ravenpaw, raising his voice. "We loners eat Clan apprentices whenever we can catch one."

The WindClan apprentices shot him a scornful look. "You don't scare us," they mewed.

"Really?" purred Ravenpaw. "Well, I guess your meat would be tough and stringy, anyway."

"How come you're such good friends with a loner?" one apprentice asked Fireheart.

"A wise warrior makes friends wherever he can,"

Fireheart replied. "If it weren't for this loner, we'd still be cold and hungry instead of dry and well fed!" He narrowed his eyes in warning and the apprentices slunk away.

"So ThunderClan thinks I'm dead," meowed Ravenpaw when they had gone. He gazed down at his paws. "Well, it's probably for the best." He lifted his eyes and looked at Fireheart and Greystripe. "I'm glad I've seen you again," he meowed warmly. Fireheart purred, and Greystripe prodded his friend affectionately with a hind paw. "But you look tired," Ravenpaw continued. "You should get some sleep. I'll keep watch tonight. I can rest tomorrow." He stood up and gently licked each of his old friends on the head. Then he padded to the entrance of the shelter, sat down, and stared out into the rain.

Fireheart looked at Greystripe. "Are you tired?"

"Exhausted," admitted Greystripe. The grey warrior rested his head on his paws and closed his eyes.

Fireheart took a final look at Ravenpaw sitting alone in the entrance. He knew now that he had made the right decision in helping Ravenpaw to leave ThunderClan. Perhaps Bluestar had been right when she'd said Ravenpaw would be better off without the Clan. *Each cat has his own destiny*, he thought. Ravenpaw was happy, and that was all that mattered.

When Fireheart woke, Ravenpaw was gone. It was past dawn. The grey rain clouds had begun to drift away. Tinged by the rosy glow of the rising sun, they looked like blossoms floating across a pond. Fireheart stared through a gap in the roof and watched them as the WindClan cats stirred and helped themselves to the leftovers of last night's catch.

A short-tailed brown tom joined Fireheart and gazed up at the clouds with him. Fireheart jumped as a curious yowl suddenly escaped the brown tom's throat. The noise brought the other WindClan cats crowding around them, murmuring and anxious.

"What is it, Barkface?" prompted Morningflower. "Has StarClan spoken to you?" Fireheart realised that this tom must be WindClan's medicine cat. He tensed instinctively at the sight of Barkface's bristling fur.

"The clouds are stained with blood!" rasped Barkface, his eyes wide and glazed. "It is a sign from our ancestors. There is trouble ahead. This day shall bring an unnecessary death."

CHAPTER 7

FOR A MOMENT, none of the cats moved or spoke. Then Deadfoot growled, "Any of the Clans could see those clouds. We can't be sure that the message is for us."

Hopeful mews spread through WindClan. Tallstar surveyed his Clan, then meowed calmly, "Whatever StarClan has planned for us, today we return to our home. I can smell more rain in the air. It's time we set off." Fireheart felt relieved at the leader's practical tone. The last thing they needed was hysteria at an ominous prophecy.

Tallstar led the way out into the chilly morning air. Fireheart and Greystripe followed. The WindClan leader was right: the wind carried the promise of more rain, and soon.

"Shall we scout ahead?" Fireheart offered.

"Yes, please," replied Tallstar. "Let me know if you see dogs, Twolegs, or rats. My Clan is stronger this morning, but we had trouble with dogs on the way out. We must stay alert." Fireheart could see from the worried look in the leader's eyes that Barkface's warning had disturbed him more than his confident words suggested. His Clan might be stronger but it was in no state to fight off attackers.

Fireheart raced away with Greystripe at his heels. They took turns going back to the Clan, telling Tallstar that the way ahead was clear, or warning him to stay back while a Twoleg passed by with a dog. The WindClan cats wordlessly obeyed their leader, plodding on heavy paws in spite of their night's rest.

By sunhigh dark clouds had gathered once more and the first drops of rain were beginning to fall. The ground began to slope upwards and when Fireheart pushed his way through a hedge, he recognised the red dirt track that led away from Twoleg territory and into WindClan's hunting grounds. His spirits soared and he met Greystripe's gaze with a look of triumph. *Nearly there!*

The muffled tramp of pawsteps sounded behind the hedge. Fireheart spun around and darted back into the field. The WindClan cats had caught up with them. Deadfoot was at the head of the group. He looked startled by Fireheart's sudden appearance.

"This way," Fireheart meowed, showing him the gap through the dripping leaves. He was eager to see WindClan's reaction when they glimpsed the uplands on the other side. With Deadfoot leading, the cats began to file slowly through.

Fireheart followed close behind the last cat, but Deadfoot and two warriors had already leaped the ditch and crossed the track and were pushing into the hedgerow on the other side. Their pace had quickened – they clearly knew where they were. Fireheart had to sprint to catch up. He followed them through the hedge and kept up with them as they bounded towards the long slope that led to the uplands and their home.

At the foot of the slope, Deadfoot and his warriors paused to wait for the rest of the Clan. They closed their eyes against the rain but held their heads high. Fireheart could see their chests rising and falling as they breathed in the familiar scents sweeping from the uplands.

Fireheart ran back to the rest of the Clan, looking for Morningflower. He spotted her walking beside a tabby warrior who held her kit in his mouth. Every few steps the tortoiseshell queen stretched her head to sniff the wet little bundle. It would not be long now before she could settle her kit into the WindClan nursery.

Fireheart fell into step beside Greystripe at the rear. They glanced happily at each other but didn't speak, too caught up in WindClan's excitement at coming home. Even the elders were moving swiftly now, keeping their bodies low and their eyes narrowed against the rain. As the Clan joined Deadfoot at the foot of the slope, the deputy got to his paws and Tallstar took the lead. Without pausing, Tallstar began to follow a narrow sheep trail through the rough grass and heather.

As the Clan neared the top, some of the warriors raced ahead again. At the brow of the hill, they made proud silhouettes against the stormy sky, while the wind sent ripples through their fur. Ahead stretched their old hunting grounds. Suddenly two apprentices charged past Fireheart and bounded away into the familiar heather.

Tallstar stiffened. "Wait!" he yowled. "There might be hunting parties from the other Clans here!"

As soon as they heard him, the apprentices skidded to a halt and pelted back to join the Clan, their eyes still bright with exhilaration.

From a rock-strewn ridge Fireheart saw the dip in the ground that concealed WindClan's camp. With a purr of delight Morningflower took her kit from the mouth of the tabby warrior and hurried towards the hollow. Tallstar flicked his tail and three warriors raced forwards to escort her as she disappeared over the edge and down into the camp.

The WindClan leader paused while the rest of his Clan rushed into the sheltering bushes below. He turned to Fireheart and Greystripe, his eyes shining. "My Clan is grateful for your help," he meowed. "You have both proved you are warriors worthy of StarClan. WindClan has returned to its rightful home, and it is time for you to return to yours."

Fireheart felt a pang of disappointment. He'd wanted to see Morningflower settled in the nursery with her kit. But Tallstar was right; there was no need for them to stay here any longer.

Tallstar spoke again. "There may be hostile hunting parties around. Onewhisker and Deadfoot will escort you to Fourtrees."

Fireheart bowed his head. "Thank you, Tallstar."

Tallstar called to his warriors and gave them their orders. Then he turned his tired eyes once more to Fireheart. "You have served WindClan well. Tell Bluestar that WindClan will not forget it was ThunderClan who brought them home."

Deadfoot padded away in the direction of Fourtrees. Fireheart and Greystripe walked after him with Onewhisker at their side. They stayed close together as they followed a narrow path through a solid mass of gorse that provided good shelter against the rain.

Suddenly Onewhisker stopped and sniffed the air. "Rabbit!" he called out joyfully before charging away into the gorse. Deadfoot stopped and waited. Fireheart could see a glint in the deputy's tired eyes. There was a rush of pawsteps in the distance and the rustle of gorse, then silence.

A moment later Onewhisker returned with a large rabbit dangling from his jaws.

Greystripe leaned towards Fireheart. "A little better than the RiverClan warriors, eh?"

Fireheart purred in agreement.

Onewhisker dropped the fresh-kill on the ground. "Anyone hungry?"

They ate the rabbit gratefully. When he'd eaten his share, Fireheart sat up and licked his lips. He felt refreshed by the meal, but a weary coldness was beginning to nag at his bones, and his paws felt sore. If he and Greystripe followed the route they'd come, past Fourtrees, they still had a long way to go. What if they took a shortcut through RiverClan's hunting grounds? After all, they were on a mission that had been agreed to, at the Gathering at least, by all the Clans. Could RiverClan really object if they passed through their territory? It wasn't as if they were going to steal prey.

Fireheart looked around at his companions and meowed tentatively, "You know, it'd be quicker if we followed the river."

Greystripe looked up from washing his paw. "But that would mean crossing into RiverClan territory."

"We could follow the gorge," Fireheart explained. "RiverClan doesn't hunt there; it's too steep for them to get down to the river."

Greystripe gently rested a damp paw on the ground. "Even my claws ache," he murmured. "I wouldn't mind taking a shorter route." He turned his yellow eyes hopefully to the WindClan deputy.

Deadfoot looked thoughtful. "Tallstar ordered us to travel with you to Fourtrees," he meowed.

"If you don't want to come with us, we'll understand," Fireheart answered quickly. "We'll only be in RiverClan territory for a blink. I can't see us meeting any trouble."

Greystripe nodded, but Deadfoot shook his head. "We couldn't let you go into RiverClan territory alone," he meowed. "You're exhausted. If you did meet trouble, you're in no state to deal with it."

"We won't meet anyone!" Fireheart had convinced himself and was determined to convince Deadfoot too.

Deadfoot gazed at him with wise old eyes. "If we did go that way," he mused, "it would let RiverClan know that WindClan is back."

Fireheart pricked his ears in understanding. "And once they've smelled fresh WindClan scent, they might not be so keen to come rabbit hunting in your territory again."

Onewhisker licked the last traces of fresh-kill from his lips and remarked, "It'll mean we'll be home before moonrise!"

"You just want to make sure you get a good nest in your den!" Deadfoot retorted. His voice was stern but there was a good-natured gleam in his eye.

"Then we're going through RiverClan territory?" Fireheart asked.

"Yes," decided Deadfoot. He changed direction and led the cats along an old badger trail that took them away from the barren uplands. Soon they were in RiverClan's territory. Even through the wind and the rain, Fireheart could hear the roaring of the river as it crashed and thundered somewhere up ahead.

The cats followed the trail towards the noise. The path shrank until it was little more than a narrow strip of grass on the very edge of a deep gorge. On one side the land stretched upwards, steep and rocky; on the other it plunged straight down. Fireheart could see the far side of the gorge only a few fox lengths away. The space looked tantalisingly narrow, and Fireheart wondered if he could leap the gap. Perhaps if he weren't so tired and hungry... His paws prickled with fear at the thought of falling, but he couldn't resist peering over the side.

Beneath his paws, the ground dropped away in a sheer cliff. Ferns clung to tiny ledges, their leaves glistening, not from rain, but from the spray of the swollen torrent that foamed at the bottom of the gorge.

Fireheart pulled back from the edge, the fur along his spine bristling with fear. Ahead of him Deadfoot, Onewhisker and Greystripe plodded steadily on, heads down. They would have to follow this path until they could cut away from it, through the small strip of forest that stood between them and ThunderClan territory.

Fireheart stumbled as he hurried to catch up. Deadfoot's ears were pricked and his tail flattened so that it almost dragged along the ground. Onewhisker was clearly nervous too; he kept looking sharply up the slope beside them as if he could hear something. Fireheart could hear nothing but the roaring of the river. He glanced anxiously over his shoulder, his eyes darting from side to side. The WindClan cats' wariness was making him uneasy.

The steep slope began to flatten out until they could

move further away from the cliff edge. The rain was still driving into their faces and the darkening sky told Fireheart that the sun was setting, but it would not be long now before they reached the forest. There would be more shelter there. The thought of food and a dry nest cheered Fireheart.

Suddenly a warning yowl rumbled in Deadfoot's throat. Fireheart stiffened and tasted the air. A RiverClan patrol! A screech sounded from behind them and the cats spun around to see six RiverClan warriors charging towards them. Fireheart's fur stood on end with horror. The deep gorge with its raging waters was still dangerously close.

A dark brown RiverClan cat landed on top of him. Fireheart rolled away from the gorge, kicking furiously with his back legs. He felt teeth bite into his shoulders and struggled under the weight of the hissing warrior. He scrabbled desperately on the sodden ground, trying to free himself. The RiverClan warrior raked his side with sharp claws. Fireheart twisted and bit into the fur of his attacker. He clamped his jaws tight and heard the warrior yowl, but the other cat's claws only raked him more fiercely. "This will be the last time you set foot in RiverClan territory," hissed the brown tom.

Around him Fireheart was aware of his companions struggling fiercely. He knew they were as exhausted as he was from the long trek. He could hear Greystripe yowling violently. Onewhisker hissed with pain and rage. Then, from the forest behind them, another sound reached Fireheart's ears. It was full of fury – yet it filled Fireheart with a surge of hope. Tigerclaw's war cry! Fireheart smelled the fast-approaching battle-scent of a ThunderClan patrol – Tigerclaw, Willowpelt, Whitestorm and Sandpaw.

Yowling and spitting, the ThunderClan cats leaped into the fray. The brown tom released Fireheart and he quickly struggled to his paws. He watched as Tigerclaw pinned a grey tabby tom to the ground, giving a warning bite to the tom's hind leg. The tom ran screeching away into the bushes. Tigerclaw whipped around and fixed his pale eyes on Leopardfur. The mottled RiverClan deputy was wrestling with Deadfoot. The lame warrior was no match for the ferocious RiverClan she-cat. Fireheart prepared to leap to the rescue, but Tigerclaw was ahead of him. The dark warrior dived forwards and grasped Leopardfur's wide shoulders. With a mighty yowl, he hauled her off the scrawny WindClan deputy.

Fireheart heard a vicious squeal behind him. He spun around to see Sandpaw locked in battle with another RiverClan she-cat. Twisting and tussling, the pair rolled over and over on the wet grass, spitting and clawing each other fiercely. Fireheart gasped. They were rolling towards the rocky edge of the gorge! One more roll and they would be over the side.

Fireheart sprang. With a mighty swipe he bundled the RiverClan warrior off Sandpaw and away from the edge.

Sandpaw skidded away, closer to the drop. Fireheart lunged forwards and grabbed her by the scruff of her neck with his teeth. She squealed with rage as he dragged her away from the gorge, her paws scrabbling on the muddy ground. She sprang to her paws as soon as he stopped and hissed at Fireheart, her eyes burning with fury, "I can win my own battles without your help!"

Fireheart opened his mouth to explain but a terrible howl made them both turn their heads. Greystripe was leaning perilously over the side of the gorge, his hind legs straining. Beside him, Fireheart glimpsed a white paw clutching at the edge. Greystripe leaned down with his mouth open, trying to get a grip on the paw, but it disappeared out of sight in a terrifying rush. Greystripe cried out after it, his wail echoing along the gorge.

All the cats stopped fighting at the sound of Greystripe's agonised call. Fireheart froze, panting with shock and exhaustion. The RiverClan cats scrambled to the edge of the gorge. Slowly Fireheart followed them and looked over the side. Far below, through the deafening spray, he saw the dark head of a RiverClan warrior sink beneath the foaming water.

With a cold feeling of horror, Fireheart recalled the words of the WindClan medicine cat: "This day shall bring an unnecessary death."

CHAPTER 8

Leopardfur lifted her head and yowled into the wind, "Whiteclaw! No!"

Greystripe scrambled backwards until all four paws were on safe ground. His wet fur was bristling and his eyes were wide with shock. "I tried to grab him... he just lost his footing... I didn't mean to..." The words tumbled out breathlessly. Fireheart bounded across to his friend and pressed his nose into his flank for comfort, but Greystripe backed blindly away.

One by one, the other cats turned away from the edge and looked at Greystripe. The RiverClan cats' eyes were narrowed with fury, their shoulders tense. Willowpelt and Whitestorm moved instinctively towards Greystripe, taking up defensive positions on either side of him.

Leopardfur growled deep in her throat, but it was a warning to her own cats. They were to stay back. The

RiverClan deputy stared Tigerclaw straight in the eye. "This has gone beyond a border fight," she murmured. "We shall return to our Clan. It has become a matter to settle at another time and in a different way."

Tigerclaw defiantly returned Leopardfur's stare. He showed no fear, but merely gave the smallest of nods. Leopardfur flicked the tip of her tail, then turned and padded away. The RiverClan cats followed her, and the whole patrol disappeared into the bushes.

Leopardfur's menacing words made Fireheart shiver. A sense of foreboding settled over his heart like a cold shadow as he realised that this battle might have started a war.

"We should leave," meowed Deadfoot, limping forwards. "Your two young warriors served us well and my Clan thanks you." But the formal words of gratitude sounded hollow after the tragedy they had just witnessed. Tigerclaw nodded, and the two WindClan warriors began to head back towards their own territory. Fireheart meowed a quiet farewell to Onewhisker as he passed. Onewhisker glanced briefly at him, and walked on.

Fireheart noticed that Sandpaw was standing at the edge of the gorge, staring down at the torrent below. Her paws seemed frozen to the ground and her eyes remained fixed on the steep drop. Fireheart guessed she had realised how close she had come to sharing Whiteclaw's fate.

Fireheart started towards her but Tigerclaw growled: "Follow me!"

The tabby warrior charged away through the trees, and the rest of his patrol followed after him, but Fireheart hesitated beside Greystripe. "Come on," he urged. "We should keep up!" Greystripe shrugged, his eyes dull and clouded with pain, and began to pad after the others, dragging his paws as if they were made of stone.

Soon the cats ahead of them were out of sight, but Fireheart was able to track them by their scent. Tigerclaw was leading them back towards ThunderClan territory, straight through RiverClan's strip of forest. Fireheart guessed there was no need to worry about RiverClan patrols right now. The damage had been done. It would be pointless to take the long way around by Fourtrees.

Tigerclaw had halted the patrol and was waiting for Fireheart and Greystripe at the border of ThunderClan's territory.

"I thought I told you to follow me," he growled.

"Greystripe was—" Fireheart began.

"The sooner Greystripe gets back to camp, the better," interrupted Tigerclaw.

Greystripe said nothing, but Fireheart bristled at the deputy's harsh tone. "Whiteclaw's death wasn't his fault!"

Tigerclaw turned away. "I know," he meowed. "But it's done. Come on, and this time keep up!" He leaped away, crossing the scent markers that bounded ThunderClan territory.

Fireheart had been looking forward to this moment since

leaving WindClan's den among the Thunderpaths. Now he hardly noticed as he pounded past the markers, keeping one eye on Greystripe.

The rain eased as they followed the familiar trail to the camp. When the patrol emerged from the gorse tunnel, some of the other Clan cats bounded out of their dens, their tails held high in greeting.

"Did you find WindClan? Are they safe?" Mousefur called. Fireheart nodded absently, but felt too hollow to reply. Mousefur's tail dropped. The other cats hung back at the edge of the clearing. The expressions on the faces of the returning cats told them that something serious had happened.

"Come with me," Tigerclaw ordered Fireheart and Greystripe, leading them towards Bluestar's den. Fireheart kept close to Greystripe so that his fur brushed against his friend. Greystripe just padded onwards, neither drawing closer to Fireheart nor moving away.

A warm mew welcomed them from the shadows beyond the lichen. The three cats pushed their way into the snug cave.

"Welcome!" Bluestar leaped up, purring. "Did you find WindClan? Did you bring them back?"

"Yes, Bluestar," Fireheart replied quietly. "They are safe in their camp. Tallstar told me to thank you."

"Good, good," meowed Bluestar. Her eyes darkened as she noticed Tigerclaw's grim expression. "What has happened?"

"Fireheart decided to return home through RiverClan territory," growled Tigerclaw.

Greystripe looked up for the first time. "It wasn't just Fireheart who decided—" he began.

Tigerclaw interrupted him. "They were found by a RiverClan patrol. If my patrol hadn't heard their yelps in time, they wouldn't have made it home at all."

"So you rescued them," meowed Bluestar, relaxing. "Thank you, Tigerclaw."

"It's not that simple." Tigerclaw snorted. "They were fighting beside the gorge. A RiverClan warrior who was battling Greystripe fell over the edge." Fireheart noticed Greystripe flinch at Tigerclaw's words.

Bluestar's eyes widened. "Dead?" she asked, looking horrified.

Fireheart meowed quickly: "It was an accident! Greystripe would never kill a cat over a border fight!"

"I doubt Leopardfur sees it that way." Tigerclaw turned on Fireheart, his tail lashing from side to side. "What were you thinking? Traveling through RiverClan territory! And with WindClan cats. You've sent a message that we are their allies, which will only drive RiverClan and ShadowClan closer together."

"WindClan was with you in RiverClan territory?" Bluestar looked even more alarmed.

"Just two warriors. Tallstar gave us an escort home; we were tired..." Fireheart murmured.

"You should not have been in RiverClan territory," Tigerclaw snarled. "Especially with WindClan cats."

"It wasn't an alliance. They were escorting us back home!" Fireheart protested.

"Does RiverClan know that?" spat Tigerclaw.

"RiverClan knew we were going to find WindClan and bring them back. They agreed to it at the Gathering. They shouldn't have attacked us – it was a special mission, like the journey to Highstones."

"They didn't agree to let you travel through their territory!" spat Tigerclaw. "You *still* don't understand Clan ways, do you?"

Bluestar stood up. Her eyes flashed as she looked around at the three cats, but her voice was calm. "You should not have entered RiverClan's hunting grounds. It was a dangerous thing to do." She looked sternly from Fireheart to Greystripe. Fireheart searched her eyes for a harsher reproach, but could find none. He felt torn between gratitude and guilt. He had caused a rift with RiverClan that might threaten the safety of his Clan for many moons.

Bluestar went on, flicking her tail uneasily. "At the same time, you did well to find WindClan and bring them back. But we will need to prepare ourselves for an attack from RiverClan. We need to start training more warriors. Fireheart and Greystripe, Frostfur tells me two of her kits are almost ready to begin their training. I want each of you to take a kit as your apprentice."

Fireheart felt stunned. What an honour! He couldn't believe Bluestar had suggested it – especially now. He glanced furtively at Tigerclaw. The deputy sat rigid as a rock.

Greystripe raised his head. "But none of Frostfur's kits are six moons yet!"

"It won't be long before they are. The divisions at the last Gathering troubled me, and today..." Bluestar's voice trailed off, and Fireheart noticed Greystripe look down at his paws once more.

Tigerclaw was staring at Bluestar, his amber eyes hard. "Wouldn't it be better to ask more experienced warriors like Longtail or Darkstripe to take on another apprentice?" he asked. "These two are hardly more than apprentices themselves!"

"I did consider that," replied Bluestar. "But Longtail will be busy enough with Swiftpaw, and Darkstripe is getting Dustpaw ready to become a full warrior."

"What about Runningwind?" Tigerclaw asked.

"Runningwind is a fine hunter and a loyal warrior," Bluestar answered. "But I don't think he has the patience for mentoring. ThunderClan has better use for his skills."

"And you think these two have got what it takes to train ThunderClan warriors?" Tigerclaw meowed scornfully.

Fireheart flinched. Tigerclaw was eyeing him alone as he spoke. *Does he think a kittypet is not fit to train Clanborn cats?* he wondered angrily.

Bluestar stared back at her deputy. "We shall find out.

Don't forget, they brought WindClan home. And of course, Tigerclaw," she added, "I am relying on you to oversee the training." Tigerclaw nodded, and Bluestar turned back to Fireheart and Greystripe. "Get something to eat," she ordered. "Then rest. We'll have the naming ceremony for the kits at moonhigh."

Fireheart led Greystripe out of the den, leaving Tigerclaw behind with Bluestar. The rain had eased to a fine drizzle.

"I'm starving," meowed Fireheart. He could smell the warm scent of fresh-kill in the clearing. "Are you coming to get something to eat?"

Greystripe stood behind him, his eyes distant and sad. He slowly shook his head. "I just want to sleep," he muttered.

Once his stomach was full, Fireheart pushed his way into the warriors' den. Greystripe was curled up in a ball, his head tucked beneath his paws. Fireheart's eyes felt heavy, but his fur was still soaked and he forced himself to wash thoroughly before settling into his warm nest.

Willowpelt woke Fireheart with a gentle prod. "Time for the ceremony," she whispered.

Fireheart lifted his head and blinked. "Thanks, Willowpelt," he meowed as she ducked out of the den.

He nudged Greystripe. "Ceremony," he hissed, then stood and stretched up on his toes until his legs quivered. He was about to become a mentor! Excitement tingled in his paws.

Greystripe stirred and uncurled slowly, like an old cat.

Suddenly Fireheart's paws seemed to remember their long journey and began to ache again.

At least the rain had stopped. In silence, Fireheart and Greystripe padded into the clearing. The moon shone above the trees, turning the wet branches silver.

"Well done for bringing WindClan home!" The cheery voice made Fireheart jump. He turned to see Halftail settling down beside him. "You must come and share the story with the elders one night."

Fireheart nodded absently, then looked back into the clearing. Frostfur was already sitting below the Highrock. A kit sat on either side of her, one smudgy grey and one ginger. The white queen twisted her head and licked behind their ears. The little grey she-kit shook her head impatiently as her mother fussed over her.

Once more, excitement made Fireheart's fur tingle.

Beside him Greystripe sat staring at the ground. "Aren't you excited?" Fireheart asked.

Greystripe shrugged.

"Greystripe" – Fireheart lowered his voice – "Whiteclaw's death wasn't your fault. It was the worst place for an attack, and the RiverClan cats would have known that. Sandpaw nearly fell over the edge too," he added.

He glanced at Sandpaw sitting nearby. Beside her, Dustpaw stared at Fireheart with raw jealousy in his eyes. Fireheart couldn't blame him. He was about to become a mentor when Dustpaw hadn't even been given his warrior name. But he flinched when Dustpaw leaned towards Sandpaw and whispered, loud enough for Fireheart to hear, "I feel sorry for Fireheart's apprentice. Imagine a Clan cat being trained by a kittypet!"

But for once Sandpaw didn't react. She just shot an uncomfortable glance at Fireheart.

Fireheart turned back to Greystripe. "Bluestar doesn't blame you," he insisted. "She knows you're a good warrior. She's giving you your own apprentice."

Greystripe lifted his eyes and replied bitterly, "She's just doing it because ThunderClan needs more apprentices. And why do we need them? Because I've given RiverClan an excuse to hate us!"

Fireheart was shocked by the harshness in Greystripe's tone. Bluestar's meow summoned them before he could say anything more. Fireheart padded towards his Clan leader, Greystripe trailing after him.

When they reached the centre of the clearing, Bluestar gazed around at the assembly of cats. "This moonhigh, we gather together to name two new apprentices. Come forward, you two."

The grey kit darted from her mother's side into the clearing, her fluffy tail held high and her blue eyes wide. The ginger kit came forwards more slowly. His ears were pricked and he frowned with seriousness as he walked to the foot of the Highrock.

Fireheart's heart began to pound in his chest – which one

of these kits would he be given? He couldn't help feeling that the solemn-faced ginger kit would be easier to train, but there was something about the grey kit's clumsy enthusiasm that reminded him of himself when he had first joined the Clan.

"From this day forward," Bluestar meowed, gazing down at the little grey kit, "until she has earned her warrior name, this apprentice will be called Cinderpaw."

"Cinderpaw!" The grey kit couldn't help mewing her new name out loud. A quietening hiss came from Frostfur, and Cinderpaw ducked her head apologetically.

"Fireheart," meowed Bluestar, "you are ready for your first apprentice. You will begin Cinderpaw's training." Pride swelled in Fireheart's chest. "You are fortunate, Fireheart, to have had more than one mentor. I expect you to pass on everything I taught you to this young apprentice" – Fireheart suddenly began to feel a bit overwhelmed. Bluestar's words carried a weight of responsibility he wasn't sure he was ready for – "and share with her the skills you learned from Tigerclaw and Lionheart."

At the mention of Lionheart, Fireheart pictured the golden warrior looking down on him from Silverpelt with warm, encouraging eyes. He lifted his head and returned Bluestar's gaze as steadily as he could.

"And this apprentice" – Bluestar turned her gaze towards the ginger kit – "will be known as Brackenpaw." Brackenpaw didn't move or make a sound.

"Greystripe, you will train Brackenpaw. Our lost friend

Lionheart was your mentor. I hope that his skill and wisdom will pass through you to your new apprentice."

Greystripe lifted his head high at Bluestar's words, and for a moment a gleam of pride showed in his eyes. He stepped forwards and touched his new apprentice's nose with his own. Brackenpaw returned the touch politely. Only his eyes, which shone like stars, gave away the fact that this young cat was as excited as his sister.

As soon as Fireheart saw the pair touch noses, he realised he should have done the same. He stepped forwards quickly. Cinderpaw jerked her head up and their noses collided painfully. Cinderpaw touched his nose again, this time less awkwardly, but Fireheart's eyes were beginning to water. He could see that Cinderpaw was trying to stop her whiskers from twitching with amusement and a flush of embarrassment washed over him. *I'm a mentor,* he reminded himself.

Fireheart looked around at the rest of the Clan. Every cat seemed to be nodding approvingly. Then his eyes found Tigerclaw. From the edge of the clearing, the deputy's amber gaze seemed to mock him.

Fireheart looked hastily down at Cinderpaw, who was staring at him with undisguised pride. Fireheart's fur suddenly began to prickle. He wanted to be a great warrior and a good mentor more than anything else, but it seemed painfully clear that Tigerclaw was just waiting for him to fail.

CHAPTER 9

FIREHEART WOKE TO find Greystripe sitting beside him, hunched on his belly like a rabbit, his shoulders stiff and his fur fluffed out. "Greystripe?" he meowed quietly.

Greystripe jumped.

"Are you OK?"

Greystripe sat up straight. "I'm fine." Fireheart suspected that his friend's cheery mew wasn't heartfelt, but at least he was trying to be more positive.

"It looks cold," Fireheart meowed. Greystripe's words had billowed out in clouds. Fireheart was still snuggled down among the warm bodies of the other warriors.

"It is!" Greystripe bent to lick his chest.

Fireheart sat up and shook his head. The air tasted of frost. "What are you going to do with Brackenpaw today?" he asked.

"Show him the forest," answered Greystripe.

"I could bring Cinderpaw and we could travel together."

"It might be better if we travel alone today," answered Greystripe.

Fireheart felt a bit hurt. They had been shown ThunderClan's hunting grounds together as apprentices. He would have liked to do it together again as mentors. But if Greystripe wanted to be by himself, then Fireheart could hardly blame him. "Fine," he mewed. "I'll see you later. We can share a mouse and compare apprentices."

"That'd be good," Greystripe meowed.

Fireheart crept out of the den. The air outside was even colder. His breath swirled from his muzzle like smoke. He shivered, ruffling out his fur, and stretched one leg at a time. The ground under his paws felt like stone as he trotted over to the apprentices' den. Cinderpaw was fast asleep inside, a fluffy grey heap that rose and fell as she breathed.

"Cinderpaw," Fireheart called quietly, and the little grey cat lifted her head at once. Fireheart backed out and in a moment Cinderpaw bounded from the den, wide awake and enthusiastic.

"What are we doing today?" she mewed, looking up at him with her ears pricked.

"I thought I'd take you on a tour of ThunderClan territory."

"Will we see the Thunderpath?" asked Cinderpaw eagerly.

"Er, yes, we will," Fireheart replied. He couldn't help thinking Cinderpaw would be disappointed when she saw what a dirty, stinking place it was. "Are you hungry?" he asked, wondering if he should tell her to eat first.

"No!" Cinderpaw shook her head.

"Oh, OK. We'll eat later," Fireheart meowed. "Well, follow me."

"Yes, Fireheart." The young cat looked up at him, her eyes sparkling. The pang of sadness that had been lingering in Fireheart's stomach since talking with Greystripe was swept away by a warm feeling of pride. He turned and padded towards the camp entrance.

Cinderpaw raced past him and charged through the gorse tunnel. Fireheart had to break into a run to catch up. "I thought I said follow me!" he called as she scrambled up the side of the ravine.

"But I want to see the view from the top," Cinderpaw protested.

Fireheart leaped after her. He overtook her easily, climbed to the top, and sat washing a forepaw, keeping an eye on her as she scrambled from rock to rock. By the time she reached the top of the camp ravine she was panting, but no less enthusiastic. "Look at the trees! They look like they're made from moonstone," she mewed breathlessly.

She was right. The trees below them sparkled white in the sunshine. Fireheart took a deep breath of cold air. "You should try to save your energy," he warned. "We have a long way to go today."

"Oh, yes. OK. Which way now?" She kneaded the ground

with impatient paws, ready to dart away into the woods.

"Follow me," meowed Fireheart. He narrowed his eyes playfully. "And this time I do mean *follow*!" He led the way to a trail along the edge of the ravine, into the sandy hollow where he had learned to hunt and fight.

"This is where most of our training sessions will be held," he explained. During greenleaf, the trees that circled the clearing filtered the sunshine into a warm dappled light. Now cold daylight streamed down on to the frozen red earth.

"A river ran here many moons ago. A stream still flows beyond that rise there," meowed Fireheart, pointing with his muzzle. "It's dry most of the summer. That's where I caught my first prey."

"What did you catch?" Cinderpaw didn't wait for an answer. "Will the stream be frozen? Let's look and see if there's ice!" She charged down into the hollow and headed towards the rise.

"You'll see it another time!" Fireheart called. But Cinderpaw kept running, and Fireheart had to race after her. He stopped beside her at the top of the rise and together they looked down at the stream. Ice had formed at the edges, but the speed of the water as it slid over its sandy bed had stopped it from freezing over completely.

"You wouldn't catch much there now," mewed Cinderpaw. "Except fish maybe."

The sight of the spot where he had caught his first prey filled Fireheart with happy memories. He watched

Cinderpaw stand at the edge of the stream and crane her neck to peer into the black water. "If I were you, I'd leave fishing to RiverClan," Fireheart warned her. "If they like getting their fur wet, then let them. I prefer dry paws."

Cinderpaw padded restlessly around in a circle. "What now?"

Her excitement, and his own apprentice memories, filled Fireheart with energy. He bounded away, calling over his shoulder, "The Owl Tree!" Cinderpaw charged after him, her short fluffy tail sticking out behind her.

They crossed the stream over a fallen tree Fireheart had used many times before. "There are stepping-stones further down, but this is a quicker route. Be careful though!" The pale white trunk was stripped of its bark. "It gets slippery when it's wet or icy."

He let Cinderpaw cross first, keeping close behind in case she lost her pawhold. The stream wasn't particularly deep, but it would be cold as ice, and Cinderpaw was still too small to cope with a soaking.

She crossed the log easily and Fireheart felt a glow of pride as he watched his apprentice jump down on to the forest floor at the far end. "Well done," he purred.

Cinderpaw's eyes shone. "Thanks," she mewed. "Now, where's this Owl Tree?"

"This way!" Fireheart bounded away through the undergrowth. The ferns had turned brown since greenleaf. By the end of leaf-fall, they would be flattened by rain and wind, but now they still stood tall and crisp. Fireheart and Cinderpaw wove their way beneath the arching fronds.

Ahead, a massive oak towered above the surrounding trees. Cinderpaw tipped her head back, looking for the top. "Does an owl really live here?" she mewed.

"Yes," replied Fireheart. "Can you see the hole in the trunk up there?"

Cinderpaw narrowed her eyes to peer through the branches. "How do you know it's not a squirrel hole?"

"Smell!" Fireheart told her.

Cinderpaw sniffed loudly but shook her head, her eyes curious as she looked up at Fireheart.

"I'll show you what squirrels smell like another time," Fireheart meowed. "You won't smell any around here. No squirrel would dare make its nest so near an owl hole. Look at the ground; what do you see?"

Cinderpaw looked down, puzzled. "Leaves?"

"Try burrowing under the leaves."

The forest floor was carpeted with brown oak leaves, crisp with frost. Cinderpaw began snuffling among them and then shoved her nose in right up to her ears. When she sat up there was something the size and shape of a pinecone in her mouth. "Yuck, smells like crowfood!" she spat. Fireheart purred with amusement.

"You knew it was there, didn't you?"

"Bluestar played the same trick on me when I was an apprentice. You'll never forget the stench."

"What is it?"

"An owl pod," Fireheart explained. He remembered what Bluestar had told him. "Owls eat the same prey as us, but they can't digest the bones and fur, so their bellies roll the leftovers into pods and they spit them out. If you find one of those under a tree, it means you've found an owl."

"Why would you want to find an owl?" squeaked Cinderpaw in alarm. Fireheart's whiskers twitched as he looked into her wide eyes, as blue as her mother's. Frostfur must have told her the elders' tale of how owls carried off young kits who strayed from their mother's side.

"Owls get a better view of the forest than we do. On windy nights, when scents are hard to follow, you can look out for owls and follow where they hunt." Cinderpaw's eyes were still wide, but the fear had left them, and she nodded. *She does listen sometimes!* Fireheart thought with relief.

"Where next?" mewed Cinderpaw.

"The Great Sycamore," Fireheart decided. They travelled through the woods as the sun rose into the pale blue sky, crossing a Twoleg path and another tiny stream. Eventually they arrived at the sycamore tree.

"It's huge!" Cinderpaw gasped.

"Smallear says he climbed to the top branch when he was an apprentice," Fireheart meowed.

"No way!" mewed Cinderpaw.

"Mind you, when Smallear was an apprentice, this tree was probably only a sapling!" Fireheart joked. He was still gazing up when a rustling sound behind him told him Cinderpaw had dashed off again. He sighed and chased after her through the bracken. His nose detected a familiar scent that made him nervous. Cinderpaw was heading towards Snakerocks. *Adders!* Fireheart picked up his pace.

He emerged from the trees and looked around anxiously. Cinderpaw was standing on a boulder at the bottom of the steep, rocky slope. "Come on; I'll race you to the top!" she mewed.

Fireheart froze, horror-struck, as she crouched, ready to spring on to the next boulder. "Cinderpaw! Get down from there!" he yowled.

He held his breath as Cinderpaw turned and scrambled down again. She stood trembling, her fur on end, as Fireheart rushed over to her. "This place is called Snakerocks," he puffed.

Cinderpaw looked up at him, her eyes huge. "Snakerocks?"

"Adders live up there. A bite from one of those would kill a cat as small as you!" Fireheart gave Cinderpaw a quick lick on top of her head. "Come on. Let's have a look at the Thunderpath."

Cinderpaw stopped shaking at once. "The Thunderpath?"

"Yep," meowed Fireheart. "Follow me!" He led Cinderpaw through the ferns, along a trail that skirted Snakerocks and took them to the part of the forest where the Thunderpath cut through like a hard, grey river of stone.

Fireheart kept one eye on Cinderpaw as they peered out from the edge of the forest. He could see from her twitching tail that Cinderpaw was desperate to creep forwards and sniff the Thunderpath ahead of them. A familiar roar was beginning to ruffle his ear fur and he could feel the ground trembling beneath his paws. "Stay where you are!" he warned. "There's a monster coming."

Cinderpaw opened her mouth a little. "Yuck!" she mewed, screwing up her nose and flattening her ears. The rumbling noise was coming closer and a shape appeared on the horizon. "Is that a monster?" she mewed. Fireheart nodded.

Cinderpaw unsheathed her claws to grip the earth as the monster roared closer. She shut her eyes tight as it charged past, stirring the air around them into a storm of wind and thunder. She kept her eyes shut until the noise had faded into the distance.

Fireheart shook his head to clear his scent glands. "Sniff the air," he meowed. "Can you smell anything apart from the Thunderpath stench?" He waited while Cinderpaw lifted her head and took several deep breaths.

After a few moments she mewed, "I remember that scent from when Brokenstar attacked our camp. And it was on the kits he took, when you brought them home. It's ShadowClan! Is that their territory, beyond the Thunderpath?"

"Yes," Fireheart answered, feeling his fur tingle at the thought of being so close to hostile Clan territory. "We'd better get out of here."

He decided to take Cinderpaw the long way home past Twolegplace, so she could see Tallpines and the Treecut place.

As they padded beneath the thin pine trees, the scents of Twolegplace made Fireheart uneasy, even though he'd lived in a place not far from there as a kit. "Stay alert," he warned Cinderpaw as she crept along behind him. "Twolegs sometimes walk here with dogs."

The two cats crouched under the trees to look at the fences that bordered the Twoleg territory. The crisp air carried a scent to Fireheart's nose that stirred an odd feeling of warmth inside him, although he didn't know why.

"Look!" Cinderpaw pointed with her nose at a she-cat padding across the forest floor. The light brown tabby had a distinctive white chest and white front paws. Her belly was swollen, heavy with unborn kits.

"Kittypet!" sneered Cinderpaw, her fur fluffed out. "Let's chase her out!"

Fireheart expected to feel the familiar rush of aggression at the sight of a stranger on ThunderClan territory, but his hackles stayed flat. For some reason he couldn't understand, he knew this cat wasn't a threat. Before Cinderpaw could attack, Fireheart deliberately brushed against a stalk of crunchy bracken.

The she-cat looked up, disturbed by the crackling noise. Her eyes widened with alarm; then she whipped around and set off at a lumbering pace, out of the trees. Within moments she was heaving herself over one of the Twoleg fences.

"Rats!" complained Cinderpaw. "I wanted to chase her! I bet Brackenpaw will have chased hundreds of things today."

"Yeah, but he probably didn't nearly get bitten by an adder," replied Fireheart, twitching his tail at her. "Now come on; I'm getting hungry."

Cinderpaw followed him through Tallpines, grumbling about the pine needles pricking her paws. Fireheart warned her to keep quiet since there was no undergrowth here to hide in and he felt every Clan cat's discomfort at being in the open. They followed one of the stinking tracks gouged out by the Treecut monster and stopped at the edge of the Treecut place. It was silent, as Fireheart knew it would be until next greenleaf. Until then, only the track marks – deep and wide and frozen into the soil – would remind ThunderClan of the monster that lived in their forest.

By the time they arrived back at camp, Fireheart was exhausted; his muscles were still weary from the long journey with WindClan. Cinderpaw looked tired too. She stifled a yawn and padded away to find Brackenpaw.

Fireheart spotted Greystripe beckoning to him from beside the nettle clump.

"Here, I've got you some fresh-kill," Greystripe meowed. He hooked a dead mouse with his claw and flung it towards Fireheart.

Fireheart caught it in his teeth and lay down next to Greystripe. "Good day?" he mumbled with his mouth full.

"Better than yesterday," answered Greystripe. Fireheart

glanced up at him, worried, but Greystripe went on: "I enjoyed it, actually. Brackenpaw's keen to learn, that's for sure!"

"So is Cinderpaw." Fireheart went back to chewing.

"Mind you," Greystripe went on with a sparkle in his eye, "I kept forgetting I was the mentor and not the apprentice!"

"Me too," Fireheart admitted.

They shared tongues until the moon rose and the coldness of the night drove them into their den. Greystripe was snoring within moments, but Fireheart felt strangely awake. The image of the pregnant she-cat kept returning to his mind. Even though he was surrounded by the familiar smells of ThunderClan, her soft kittypet scent lingered in his nostrils.

He fell asleep at last, but his dreams all carried the same scent, until finally he dreamed of his days as a kit. He remembered lying beside his mother's belly, curled in a bed softer than any forest moss with his brothers and sisters. And still the scent of the she-cat lingered.

Fireheart opened his eyes, suddenly jolted out of his sleep. Of course! The she-cat he had seen in the woods... was his sister!

CHAPTER 10

FIREHEART WOKE AT dawn with the image of his sister still clear in his mind. He pushed his way out of the den, hoping the routine of the day would distract him. It was another cold, frosty morning. Whitestorm and Longtail were waiting near the camp entrance, preparing to leave on patrol. Mousefur padded past on her way to join them and greeted Fireheart with a cheery mew. Whitestorm called for Sandpaw, who came racing out of her den just in time to follow the patrol as it pounded out of the camp. It was a scene Fireheart had watched many times, but for once he didn't yearn to join them as they thundered away into the morning-fresh forest.

He padded across the clearing, wondering if Cinderpaw was awake yet. Brindleface was just squeezing out of the narrow nursery entrance. A speckled kit followed her, then one more. A third kit, pale grey with darker flecks like the other, tumbled out and fell on to the ground.

Brindleface picked it up by its scruff and placed it gently back on its paws. The tenderness of Brindleface's action brought Fireheart's dream flooding back. His mother had probably done the same for him. He knew that Brindleface's fourth kit had died soon after it was born and she seemed to love the remaining kits even more fiercely now.

Fireheart was overwhelmed by a pang of envy at the thought that the other cats here all shared something he did not – *they were all Clanborn*. Fireheart had always been proud of his loyalty to the Clan that had taken him in and given him a life he would never have known as a kittypet. He still felt that loyalty – he would die to protect ThunderClan – but no one in the Clan understood or even respected his kittypet roots. Fireheart felt certain the she-cat he had seen yesterday would. With an ache in his heart, he wondered what memories they might share.

Fireheart heard Greystripe's heavy pawsteps behind him. He turned to greet his friend, stretching his head to touch Greystripe's nose. "Could you take Cinderpaw for the day?" he asked.

Greystripe looked curiously at Fireheart. "Why?"

"Oh, it's nothing important," replied Fireheart as casually as he could. "I just wanted to check out something I saw yesterday. Watch out for Cinderpaw, though; she doesn't listen to orders very well. Don't take your eyes off her or she'll be charging off in every direction."

Greystripe's whiskers twitched with amusement. "She sounds like a pawful! Still, it'll be good for Brackenpaw. He never charges off anywhere without thinking about it carefully first."

"Thanks, Greystripe!" Fireheart bounded away towards the camp entrance before his friend could ask him where he was going.

As the Twolegplace came into view through the trees, Fireheart dropped into a crouch. He opened his mouth and breathed in the cold morning air. No sign of a ThunderClan patrol, and no Twoleg scents either. He relaxed a little.

Slowly he approached the Twoleg fence where he had seen the she-cat disappear. He hesitated at the bottom and looked around, sniffing the air once more. Then he leaped, landing on a fence post in one easy jump. No Twolegs to be seen – just an empty garden with its strongly scented plants.

Fireheart felt exposed on the post. The branch of a tree hung low overhead. Its leaves had gone, but it would be easier to hide there. Silently he pulled himself up and lay down to wait, flattening himself against the rough bark.

Fireheart could see a swinging flap in the entrance to the Twolegplace. He had used one just like it as a kit. He fixed his gaze on the flap, hoping his sister's face would appear at any moment. The sun rose slowly into the morning sky, but Fireheart started to feel cold. The damp branch was drawing the heat from his body. Perhaps the Twolegs were keeping his sister shut in. After all, her kitting would be soon. Fireheart licked a paw and wondered if he should go back to the camp.

Suddenly he heard a loud clatter. Fireheart looked up and saw his sister pop out through the swinging flap. The fur along his spine rippled with anticipation and Fireheart fought to stop himself leaping down into her garden straightaway. He knew he would frighten her, as he had done yesterday. He smelled like a forest cat now, not a friendly kittypet.

Fireheart waited until his sister had reached the end of the grass; then he crept to the tip of the branch and slipped down on to the fence. Quietly he jumped into the bushes below. The she-cat's scent brought his dream flooding back to him.

How could he get her attention without frightening her? Desperately he searched his mind, trying to think of the name his sister had been given. He could remember only his own kittypet name. Fireheart called softly from the bushes, "It's me, Rusty!"

The she-cat stopped dead and looked around. Fireheart took a deep breath and crept out from the bushes.

The cat's eyes widened with terror. Fireheart knew how he must appear to her – lean and wild, with the sharp forest scents on his pelt. The she-cat raised her hackles and hissed ferociously. Fireheart couldn't help feeling impressed by her courage.

In a flash he remembered his sister's name. "Princess! It's me, Rusty, your brother! Do you remember me?"

Princess remained tense. Fireheart guessed she was wondering how this strange cat could know these names. He dropped into a submissive crouch, hope soaring in his chest as he watched his sister's expression slowly change from fear to curiosity.

"Rusty?" Princess sniffed the air, wide-eyed and wary. Fireheart took a careful step forwards. Princess did not move, so Fireheart edged closer. Still, his sister held her ground until Fireheart was standing only a mouse length away.

"You don't smell like Rusty," she mewed.

"I don't live with Twolegs any more. I've been living in the forest with ThunderClan. I carry their scent now." *She's probably never heard of the Clans*, Fireheart realised, remembering his own innocence before he'd met Greystripe in the woods.

Princess stretched her nose forwards and rubbed her muzzle cautiously along his cheek. "But our mother's smell is still there," she murmured, half to herself. Her words filled Fireheart with happiness, until her eyes narrowed and she took a step backwards, her ears flat with distrust. "Why are you here?" she asked.

"I saw you yesterday, in the woods," Fireheart explained. "I had to come back to speak with you."

"Why?"

Fireheart looked at her in surprise. "Because you're my sister." *Surely she must feel something for him?*

Princess studied him for a moment. To Fireheart's relief, her guarded expression lifted. "You're very thin," she mewed critically.

"Thinner than a kittypet, maybe, but not thin for a Clan – a forest – cat," Fireheart replied. "Your scent was in my dreams last night. I dreamed of you and our brothers and sister and..." Fireheart paused. "Where is our mother?"

"She's still with her housefolk," answered Princess.

"What about...?"

Princess guessed what he was going to ask. "...our brothers and sisters? Most of them live near here. I see them in their gardens from time to time."

They sat silently for a moment; then Fireheart asked, "Do you remember the soft bedding of our mother's basket?" He felt a flicker of guilt about longing for such kittypet softness, but Princess purred, "Oh, yes. I wish I could have it for my own kitting."

Fireheart's discomfort faded. It felt good to be able to talk of such a tender memory without shame. "Will this litter be your first?"

Princess nodded, uncertainty showing in her eyes. Fireheart felt a wave of sympathy. Even though they were the same age, she seemed to him very young and naive. "You'll be fine," he mewed, remembering Brindleface's kitting. "You look as if your Twolegs treat you well. I'm sure your kits will be healthy and safe."

Princess moved closer to him, pressing her fur against

his flank. Fireheart felt his heart swell with emotion. For the first time since he was a kit, he caught a glimpse of what the Clan cats must take for granted: the closeness of kinship, a common bond determined by birth and heritage.

Suddenly Fireheart wanted his sister to know about the life he led now. "Do you know about the Clans?"

Princess gazed at him, mystified. "You mentioned a ThunderClan."

Fireheart nodded. "There are four Clans altogether." He went on, the words tumbling out. "In the Clan, we take care of each other. Younger cats hunt for elders, warriors protect the hunting grounds from other Clans. I trained all greenleaf to become a warrior. Now I have an apprentice of my own." Fireheart could see by her bemused expression that his sister couldn't understand everything he was telling her, yet her eyes brightened with pleasure as he spoke.

"It sounds as if you enjoy your life," she mewed in awe.

A Twoleg voice called from the house. Fireheart instantly darted under the nearest bush.

"I should go," Princess mewed. "They'll be worried if I don't go back, and I have many tiny mouths to feed. I can feel them moving inside me." She glanced at her swollen belly, her eyes soft.

Fireheart looked out from beneath the bush. "Go, then. I have to return to my Clan anyway. But I'll come back and see you."

"Yes, I'd like that!" Princess called over her shoulder. She was already trotting back towards her Twoleg nest. "Goodbye!"

"See you soon," Fireheart called. His sister disappeared from view, and he heard the swinging flap slap shut behind her.

Once the garden was silent, Fireheart crept through the bushes to the fence. He jumped over it and ran into the forest. Memories of kithood scents crowded his mind, suddenly more real than the scents of the forest around him.

Fireheart paused at the top of the ravine and looked down at the ThunderClan camp. He didn't feel ready to go back yet. He was worried that it would all seem strange to him. *I'll go and hunt*, he thought. Cinderpaw would be safe with Greystripe for a while longer, and the Clan would welcome any extra fresh-kill. He turned away and headed back into the forest.

When he finally returned to camp, he carried a vole and a wood pigeon in his mouth. The sun was setting and the Clan cats were gathering for their evening meal. Greystripe sat alone beside the nettle clump, a fat chaffinch at his paws. Fireheart nodded to him as he padded across the clearing to the pile of fresh-kill that had already been collected.

Tigerclaw was sitting below the Highrock, his amber eyes narrow. "I noticed that Cinderpaw spent the day with Greystripe," he meowed as Fireheart dropped his catch on to the pile. "Where were you?"

Fireheart returned Tigerclaw's gaze. "It seemed a good day for hunting – too good to waste," he replied, his heart thudding in his chest. "The Clan needs all the fresh-kill it can get at the moment."

Tigerclaw nodded, suspicion darkening his eyes. "Yes, but we also need warriors. Cinderpaw's training is your responsibility."

"I understand, Tigerclaw," Fireheart meowed. He dipped his head respectfully. "I'll take her out tomorrow."

"Good." The deputy turned his head and looked around the camp. Fireheart picked up a mouse and carried it over to eat next to Greystripe.

"Find what you were looking for?" asked Greystripe absently.

"Yes." Fireheart felt a pang of sorrow for the pain in his friend's eyes. "Are you thinking about that RiverClan warrior?"

"I do try not to," answered Greystripe quietly. "It's just when I'm alone I can't help remembering Barkface's prediction of an unnecessary death and trouble ahead—"

"Here," Fireheart interrupted, and pushed his mouse towards Greystripe. "That chaffinch looks like it'll be half feathers, and I'm not that hungry. Want to swap?" Greystripe shot him a grateful glance, and the two friends exchanged prey and began to eat.

As he crunched on the chaffinch, Fireheart scanned the clearing. He could see Sandpaw and Dustpaw outside the apprentices' den. Dustpaw was busy ripping apart a rabbit. Fireheart caught Sandpaw's eye but she looked away.

Cinderpaw lay beside the old tree stump where he'd shared many meals as an apprentice. She was chatting enthusiastically to Brackenpaw, who nodded from time to time while plucking the feathers from a sparrow. Seeing the two young cats – brother and sister – lying together, so at ease, reminded Fireheart once more of Princess, and for the first time the familiar sights of his clan made Fireheart feel uneasy. He had been careful to lick his sister's smell from his fur before returning to camp, but it was her scent that lingered in his nostrils as the sun disappeared over the distant horizon. He had found the closeness he had missed, but it had given shape to a sense of loneliness that, until now, had lain vague and nameless in his heart. *Were the deep-rooted memories he shared with Princess stronger than his loyalty to the Clan?*

CHAPTER 11

"ANOTHER DAY OF sunshine!" Fireheart purred to Greystripe, feeling his flame-coloured pelt glow in the weak morning sun. Thanks to the fine weather, he had visited Princess nearly every day recently, slipping away to see her between patrols, hunting, and training sessions. Now he walked with his friend along the short trail to the sandy hollow where Cinderpaw and Brackenpaw would be waiting.

"Let's hope it stays clear for the rest of leaf-bare," Greystripe meowed. Fireheart knew how much his thick-coated friend hated rain – when Greystripe's fur got wet, it clung to him and stayed damp long after Fireheart's shorter fur had dried off.

The two warriors arrived at the edge of the hollow just as Cinderpaw pounced on a pile of frosty leaves, sending them flying in all directions. She leaped and twisted to catch one as it fluttered back to the ground.

Fireheart and Greystripe glanced at each other, amused.

"At least Cinderpaw will be warmed up and ready for today's assignment," Greystripe observed.

Brackenpaw jumped to his paws and looked up at his mentor, his eyes wide. "Good morning, Greystripe," he meowed. "What *is* today's assignment?"

"A hunting mission," Greystripe told him. He padded down into the hollow, followed by Fireheart.

"Where?" mewed Cinderpaw, dashing towards them. "What are we going to catch?"

"We're going to Sunningrocks," Fireheart replied, suddenly sharing her enthusiasm. "And we'll catch whatever we can."

"I'd like to catch a vole," declared Cinderpaw. "I've never tasted vole."

"I'm afraid everything we catch today goes straight back to the elders," Greystripe warned. "But I'm sure if you asked one of them nicely, they'd be happy to share."

"OK," mewed Cinderpaw. "Which way is Sunningrocks?" She bounded up one side of the hollow and peered into the forest, her tail sticking straight up.

"This way!" meowed Fireheart, leaping up the opposite side.

"OK." Cinderpaw raced down the slope, across the hollow, and up to Fireheart's side, sending fallen leaves flying everywhere.

Greystripe leaped up and caught one as it drifted past his nose. He pinned it to the ground with a purr of satisfaction and saw Brackenpaw staring at him. "Er, never miss a chance to practise your hunting skills," Greystripe told him quickly.

The four cats made their way along the familiar scent-trails to Sunningrocks. The sun was above the trees by the time they emerged into open territory. Ahead of them, a slope of rock rose out of the soft earth, its smooth surface lined with cracks. The cats had to narrow their eyes as they looked at it. After the shade of the woods, the flat rock face reflected the sun with dazzling glare.

"This is Sunningrocks," Fireheart announced, blinking. "Come on!"

"Mrrrr! It feels nice!" mewed Cinderpaw as she raced up the stone slope behind him. Fireheart realised she was right. The stone felt comfortingly warm and smooth after the ice-cold forest floor.

They rested at the top, where the far side fell away steeply to the forest. Fireheart listened for the gentle bubbling of the river that followed the RiverClan border, flowing down from the uplands. It touched the Sunningrocks before turning to run deeper into RiverClan territory. He could barely hear it – perhaps the water was low after the dry weather.

Fireheart stretched out, enjoying the warmth of the rock beneath him and the soft heat of the sun on his pelt. He closed his eyes, feeling proud to be lying here, a place where generations of ThunderClan cats had come to warm themselves, and which they had battled hard to keep.

Greystripe joined him. "Come on," he meowed to the two apprentices. "Make the most of the sun while it's here. There are enough cold, damp days ahead of us." The two apprentices lay down beside their mentors and purred as the warmth seeped into their fur.

"Is this where Redtail died?" asked Brackenpaw.

"Yes," Fireheart answered cautiously.

"And where Tigerclaw avenged his death by killing Oakheart?" Cinderpaw piped up.

Fireheart's fur prickled as he remembered Ravenpaw's account of the fight – that *Redtail* had been responsible for Oakheart's death and then Tigerclaw had killed Redtail, the deputy of his own Clan. Fireheart pushed away the disturbing thoughts and replied simply, "This is the place." The two apprentices fell silent and looked down the slope in awe.

Suddenly Fireheart heard a noise. He pricked his ears. "Hush," he hissed. "What can you hear?"

The two apprentices strained their ears forwards.

"I think I can hear some scrabbling," Brackenpaw whispered.

"It might be a vole," murmured Greystripe. "Can you tell where it's coming from?"

"Over there!" mewed Cinderpaw, leaping to her paws.

The scrabbling noise became more furious and then disappeared.

"I think it heard you," Fireheart remarked. Cinderpaw looked crestfallen. Brackenpaw purred with amusement at his sister's clumsiness.

"Never mind," meowed Greystripe. "Now you know that it's better to creep up slowly, especially on voles. They're fast!"

"Sit still and listen," Fireheart advised. "Next time we hear something, work out where it is and then begin to move towards it very slowly. A mouse could probably hear even the rustling of your fur, so let him think it's just the wind blowing across the rock."

The cats remained where they were, no one daring to move until they heard the scrabbling sound again. His ears pricked, Fireheart rose and crept forwards, placing each paw noiselessly in front of the other until he reached the edge of a small crack that ran across the rock face. He paused. The scrabbling noise continued. Fireheart lunged forwards and reached down into the crack with a forepaw. He scooped out a fat vole that had been hiding in the shadows and flung it on to the bright stone. It squealed as it landed, but the hard ground stunned it and Fireheart finished it off quickly.

"Wow!" mewed Cinderpaw. "I want to do that!"

"Don't worry; you'll have plenty of chances. For now, let's get back to the forest," meowed Greystripe.

"Aren't we going to catch anything else?" Cinderpaw protested.

"Did you hear that vole squeal?" meowed Fireheart. Cinderpaw nodded. "Well, so did every other creature around here. The prey will be hiding for a while. I should have caught it and killed it before it could make a sound."

Greystripe's whiskers twitched with amusement. "I wasn't going to say a word," he purred.

Fireheart picked up the dead vole in his mouth and together the cats headed down the slope and began to trek onwards through the forest. After the open warmth of Sunningrocks, the woods seemed chilly, even though sunhigh was approaching. Fireheart smelled fresh markers at the RiverClan border. Beyond them the ground sloped down to meet the river.

A leaf fluttered down towards Brackenpaw. The young cat immediately leaped up and caught it between his paws. He landed, looking pleased with himself.

"Well done!" called Greystripe. "You'll have no trouble with voles!" Brackenpaw looked doubly pleased.

"Nice catch, Brackenpaw!" Cinderpaw mewed. She nudged her brother's shoulder with her nose before turning to stare down the wooded slope.

"The river's quiet today," Fireheart mumbled through his mouthful of vole.

"That's because it's frozen," mewed Cinderpaw excitedly. "I can see it through the trees!"

Fireheart dropped the vole. "Frozen? Completely?" He stared down the wooded slope. The river glittered at the bottom, frosty and still. Could Cinderpaw be right? Fireheart's paws tingled with excitement. He had never seen the river frozen over.

"Can we have a look?" asked Cinderpaw. Without waiting for an answer, she bounded past the scent-markers. Fireheart's excitement turned to panic as he saw the small grey cat disappear into RiverClan territory. He couldn't call after her – he didn't want to alert any RiverClan patrols that might be in the area. But he had to get her back. He left the vole where he'd dropped it and tore after her, Greystripe and Brackenpaw close behind him.

They caught up with Cinderpaw at the edge of the river. It was almost totally frozen, apart from a narrow channel of dark water that flowed swiftly between two wide fringes of ice. Fireheart remembered Whiteclaw with a shudder. He was about to suggest they leave when he noticed Greystripe's ears were pricked.

"Water vole," the grey warrior hissed. Sure enough, a small vole was scampering along the ice, near the bank.

Fireheart glanced at Cinderpaw and Brackenpaw, afraid that they might try to catch this tiny piece of prey. But neither apprentice moved. Fireheart felt relieved for a moment, and then his heart lurched as Greystripe dashed out on to the ice at hunting speed.

"Come back!" Fireheart hissed.

It was too late. The ice beneath Greystripe's paws gave a terrifying crack and broke. With a startled yowl, Greystripe fell into the water. He paddled madly for a moment before disappearing into the cold, dark depths of the river.

Brackenpaw stared in horror and Cinderpaw gave a desperate mew. Fireheart didn't quiet her. He was rigid with fear, staring into the water after his friend. Was Greystripe trapped underneath the ice? Fireheart stepped on to the ice. It felt cold and slippery beneath his paws, impossible to run on. He jumped back on to the bank. Panic gripped him, then a blaze of relief as a drenched grey head appeared in the water further along.

But relief turned to alarm as Fireheart saw that Greystripe was being carried downriver, turning and bobbing in the freezing waters. His paws thrashed helplessly, all his instincts to swim thwarted by the fierce current. Fireheart bounded along the bank, forcing his way through the bracken, but Greystripe was swept further and further away.

Suddenly Fireheart heard a yowl from the opposite bank and stopped. A slender silver tabby had leaped on to the ice further downstream. She padded lightly over the frozen sheet and slid into the river ahead of Greystripe. Amazed, Fireheart watched the she-cat swim strongly against the current, holding her position in the icy water with confident churning paws. As Greystripe was swept past, the tabby grabbed a mouthful of his fur between her teeth.

But to Fireheart's horror, Greystripe's weight pulled both cats under. He started running again, his eyes fixed on the river. Where were they? Then a silver-striped head appeared amid the rolling waters, pushing through the waves. The tabby was swimming against the current, dragging Greystripe with her. Fireheart could hardly believe that such a slender cat could swim with such a weight. The tabby grabbed the ice on Fireheart's side of the river with her forepaws, her neck craning awkwardly as she held Greystripe between her teeth. Slipping and sliding, she hauled herself out of the river. Greystripe hung limply in the water, twisting and turning as the current dragged at his fur, but the tabby kept a firm grip.

Fireheart slid down the bank, raced across the ice, and skidded to a halt beside her. Without a word he reached forwards and took hold of Greystripe in his teeth. Together the two cats heaved his soaking body out of the water and dragged him to the safety of the riverbank.

Fireheart bent over his friend to see if he was breathing. He felt dizzy with relief as he saw Greystripe's slick grey flank rising and falling. Greystripe coughed and spluttered and spat out a mouthful of river water. Then he lay still.

"Greystripe!" Fireheart meowed urgently.

"I'm OK," wheezed Greystripe. His mew was breathless but reassuring.

Fireheart sighed and sat down. He looked closely at the silver tabby. She carried the scent of RiverClan on her. After seeing her swim, Fireheart wasn't surprised. The tabby returned his gaze coldly, shook herself, and sat down, her sides heaving as she got her breath back. Water streamed from her glossy fur as if her pelt were made from duck feathers.

Greystripe turned his head and looked at his rescuer. "Thanks," he croaked.

"You idiot!" she spat, flattening her ears. "What are you doing in my territory?"

"Drowning?" replied Greystripe.

The silver tabby flicked her ears, and Fireheart saw a glimmer of amusement in her eyes. "Can't you drown yourself in your own territory?"

Greystripe's whiskers twitched. "Ah, but who would rescue me there?" he rasped.

There was a tiny mew behind Fireheart. He turned to see Cinderpaw crouching by a clump of grass further up the bank. "Where's Brackenpaw?" he asked.

"Just coming," answered Cinderpaw, pointing with her nose. Her brother was creeping nervously along the bank towards them.

Fireheart sighed and turned to his friend. "Look, Greystripe, we've got to get out of here."

"I know." Greystripe pushed himself to his paws and turned to the silver tabby. "Thanks again."

She dipped her head graciously, but hissed, "Hurry, go now!" She looked over her shoulder. "If my father knew that

I'd rescued a ThunderClan intruder he'd shred me for kit bedding!"

"Why'd you save me then?" teased Greystripe.

The tabby looked away. "Instinct. I couldn't watch any cat drown. Now go away!"

Fireheart stood up. "Thanks. I'd have missed this furball if he'd drowned." He nudged Greystripe. His friend hadn't even shaken the icy water from his fur and he was soaked to the skin. "Come on, let's get back to camp. You're freezing!"

"OK, I'm coming!" Greystripe meowed. But before he followed Fireheart up the slope, he turned back to the silver she-cat. "What's your name? Mine's Greystripe."

"Silverstream," she replied, and bounded away, back on to the ice and over the channel of water to the far side.

Fireheart and Greystripe led their apprentices through the bracken, towards the border. Fireheart couldn't help noticing that Greystripe looked back over his shoulder more than once.

Cinderpaw noticed too. The little grey cat glanced up, mischief dancing in her eyes. "What a pretty RiverClan cat she was!"

Greystripe gave her a playful cuff around the ear and she ran on ahead.

"Stay with us," Fireheart warned in a loud hiss. They were still in RiverClan territory. He flashed Cinderpaw an angry look as she stopped and waited for them. If it weren't for her, they wouldn't be here at all, and Greystripe wouldn't have nearly drowned. He looked at his wet friend. Even though the grey warrior had shaken as much of the water from his fur as he could, his coat was still dripping and ice was beginning to form on the ends of his whiskers.

Fireheart quickened the pace. "Are you OK?" he asked Greystripe.

"F-f-fine!" replied Greystripe, through chattering teeth.

"Sorry," mewed Cinderpaw softly as she fell into step behind Fireheart.

He sighed. "It's not your fault." He felt weighed down with worry. How were they going to explain this to the Clan? No fresh-kill for the elders – there wasn't time to go back for the vole now – and a soaked Greystripe. Fireheart shuddered as he thought how close he had come to losing his closest friend. Thank StarClan that Silverstream had been there to save him.

"The stream near the training hollow is still running with water," Brackenpaw meowed thoughtfully from the back.

"What?" asked Fireheart, puzzled out of his gloomy thoughts.

"The Clan will probably assume that Greystripe fell in there," continued the young apprentice.

"We could say he was showing us how to catch fish," Cinderpaw added.

"I'm not sure any cat would believe Greystripe would

get his paws wet on purpose in this weather," Fireheart pointed out.

"Well, I don't want the rest of the Clan to know I had to be rescued by a RiverClan cat!" meowed Greystripe with a flash of his old spirit. "And we can't let them know we were in RiverClan's territory again."

Fireheart nodded. "Come on," he meowed. "Let's run the rest of the way; it'll help Greystripe warm up."

The cats raced across the RiverClan border and past Sunningrocks. As the sun began to dip behind the treetops, they arrived back outside the camp.

Greystripe's fur had dried a little, but frozen droplets hung on his whiskers and tail.

Fireheart led the way through the gorse entrance. His heart sank when he saw Tigerclaw sitting in the clearing watching them.

The deputy fixed his sharp eyes on Fireheart. "No fresh-kill?" he growled. "I thought you were meant to be teaching these two how to hunt today. You look half-drowned, Greystripe. You must have fallen into a river to get that wet." His nostrils flared and he drew himself up to his full height. "Don't tell me you've been into RiverClan territory again!"

CHAPTER 12

Fireheart lifted his head, about to speak, but Cinderpaw beat him to it.

"It's my fault, Tigerclaw." She stared boldly up at the great tabby. "We were hunting on the frozen stream by the training hollow, on the bend by the deep pool. Even that bit was frozen. I slipped and Greystripe came to help me, but the ice wasn't thick enough for him and it cracked and he fell into the water." Tigerclaw looked into her clear, bright eyes as she added, "It really is deep there. Fireheart had to pull him out."

Fireheart cringed, remembering how he had stood motionless with terror at the sight of Greystripe disappearing into the river.

Tigerclaw nodded and looked at Greystripe. "You'd better get yourself to Yellowfang before you freeze to death."

The ThunderClan deputy stood up and stalked away, and Fireheart breathed a sigh of relief.

Greystripe didn't hesitate. The long run home hadn't stopped his teeth from chattering. He bounded away to Yellowfang's den. Brackenpaw glanced at Cinderpaw and padded off to his nest, his tail drooping with exhaustion.

Fireheart looked at Cinderpaw. "Aren't you even a bit frightened by Tigerclaw?" he asked curiously.

"Why should I be?" replied Cinderpaw. "He's a great warrior. I admire him."

Of course, why shouldn't she? Fireheart thought. "You lie very well," he growled sternly, trying his best to act like a mentor.

"Well, I try not to," mewed Cinderpaw. "I just thought the truth wouldn't be very helpful here."

Fireheart had to admit she had a point. He shook his head slowly. "Go and get warm."

"Yes, Fireheart!" Cinderpaw dipped her head and charged after Brackenpaw.

Fireheart padded over to the warriors' den. He was worried at how easily the story about Greystripe's soaking had tumbled from Cinderpaw's mouth. But he also believed she was a well-meaning and honest cat. He thought of Ravenpaw, another good cat. Had the story he'd told about Tigerclaw killing Redtail simply been just that – a story that tumbled from his mouth in the heat of the moment? Fireheart shook the thought away. Ravenpaw had been terrified when he spoke to Fireheart. He obviously believed his own story. Why else would he have been frightened enough to leave the Clan?

Fireheart chose a few pieces of fresh-kill and carried them over to the nettle clump. He settled himself beside it and began to gnaw thoughtfully on a mouse. The admiration in Cinderpaw's voice when she had spoken of Tigerclaw worried him. It seemed as though he alone suspected there was more to the ThunderClan deputy than met the eye. Bluestar's attitude towards Tigerclaw certainly hadn't changed. She had been treating him with the same trust and respect that she had always shown him. With a flash of frustration, Fireheart ripped another mouthful from his meal.

A loud sneeze made him look up. Greystripe was heading towards him.

"How are you?" Fireheart asked as Greystripe arrived, smelling of one of Yellowfang's herbal concoctions.

Greystripe sat down heavily and coughed.

"I've saved you some food," Fireheart meowed, pushing a plump thrush and a vole towards his friend.

"Yellowfang says I have to stay in camp. She says I have a chill," Greystripe meowed thickly.

"I'm not surprised. What did she dose you with?"

"Feverfew and lavender." Greystripe lay down and began to nibble at the thrush. "This'll be enough for me," he mumbled. "I'm not very hungry."

Fireheart looked at his friend in amazement. That wasn't something he had ever thought he'd hear Greystripe say. "You sure?" he asked. "There's plenty here."

Greystripe stared down at the thrush and didn't reply.

"Are you sure?" Fireheart repeated.

"What?" Greystripe turned his faraway gaze on Fireheart. "Uh, yeah," he meowed.

He must have a fever, Fireheart decided, shaking his head. Oh, well, at least he was still here, thanks to that RiverClan cat.

A few days later Fireheart woke to find the first fog of leaf-bare filling the den. When he crept outside, he could barely see the other side of the clearing. He heard pawsteps hurrying towards him and Mousefur appeared out of the gloom.

"Tigerclaw wants to see you," she meowed.

"Right, thanks," answered Fireheart. Alarm shot through him. He'd slipped away to visit Princess yesterday. Had Tigerclaw noticed?

"What was that?" Greystripe's voice wheezed behind him. He sat down beside Fireheart, sneezed and yawned.

"Tigerclaw wants to see me." Fireheart looked at his friend. "You should be asleep." He was beginning to worry about Greystripe. He ought to have recovered by now. "Did you rest up yesterday?" he asked.

"As much as I could between coughing and sneezing," complained Greystripe.

"Then why weren't you in your nest when I got back from" – Fireheart hesitated, remembering he'd spent the afternoon talking with Princess – "training?"

"Do you think I get any peace and quiet in there?" Greystripe flicked his head back at the den. "Warriors trooping in and out all day! I found somewhere quieter, that's all."

Fireheart was about to ask where, but Greystripe spoke first. "I wonder what Tigerclaw wants?"

Fireheart's paws prickled. "I'd better go and find out."

He could just see the shapes of Tigerclaw and Whitestorm through the mist, sitting below the Highrock. As Fireheart padded over to them, they stopped talking and Tigerclaw turned to him. "It's time Cinderpaw and Brackenpaw were assessed," he growled.

"Already?" Fireheart meowed in surprise. The apprentices had not been training long.

"Bluestar wants to see how their training is progressing. Especially with Greystripe being too ill to train Brackenpaw. If Brackenpaw is falling behind, she needs to know so she can appoint another mentor for him."

Fireheart's tail twitched with annoyance. Surely Greystripe would recover soon. It would be unfair to entrust his first apprentice to someone else. "I've been taking Brackenpaw out with me and Cinderpaw every day," he meowed quickly.

Tigerclaw glanced at Whitestorm and nodded. "Yes, but

this is your first time as a mentor. It's a lot for you to take on, and ThunderClan needs well-trained warriors."

I know, and I'm just a kittypet, not a Clanborn warrior, Fireheart thought bitterly. He looked down at his paws, stinging with resentment. No one had asked him to take on Brackenpaw and he'd been putting in a lot of effort with both apprentices.

Tigerclaw went on. "Send Brackenpaw and Cinderpaw on a hunting mission through Tallpines, as far as Twolegplace. Keep an eye on them, watch them hunt, and report to me. I'll be interested to see how much fresh-kill they add to the pile."

Whitestorm added, "If Cinderpaw's skills match her enthusiasm, there should be plenty to eat tonight. I hear she is a keen apprentice."

"Yes, she is," Fireheart agreed, though he was barely listening. Tigerclaw's words had set his heart racing. *Why was Tigerclaw sending him to Twolegplace again?* His own hunting assessment had been held over exactly the same route, and Tigerclaw had seen him sharing words with an old kittypet friend; he'd reported it to Bluestar and she had questioned Fireheart's loyalty to the Clan. Fireheart felt the fur along his spine begin to prickle. Was this Tigerclaw's way of warning him that he had been spotted talking to Princess?

Fireheart twisted his head and gave his back a quick lick, brushing his bristling hairs flat with his tongue. He sat up straight again and calmly suggested, "The Sunningrocks would be an equally good place to test their skills. The sun there might have burned away some of this mist, too."

"No," growled Tigerclaw. "The dawn patrol reported scenting RiverClan at Sunningrocks. They may have started hunting there again." Anger flared in his eyes and his lip curled to reveal sharp teeth. "They will need to be warned off before we do training there. For now, Tallpines would be much safer for the assessment."

Whitestorm nodded in agreement while Fireheart's ears twitched uncomfortably at this news. RiverClan at Sunningrocks! It was lucky they hadn't been spotted by enemy patrols when Greystripe fell into the river.

"As for the fog," Tigerclaw continued smoothly, "hunting in difficult conditions will make the test more interesting."

"Yes, Tigerclaw," meowed Fireheart, ducking his head respectfully to the two warriors. "I'll tell Cinderpaw and Brackenpaw. We'll get started right away."

When Fireheart explained the assessment to the apprentices, Cinderpaw flicked up her tail and ran in an excited circle. "An assessment! Do you think we're ready?"

"Of course," Fireheart meowed, hiding his doubts. "You've been working hard and learning quickly."

"But won't the fog make hunting difficult?" asked Brackenpaw.

"There are advantages to the stillness of the air," Fireheart replied.

Brackenpaw looked thoughtful, then his eyes began to shine and he mewed, "It'll be harder to sniff out prey, but it'll also make it harder for the prey to smell us."

"Exactly," Fireheart agreed.

"Shall we go now?" Cinderpaw asked.

"As soon as you like," answered Fireheart. "But take your time; it's not a race..." His words were wasted on Cinderpaw, who was already charging towards the camp entrance. "You've got till sunset," he called after her. Brackenpaw glanced at Fireheart and turned to follow his sister with a small sigh.

Fireheart tracked the two apprentices through the Tallpines. The springy layer of pine needles underpaw felt strangely soft after the frozen ground in the rest of the forest. He followed Cinderpaw's trail until he could see her stalking eagerly through the forest. Then he picked up Brackenpaw's scent and followed that. The trails crossed here and there. Fireheart could smell where the apprentices had run fast, where they had sat down, even where they had lingered together at one point.

Before long Fireheart found a spot where Cinderpaw had made a kill. She had taken it with her – as he followed her trail, he could smell the scent of her catch mingling with her own. Then he discovered where Brackenpaw had caught a thrush. The feathers were scattered everywhere. The apprentices were hunting well. Fireheart knew this for sure when he detected a scent thick with fresh-kill. He dug down among the needles at the roots of a pine. There was a stash of prey hidden underneath it, left by Cinderpaw to pick up later. Fireheart felt a small glow of pride at her work. She had caught plenty, and now she was heading for the oak woods behind the Twolegplace.

Fireheart followed. Just beyond the edge of the pine forest, he picked up Brackenpaw's scent. It was strong, which meant the apprentice was nearby. Fireheart crept forwards and peered around a young oak. The apprentice was crouching beneath a tangle of brambles, well disguised among its shadows. Fireheart could just see his tail moving as it twitched from side to side.

Brackenpaw had his eyes fixed on a wood mouse that was scrambling around the roots of a tree. Brackenpaw was taking his time. *Good*, thought Fireheart. He watched Brackenpaw draw himself forwards, one step at a time. The leaves beneath his paws hardly made a sound. He was as quiet as the mouse itself, which continued to hunt for food, suspecting nothing. Fireheart watched breathlessly, remembering his first hunting mission.

Brackenpaw closed in. The soft rustle of his paws on leaves melted into the background sounds of the forest. Fireheart found himself willing the apprentice on. Brackenpaw was only a rabbit length away from the mouse now, his body pressed flat against the forest floor. The mouse scampered on to a root and looked around. It froze. Something was wrong.

Now! thought Fireheart. Brackenpaw sprang and landed on the mouse, grasping it in his front paws. The mouse didn't have time to struggle. It was over in a single bite.

Brackenpaw raised his head. Fireheart saw the satisfied expression on the young cat's face as he breathed the scent of his fresh-kill. Then Brackenpaw darted away between the trees. Fireheart realised he was looking forwards to reporting back to Tigerclaw about his apprentices.

"Hi!" The small voice behind him made Fireheart jump into the air. He spun around.

"How are we doing?" asked Cinderpaw, looking up at him with her head to one side.

"You're not meant to ask that!" Fireheart spat, and licked his ruffled fur. "You're not supposed to speak to me at all. I'm assessing you, remember?"

"Oh!" mewed Cinderpaw. "Sorry."

Fireheart sighed. He would never have dared to approach Tigerclaw during his own assessment. He didn't want to scare Cinderpaw into obedience, as Tigerclaw had done with Ravenpaw, but he wouldn't mind a little respect every now and then. Sometimes he didn't feel like Cinderpaw's mentor at all.

Cinderpaw looked at the ground for a moment, then glanced up at him, a puzzled expression on her face. "Were you really born over there, in Twolegplace?"

The question caught Fireheart off guard. He glanced nervously in the direction of the Twoleg fence, praying that the strange scents of Cinderpaw and Brackenpaw would keep Princess inside her own garden today. "Why d'you ask?" he mewed, stalling.

"Tigerclaw mentioned it, that's all," answered Cinderpaw. She seemed genuinely curious, but Fireheart felt a dark quiver of menace at the mention of Tigerclaw's name. What else had Tigerclaw been telling Cinderpaw about him?

"I was born a kittypet," Fireheart meowed firmly. "But I'm a warrior now. My life is with the Clan. My old life wasn't bad, but it's over, and I'm glad."

"Oh, OK," mewed Cinderpaw, sounding unconcerned. "See you later!" She spun around and charged off into the trees.

Fireheart stood alone in the woods, his heart thudding as he stared at the Twoleg fence. A moon ago, his words to Cinderpaw about being glad his old life was over would have been utterly true. Now he was not so sure. His fur tingled with the knowledge that some of his happiest moments recently had been spent sharing memories with his gentle kittypet sister.

CHAPTER 13

As the sun sank into the forest, Fireheart waited beside the pine tree where Cinderpaw had buried her first lot of fresh-kill. He heard pawsteps and turned to see Cinderpaw and Brackenpaw padding towards him. Prey dangled from their mouths. Brackenpaw could barely hold his catch, it was so big. Fireheart felt a surge of relief. Even Tigerclaw couldn't criticise the apprentices' efforts.

"I'll help carry this lot back," Fireheart offered, flicking away the covering of pine needles from Cinderpaw's stash. He dug it up, grasped the fresh-kill between his teeth, and set off back to the camp.

When they arrived in the camp clearing, some of the Clan cats were already taking their share of fresh-kill from the pile. Tigerclaw must have been looking out for their return, because he padded over to them as they dropped their catch near the rest.

"They caught all this themselves?" he asked, nudging the pile with a massive paw.

"Oh, yes," Fireheart replied.

"Good," meowed Tigerclaw. "Come and join me and Bluestar. Bring some fresh-kill for yourself; we're already eating."

Cinderpaw and Brackenpaw looked at Fireheart with admiring stares – it was a privilege to eat with the Clan leader and deputy. Fireheart didn't share their excitement. He'd hoped that he would report to Bluestar alone. The last cat he wanted to share his meal with was Tigerclaw.

"By the way, have you seen Greystripe?" asked Tigerclaw. Fireheart felt a pang of concern as Tigerclaw continued: "He's supposed to stay in camp while he has this cold, but I haven't seen him since sunhigh."

Fireheart shifted his paws. Had Greystripe gone off looking for peace and quiet again? "No," he admitted. "Perhaps he's with Yellowfang?"

"Perhaps," echoed Tigerclaw, and padded away to where Bluestar was gnawing a fat pigeon.

Fireheart followed, trying to push away his growing worry about Greystripe's disappearances. He selected a small chaffinch from the pile of fresh-kill as he passed, then wished he'd chosen a vole. How was he going to give his report with a mouthful of feathers?

"Welcome, Fireheart," meowed Bluestar as Fireheart sat

down in front of her. He placed the chaffinch on the ground, but decided not to start eating.

"Tigerclaw tells me your apprentices caught plenty of prey." Bluestar's gaze was friendly. Tigerclaw, sitting up beside her, glared at him more critically, making Fireheart's tail twitch.

"Yes. They've never hunted in the mist before, but it didn't seem to put either of them off," Fireheart meowed. "I watched Brackenpaw catch a wood mouse. His stalking was excellent."

"And what about Cinderpaw?" asked Bluestar.

Fireheart noticed a steely glint appear in her eyes. Was she worried about Cinderpaw's abilities? Fireheart replied, "Her hunting skills are developing well. She has lots of enthusiasm, that's for sure, and she doesn't seem to be scared of anything."

"Aren't you worried that might make her reckless?" asked Bluestar.

"She's quick and inquisitive, which makes her a good learner. I think that will make up for her" – Fireheart searched anxiously for the right word – "eagerness."

Bluestar flicked her tail. "Her *eagerness*, as you say, worries me," she meowed, flashing a glance at Tigerclaw. "She will need careful guidance in her training." Fireheart's spirits plummeted. Was Bluestar unhappy with his mentoring?

Bluestar's eyes softened. "She was always going to be a challenge. But she is clearly turning into a fine hunter. You have done good work with her, Fireheart. With both of them, in fact." Fireheart brightened immediately, and Bluestar went on. "I've noticed how you've taken over Brackenpaw's training without being asked, and I want you to carry on mentoring them both for the time being."

Tigerclaw turned his gaze away, but Fireheart didn't miss the anger that flashed in his eyes. "Thank you, Bluestar," he meowed.

"I see your missing friend has returned," Tigerclaw growled without turning his head.

Fireheart spun around to see Greystripe appearing from behind the nursery. "He was probably just getting some peace and quiet," he suggested. "He's still feverish, and it can't be easy being stuck in the camp all day."

"Easy or not, he should be concentrating on getting better," meowed Tigerclaw. "Leaf-bare is no time for sickness in the camp. Mousefur was coughing on patrol this morning. I just hope StarClan protects us from greencough this season. We lost five kits to it last year."

Bluestar nodded her grey head solemnly. "Let's pray this leaf-bare isn't as long or as hard. It's never an easy time for the Clans." She looked wistful for a moment, then told Fireheart, "Take that chaffinch and share it with Greystripe. He'll want to know how his apprentice did in the assessment."

"Yes, Bluestar. Thanks," meowed Fireheart. He picked up the chaffinch and bounded over to the nettle clump where

Greystripe had settled himself with a large wood mouse. Greystripe had eaten half of it by the time Fireheart arrived. Perhaps his cold was on the mend.

As Fireheart dropped the chaffinch beside his friend, Greystripe sneezed.

"Cold no better?" asked Fireheart sympathetically.

"Nope," replied Greystripe with his mouth full. "I guess I'll have to stay in camp a while longer."

Fireheart thought his friend sounded a lot more cheerful than he had before, but he didn't want to betray his growing suspicion that Greystripe was up to something.

"Brackenpaw did really well in his assessment today," he meowed.

"Really?" Greystripe took another bite of mouse. "That's good."

"Yeah, he's a great hunter." Fireheart started to eat his chaffinch. "Greystripe," he meowed after a long silence, "have you been out of the camp the past few days?"

Greystripe stopped chewing. "Why do you ask?"

Fireheart's tail twitched uncomfortably. "Well, you weren't here when I got in from last night's patrol, and Tigerclaw said he hadn't seen you since sunhigh today."

"Tigerclaw?" Greystripe sounded worried.

"I told him you were probably out looking for peace and quiet, or that you might be with Yellowfang," Fireheart meowed. He took another bite of chaffinch. "Were you?" he asked through the feathers, suddenly desperate for

Greystripe to say yes, to stop the suspicion that Greystripe might be keeping a secret from him.

But Greystripe ignored Fireheart's query. "Well, thanks for covering for me." He carried on chewing.

Fireheart didn't ask any more questions, even though he was burning with curiosity. When Greystripe got to his paws and announced he was going to the den, Fireheart was still no wiser about what was on Greystripe's mind.

"OK," he meowed. "I think I'll stay here a bit longer." Greystripe gave him a brief nod and padded away. Fireheart rolled on to his back for a long stretch, scratching the ground above his head with his claws. He lay on his back for a while, thinking. From the smell of him, Greystripe had given himself a good wash very recently. Was he trying to hide some scent? Fireheart realised that Greystripe had pretty much admitted he had left the camp. But where could he have gone that he couldn't, or wouldn't, tell Fireheart? Suddenly his paws prickled – what about his own visits to Princess, in Twoleg territory, of all places! He'd washed himself thoroughly before returning to camp too, and never mentioned the meetings to Greystripe.

Fireheart flipped over and sat up. There was something caught under one of his claws. He lifted his paw and tugged out the piece of dirt with his teeth. It was a catkin, old and shrivelled, but definitely a catkin. What was this doing here? Willow trees didn't grow in ThunderClan's part of the forest – in fact, the only willows Fireheart had ever seen grew close to the river, in RiverClan territory. Fireheart held his breath as his heart began to pound. Had this come from Greystripe's coat?

He crept into the warriors' den. Greystripe was already asleep. Fireheart lay awake beside him and wondered if Greystripe had really been foolish enough to return to RiverClan territory. The look in Leopardfur's eyes after Whiteclaw's death had shown that there was a score to be settled. Fireheart shuddered as he resolved to find out exactly where Greystripe was going, and why.

When Fireheart awoke the den felt damp and chilled. One sniff of the air told him rain was on the way. He pushed his way outside, yawning. He hadn't slept well, worrying about Greystripe. Even now, the thought of his friend alone in RiverClan territory sent a shiver through him.

"Chilly, eh?" Runningwind's voice startled Fireheart. Fireheart looked over his shoulder, his tail twitching. The lean tabby warrior was padding out of the den.

"Er, yeah," Fireheart agreed.

"Are you OK?" asked Runningwind. "Not caught your friend's cold, have you? Mousefur's streaming with it this morning, and Longtail said Swiftpaw sneezed all through training yesterday."

Fireheart shook his head. "I'm fine. Just tired after yesterday's assessment."

"Ah. Bluestar thought you might be. That's why she

asked me to help you with Cinderpaw and Brackenpaw's training today. Is that OK with you?"

"Yeah, thanks," Fireheart meowed.

"Right, then," Runningwind decided. "I'll meet you in the hollow after I've eaten. If Swiftpaw's coming down with a cold, we should have the place to ourselves. Are you hungry?" Fireheart shook his head, and Runningwind trotted away to pick through the leftovers from last night's fresh-kill.

Fireheart went straight to the training hollow and waited for the others to arrive. His mind was not on training; he was still thinking about Greystripe. He felt sure his friend would slip out of camp again today.

A rain-laden wind was beginning to sway the leafless branches above the hollow when Cinderpaw and Brackenpaw arrived, followed by Runningwind.

"What are we doing today?" asked Cinderpaw, scampering down into the hollow. Fireheart stared at her blankly. He hadn't thought about it at all.

"Hunting?" Brackenpaw mewed hopefully as he trotted after Cinderpaw.

Runningwind padded across the hollow and joined them. "How about practising some stalking techniques?" he suggested.

"Good idea," Fireheart agreed quickly.

"Not the old 'rabbit hears you, mouse feels you' lesson again!" Cinderpaw moaned.

Runningwind silenced her with a look and turned to Fireheart.

Fireheart realised with a jump that Runningwind was waiting for him to start. "Er, I'll start by showing you the best way to stalk rabbit," he stammered. He dropped into a crouch and began to move forwards, fast and light, until he reached the end of the hollow. He stood and turned to find the other three cats staring at him quizzically.

"Are you sure that'd fool a rabbit?" mewed Cinderpaw, her whiskers twitching.

Fireheart felt confused for a moment until he realised he'd just demonstrated his best bird-stalking technique. A rabbit would have heard the swish of his fur through the undergrowth three fox lengths away.

Fireheart looked at Runningwind, embarrassed. The tabby warrior frowned. "How about I show you two how to creep up on a shrew?" Cinderpaw turned her bright gaze from Fireheart to Runningwind. Fireheart sighed and padded over to watch.

By sunhigh, Fireheart was still finding it difficult to concentrate on the training session. He kept imagining Greystripe sneaking out of the camp, and longed to follow him. Eventually his restlessness overwhelmed him. He went over to Runningwind and spoke quietly into his ear. "I have a bellyache," he meowed. "Can you take over the training for the rest of the day? I want to see if Yellowfang has anything for it."

"I thought you seemed a little distracted," Runningwind replied. "You go back to camp. I'll take this pair out hunting."

"Thanks, Runningwind," meowed Fireheart, feeling a pang of shame that Runningwind had believed him so easily.

He limped across the hollow, trying to look as if he were in pain. As soon as he was safely among the trees, he broke into a run and raced back to the camp. When Greystripe had returned yesterday, he'd appeared from behind the nursery. Fireheart knew from experience that this was the best place to slip through the camp boundary without being noticed – it was where Yellowfang had escaped from the camp when the Clan had suspected the old medicine cat of Spottedleaf's murder.

Fireheart padded around the outside of the camp and sniffed at the wall of bracken. His heart sank as he picked up Greystripe's scent. Greystripe had definitely been sneaking out of the camp this way, and often by the smell of it. At least the scent was stale, which meant he hadn't been this way today.

Fireheart crouched behind a nearby tree and settled down to wait. The wood was growing darker as rain clouds began to push across the sky. The shadows hid him perfectly, and he made sure he was downwind so Greystripe wouldn't detect him. His belly really was aching now, tense with guilt and apprehension. He half hoped Greystripe wouldn't come, half hoped he would just lead him to some quiet spot within ThunderClan's borders.

Fireheart's heart lurched as he heard a rustling in the bracken wall. A grey nose was pushing its way through the fronds. Fireheart ducked his head as Greystripe looked around cautiously. After a few moments, the warrior leaped out and set off at a trot towards the training hollow.

Hope flared in Fireheart's chest. Perhaps Greystripe's cold was better and he'd decided to join the training session. He set off after him, keeping a safe distance behind, relying on scent rather than sight to track his friend.

But when the trail veered away from the path that led to the training hollow, Fireheart knew that his hope had been in vain. With an ominous sense of dread, he saw the distinctive grey rock loom ahead through the trees: Sunningrocks. Fireheart pricked his ears and opened his mouth, testing the breeze for the smell of enemy cats. At the edge of the trees, he caught a glimpse of a broad-shouldered grey cat slipping past the rocks, towards the RiverClan border. There was no doubt now where Greystripe was heading.

As soon as his friend was out of sight, Fireheart padded forwards and peered down the slope to the river. By the swaying of the undergrowth, Fireheart could guess where Greystripe was. He just hoped there weren't any RiverClan warriors watching too.

Fireheart made his way down through the fronds. The river wasn't frozen any more – he could hear the water lapping at the bank and splashing over the boulders. He slowed his pace as he reached the edge of the bracken and peered out at the open shore.

Greystripe was sitting on the pebbles. The grey warrior was looking around, his ears pricked, but Fireheart could tell from the relaxed slope of his shoulders that he wasn't listening for prey.

A strange cat's call sounded in the distance. A RiverClan patrol? Fireheart's fur prickled and his muscles instinctively tensed, but Greystripe didn't move. Then Fireheart heard a rustle in the bracken beyond the river. Still Greystripe stayed where he was. Fireheart held his breath as a face appeared on the far riverbank. With barely a sound, the silver she-cat emerged from the undergrowth and slipped into the river. Fireheart felt his heart miss a beat. It was Silverstream, the she-cat who had rescued his friend!

She swam easily across the river. Greystripe stood up and mewed with delight, kneading the pebbles with his paws in anticipation. Holding his tail high, he padded to the edge of the water as she climbed on to the shore.

Silverstream shook the drops from her fur and the two grey cats touched noses gently. Greystripe rubbed his muzzle along her jaw and she lifted her chin happily. Then Silverstream stood on tiptoe and wound her slender body around his. For once Greystripe didn't seem to mind getting wet at all, because he purred loud enough for Fireheart to hear as Silverstream pressed her damp fur against him.

CHAPTER 14

FIREHEART'S HACKLES BRISTLED with horror. How could Greystripe be so stupid? He was breaking every part of the warrior code by meeting this cat from another Clan.

"Greystripe!" Fireheart hissed as he sprang from the bushes.

The two cats spun around to face him. Silverstream's ears flattened angrily. Greystripe just stared at him, startled. "You followed me!"

Fireheart ignored his stunned meow. "What are you doing? Don't you know how dangerous this is?"

Silverstream spoke up. "It's OK. There won't be a patrol here till after sunset."

"You can be sure of that, can you? As if you know all your Clan's movements!" Fireheart growled.

Silverstream lifted her chin. "Actually, I do. My father is

Crookedstar, the leader of RiverClan."

Fireheart froze. "What are you playing at?" he spat at Greystripe. "Could you have chosen worse?"

Greystripe met Fireheart's eyes for an instant, then turned to Silverstream. "I'd better go," he mewed.

Silverstream blinked slowly and stretched her head forwards to touch his cheek. They closed their eyes and remained still for a moment. Fireheart watched, his paws prickling with alarm. Silverstream whispered something into Greystripe's ear and the two cats stepped apart. The RiverClan she-cat raised her head and stared challengingly into Fireheart's eyes before slipping back into the river.

Greystripe bounded over to Fireheart's side. The two friends didn't speak as they raced out of RiverClan territory and back past Sunningrocks. As they approached the camp, Greystripe slowed his pace.

Fireheart slowed too. "You must stop seeing her," he panted. His panic had lessened now they were well away from the RiverClan border, but he was still angry.

"I can't," replied Greystripe hoarsely. He coughed, his sides heaving.

"I don't understand," Fireheart meowed. "RiverClan is completely hostile to ThunderClan at the moment. You heard Leopardfur after Whiteclaw died." Fireheart winced, knowing that the reminder would be painful for his friend, but he couldn't stop now. "How do you even know you can trust this RiverClan cat?"

"You don't know Silverstream," Greystripe spat back. He stopped and sat down. His eyes glazed with pain. "And there's no need to remind me about Whiteclaw. Do you think it's easy knowing I'm responsible for the death of one of Silverstream's Clan mates?" Fireheart snorted impatiently – Whiteclaw was an enemy warrior, not a *Clan mate*! But Greystripe went on. "Silverstream understands it was an accident. The gorge was no place for a battle. Any cat could have fallen there!"

Fireheart paced around him as Greystripe began to lick the scent of Silverstream from his fur. "It doesn't matter what Silverstream thinks! What about your loyalty to ThunderClan?" he demanded. "You're breaking the Clan code by seeing her!"

Greystripe stopped washing. "You think I don't know that?" he hissed. "Do you doubt my loyalty to ThunderClan?"

"What else can I think? You can't see her without lying to the Clan. And what if we have a battle with RiverClan? Have you thought about that?"

"You worry too much," Greystripe snapped. "It won't come to that. Now that Brokenstar's gone and WindClan is back, the Clans will be at peace."

"RiverClan doesn't seem to be acting very peacefully," Fireheart pointed out. "You know they've been hunting on Sunningrocks, in our territory."

"They've been hunting on Sunningrocks since before I was kitted," scoffed Greystripe, twisting to wash the base of his tail.

Fireheart carried on pacing. Greystripe just didn't seem to understand what he was doing. "OK. What if a RiverClan patrol catches you?"

"Silverstream won't let that happen," answered Greystripe between long licks along his bushy tail.

"For StarClan's sake, aren't you even a bit worried?" Fireheart burst out, exasperated.

Greystripe stopped washing and looked up at his friend. "You don't get it, do you? StarClan must have planned this. Look, Silverstream wants to see me – *even after what happened to Whiteclaw*. We share the same thoughts; it's as if we were born into the same Clan."

Fireheart realised it was pointless to argue any more. "Come on," he meowed heavily. "We'd better get back before you're missed again."

Greystripe got to his paws. Side by side, he and Fireheart walked to the top of the ravine and looked down at the camp. Over and over, one thought echoed in Fireheart's mind – how could Greystripe love Crookedstar's daughter, but remain loyal to ThunderClan?

He glanced at Greystripe and they began to climb down the steep slope home. They crept back into the camp the same way Greystripe had left it. Fireheart held his breath as he squeezed through the boundary wall, angry with Greystripe for making him sneak around like this. His heart sank as they rounded the nursery to find Whitestorm approaching them.

"Greystripe, you should be resting, not hanging around

here. That cough of yours has already begun to spread. We don't want it getting into the nursery!" warned the warrior. Greystripe nodded and padded back towards the warriors' den. "And you" – Fireheart's ears flicked nervously as Whitestorm turned to him – "shouldn't you be training your apprentices?"

"I came back to get something from Yellowfang for a bellyache," Fireheart mumbled.

"Well, go and get it then," replied Whitestorm. "And once you have, you can make yourself useful and find some fresh-kill. It's leaf-bare – we can't have young warriors hanging around the camp doing nothing!"

"Yes, Whitestorm," meowed Fireheart. He turned away, relieved to escape questions, and ran towards Yellowfang's den.

Yellowfang was busy mixing herbs. There were several heaps of leaves gathered in front of her. Fireheart stood and watched her for a moment without speaking. He felt sad, drained after the row with Greystripe. He couldn't help wishing it were Spottedleaf here mixing herbs instead of Yellowfang.

Yellowfang glanced up at him. "My supplies are running low. I might need help to restock."

Fireheart didn't reply. He was just wondering if he should confide his worries about Greystripe when she interrupted his thoughts.

"It looks like there's whitecough in the camp," she growled, prodding impatiently at a dried leaf. "Two cases this morning."

"Swiftpaw?" asked Fireheart.

The old medicine cat shook her head. "Swiftpaw's just got a cold. It's Speckletail's kit. And Patchpelt. Not serious at the moment, but we need to concentrate on getting the Clan strong. Leaf-bare always brings the threat of greencough." Fireheart understood her concern. Greencough was a killer. Yellowfang looked up again. "What do you want?"

"Oh, nothing, just a bellyache, but it doesn't matter if you're busy."

"Bad?" she meowed.

"No," Fireheart admitted, unable to meet her gaze.

"Then come back when it is." The medicine cat went back to her mixing. Fireheart turned to leave, but Yellowfang called him back. "Make sure Greystripe stays in his den, will you? He's a strong young warrior. If he were resting, his cough would be better by now."

Fireheart's tail twitched nervously. Had she guessed that Greystripe had been slipping out of the camp? He waited, his heart thudding, in case she was going to say more, but Yellowfang was frowning at the herbs again, so he padded quietly away.

It was getting dark and Fireheart knew he had only a short time left for hunting. He quickly caught a shrew, a chaffinch and a mouse, but hesitated before returning to camp. His fears for Greystripe felt more important than anything Whitestorm might say if he didn't add something to the fresh-kill pile in time. Fireheart came to a decision – if

Greystripe wouldn't listen to reason, maybe Silverstream would.

He stashed his catch beneath a tree root and covered it with leaves. For the second time that day, he turned towards Sunningrocks. The rain that had been threatening all day finally began to fall. It was drumming steadily on the bracken by the time Fireheart crept down the shadowy slope towards the river.

Even in the rain, Silverstream's scent was easy to find. Fireheart followed the trail to the place where he had found Greystripe and Silverstream together. Hyper-alert, he padded on to the shore. The dark water rushed past relentlessly, sending a shiver down Fireheart's spine. He had no desire to swim across. His fur did not have the oily protection from the water that the pelts of the RiverClan cats had, and leaf-bare was no season to get a soaking.

Suddenly Fireheart froze. He smelled RiverClan warriors!

He dropped to a crouch and looked across the river to see Silverstream pushing her way through the trailing branches of a willow. Behind her came two of her Clan, one of them a warrior with massive shoulders and battle-torn ears. The warrior sniffed the air suspiciously and peered around.

Fireheart heard the blood roaring in his ears. Had the warrior picked up his scent?

CHAPTER 15

VERY, VERY QUIETLY, Fireheart backed into the bracken. The RiverClan warrior had stopped smelling the air, but he was still looking around.

Fireheart turned, still crouching, and began to creep away. He heard a small splash behind him. A cat had slipped into the river. Fireheart glanced over his shoulder, his heart pounding. Through the bracken he could see a silver head bobbing towards him. Silverstream! But where were the two other cats? He circled cautiously, tasting the air with an open mouth. No scent of them nearby. They must have moved on. He looked back at Silverstream, swimming determinedly across the river. For a moment Fireheart wondered if this was a trap, wondered if he should run, but his concern about Greystripe made him stay.

The silver tabby climbed on to the bank and hissed quietly, "Fireheart, I know you're there. I can smell you! It's OK, Stonefur and Shadepaw have gone."

Fireheart didn't move.

"Fireheart, I wouldn't let anything happen to Greystripe's closest friend!" She sounded impatient. "Believe me, for StarClan's sake!"

Fireheart crept slowly from his hiding place.

Silverstream stared at him, her tail twitching. "What are you doing here?"

"I was looking for you," he whispered, painfully aware he was in enemy territory.

Silverstream flicked her ears in alarm. "Is Greystripe OK? Has his cough got worse?"

Fireheart was irritated by her concern. He didn't want to know how much this she-cat cared for his best friend. "He's fine!" he growled, his caution swept away by anger. "But he won't be if he carries on meeting you!"

Silverstream bristled. "I won't let anything bad happen to Greystripe!"

"Oh, really?" Fireheart snorted. "And what could you do to protect him?"

"I am a Clan leader's daughter," meowed Silverstream.

"Does that give you the power to control your father's warriors? You're hardly more than an apprentice!"

"Like you!" she hissed indignantly.

"Yes, that's true," Fireheart admitted. "And that's why I'm

not sure I could protect Greystripe from the anger of his own Clan – or yours – if they find out you're seeing each other."

Silverstream tried to glare at him, but her eyes were clouded with emotion. "I can't stop seeing him," she meowed. Her voice softened to a whisper. "I love him."

"But the tension between our Clans is bad enough already!" Fireheart was too angry to feel any sympathy. "We know RiverClan is hunting in our territory..."

The defiant gleam returned to Silverstream's eyes. "If ThunderClan understood why, they wouldn't begrudge what we catch there!"

"Why?" Fireheart flashed back at her.

"My Clan is hungry. Our kits cry because their mothers have no milk. The elders are dying for lack of decent prey."

Fireheart stared, taken aback. "But you've got the river!" he protested. Every cat knew that RiverClan enjoyed the best hunting of all – fish from the river, as well as woodland prey in the fields beyond.

"It's not enough. Twolegs have taken over our territory downstream. They built a camp there all greenleaf and stayed as long as the fish were plentiful. By the time they went, the fishing was scarce. And the damage they've done to the forest means that even woodland prey is harder to find."

Fireheart felt a pang of pity in spite of his anger. He could guess how serious this must be for RiverClan. They were used to their rich diet of fish, and grew fat on it every greenleaf so that they could endure the harsh moons of leaf-bare. He stared at the she-cat with new eyes. She wasn't slim, he realised – she was skinny. As her wet coat clung to her, he could see her ribs. Suddenly he understood Crookedstar's hostility to Bluestar's plan at the Gathering. "That's why you didn't want WindClan to come home!"

"Rabbits run on the moorlands all year round," Silverstream explained. "They were our only hope of making it through leaf-bare without losing kits." She shook her head slowly before lifting her gaze back to Fireheart.

"Does Greystripe know all this?" he asked.

Silverstream nodded. Fireheart looked at her, perplexed for a moment. But he couldn't let these feelings get in the way of the warrior code – and neither could his friend. "Whatever problems your Clan has, you still have to stop seeing Greystripe," he mewed.

"No," answered Silverstream, lifting her chin. Her eyes flashed. "How can our love do any harm?"

Fireheart returned her stare. Another shiver ran down his back as the cold rain seeped through his thick pelt.

Suddenly Silverstream hissed, making Fireheart jump. "You must leave, the patrol's coming."

Fireheart heard a faint rustle on the other side of the river. It would be pointless – and dangerous – to stay any longer. The rustling noise was growing closer. Without saying goodbye, he bounded back into the wet bracken and headed home.

He raced back towards the stash of fresh-kill he'd left beneath the oak tree. Halfway home, the scent of a fresh Twoleg trail stopped him in his tracks, reminding him of Princess. He wondered whether there was time to follow the trail back to Twolegplace. He wanted to know if she had kitted yet. But Princess would probably be safely tucked up in her Twoleg nest by now, and the Clan needed fresh-kill. With an uneasy twinge, Fireheart realised that Greystripe wasn't the only one with divided loyalties.

Rain began to drip from the end of his whiskers. He shook the drops away and bounded on towards his hoard of fresh-kill.

The camp was silent by the time he arrived, the cats sheltering in their dens. Fireheart crossed the muddy clearing and dropped his catch on the pile. Taking a piece for himself, he trotted towards the warriors' den. There was no way he was eating outside tonight.

He pushed his head inside. Greystripe was dozing, to Fireheart's relief. He might actually get better if he wasn't charging through the forest, looking for Silverstream.

"Yellowfang hasn't taken any fresh-kill yet." Whitestorm's meow sounded from the shadows. "She's been too busy. I think she would appreciate that mouse you're carrying."

Fireheart nodded and backed out again. If Yellowfang was too busy to fetch food, it must mean the sickness in the camp was getting worse. Fireheart raced across the clearing, stopping only to pick up another mouse before hurrying through the fern tunnel.

A tabby kit lay in a nest of moss in the bracken at the edge of the clearing. Yellowfang crouched beside it, trying to persuade it to eat some herbs. The kit snuffled pitifully, blinking up at her with streaming eyes and nose. Fireheart realised this must be the kit with whitecough.

Yellowfang turned when she heard Fireheart arrive. "Is that for me?" she meowed, looking at the mice hanging from Fireheart's mouth. He nodded and dropped them on the ground. "Thanks. Now that you're here, why don't you see if you can persuade this kit to take his medicine?" She padded over to the mice, moving stiffly from her old shoulder injury, and began to gnaw on one hungrily.

Fireheart approached the kit. It looked up at him, opening its tiny mouth in a rasping, painful cough. Fireheart gently pushed a small green herb towards it. "If you want to be a warrior, you'll have to get used to swallowing these horrible things," he mewed. "When you make your trip to the Moonstone, you have to eat herbs far worse than this."

The kit looked wonderingly at him.

"Think of it as practice," Fireheart urged. "Practice for when you become a warrior."

The kit reached forwards and took a tentative mouthful. Fireheart gave it an encouraging purr.

Yellowfang appeared at his side. "Well done," she

meowed. She gestured with her nose, and Fireheart understood she wanted to talk to him. He followed her to the shelter of the tall rock where she slept. The rain was still falling, and Yellowfang's matted grey fur was soaked, her sodden tail dragging in the dirt.

"Bluestar has whitecough," she meowed gravely.

"But whitecough isn't that serious, right?"

Yellowfang shook her head. "It came on very quickly," she meowed, "and it's affected her badly." Fireheart's stomach tightened as he remembered the dwindling number of lives left to the Clan leader. "I warned her to stay away from the other sick cats, but she wanted to see them," Yellowfang went on. "She's sleeping in her den at the moment. Frostfur is with her."

The fear in Yellowfang's eyes made Fireheart wonder if she knew the truth about Bluestar's lives. Fireheart had assumed he was the only cat in the camp whom Bluestar had shared her secret with. The rest of the Clan thought she had three lives left, but perhaps a medicine cat could sense these things instinctively.

The truth was, if Bluestar lost this life, she would have only one more left.

CHAPTER 16

THE RAIN CONTINUED through the night and into the next morning. But by sunhigh, the clouds began to clear. A sombre air hung over the clearing as the Clan waited for news of their leader.

Fireheart crept out from the patch of brambles by the boundary wall, where he'd sheltered since dawn. He padded over to Bluestar's den in the side of Highrock. There was no sound from inside. As he turned away, he ran into Willowpelt carrying food to the nursery. She tipped her head questioningly to one side.

Fireheart knew she was hoping for news of Bluestar. "Nothing to report, I'm afraid." He shrugged.

Fireheart had given Cinderpaw and Brackenpaw a day's rest from training. He could see them now, lounging outside their den, looking bored. Fireheart knew he had let them down, but he wanted to stay in camp while Bluestar was sick. At least Tigerclaw wasn't here to criticise his decision. The great deputy had taken out the dawn patrol.

Suddenly the lichen at Bluestar's den twitched and Frostfur burst through. She raced across the clearing to Yellowfang's den and reappeared within moments with the medicine cat behind her.

Fireheart bounded over to Bluestar's den just as Frostfur and Yellowfang pushed through the hanging lichen. He stopped outside and sat down, his heart racing. Frostfur peered out.

"What's wrong?" Fireheart asked, his voice trembling.

Frostfur closed her eyes. "She has greencough," she told him bleakly. "Stand watch and make sure no one comes in." She ducked back inside.

Fireheart sat motionless as shock flooded through him. Greencough! Bluestar really was in danger of losing another life.

A sharp yowl outside the camp made him turn and look towards the gorse tunnel. Dustpaw exploded into the clearing and skidded to a halt beside Fireheart. "I've come from Tigerclaw," he panted. "I have a message for Bluestar."

"She's sick," Fireheart replied. "You can't go in."

Dustpaw flicked his tail impatiently. "Tigerclaw needs to see her at the Thunderpath. It's very urgent."

"What's wrong?"

Dustpaw glared at him. "Tigerclaw asked for Bluestar," he sneered. "Not some kittypet pretending to be a warrior!"

Fury shot through Fireheart and he unsheathed his claws. "Bluestar can't leave the camp," he growled. He flattened his ears and moved so that he blocked the entrance to his leader's den.

"Fireheart is right." Yellowfang's rough meow sounded behind him. She had come out of Bluestar's den.

Dustpaw looked at the medicine cat, shrinking beneath her orange gaze. "Tigerclaw has found evidence of ShadowClan warriors in our territory," he meowed. "They've invaded our hunting grounds!"

In spite of his fear for Bluestar, Fireheart felt his lip curl in anger. How dare they? After what ThunderClan had done for them!

But Yellowfang wasn't interested in Dustpaw's report. She turned to Fireheart, her eyes filled with urgency. "Fireheart," she meowed. "Tell me, do you know whether there is any catnip in the Twolegplace?"

"Catnip?" Fireheart echoed.

"I need it for Bluestar," Yellowfang explained. "It's a herb I haven't used for moons, but I think it will help her." The medicine cat had Fireheart's full attention now. She continued, "It has soft leaves and an irresistible scent—"

Fireheart interrupted her. "Yes, I know where to find some!" He had never seen it in the woods, but as a kit he had rolled in a patch in his Twoleg home.

"Good," replied Yellowfang. "I need as much as you can carry, and fast."

"What about Tigerclaw?" demanded Dustpaw.

"Tigerclaw will have to deal with it on his own for the moment!" Yellowfang snapped.

Cinderpaw had been watching them from the tree stump. She bounded up. "Deal with what himself?" she mewed excitedly. Fireheart signalled her to be quiet with an urgent flick of his tail.

Dustpaw ignored the apprentice. "ShadowClan could be in our territory by now!" he hissed.

Cinderpaw's eyes widened but she held her tongue.

Yellowfang paused to think. "Where's Whitestorm?" she asked.

"Patrolling Sunningrocks with Sandpaw and Mousefur," Dustpaw answered.

Yellowfang nodded. "With Bluestar sick and Fireheart fetching catnip, we can't risk sending warriors out of the camp. If ShadowClan *is* in our territory, they might attack here. They've done it before," she reminded him grimly.

"If I'm quick getting the catnip," Fireheart put in, "I could meet Tigerclaw afterwards and bring back his message for Bluestar."

Dustpaw's eyes flashed. "But he wants Bluestar to see the evidence for herself. ShadowClan has left the remains of fresh-kill on our side of the Thunderpath!"

Yellowfang silenced him with a growl. "Bluestar doesn't

need to see the evidence," she rasped. "The word of her deputy ought to be enough."

"Tigerclaw just needs to be told that Bluestar can't come," meowed Fireheart. "I'll take the message to him after I've fetched the catnip. Where is he?"

"I'll go!" Dustpaw spat. "Do you think you're a better messenger than me because you're a warrior and I'm just an apprentice?" He threw Fireheart a look of pure hatred.

But Yellowfang had no time for quarrels. "The Clan will need protecting while Fireheart is gone!" she hissed at Dustpaw, flattening her ears. "Isn't that duty important enough for you? Now, where is Tigerclaw?"

"Beside the burned ash tree that overhangs the Thunderpath," Dustpaw replied sulkily.

"Right," Yellowfang growled. "Go now, Fireheart! Quickly!"

As Fireheart sped away across the clearing, he heard small pawsteps sprinting after him. "Fireheart, wait!"

"Go back to your den, Cinderpaw," he meowed over his shoulder without slowing down.

"But I could go and give Tigerclaw the message while you get the catnip!"

Fireheart stopped in his tracks and turned to face his young apprentice. "Cinderpaw, if there are any ShadowClan warriors around, you need to stay in camp." Cinderpaw looked crushed, but Fireheart didn't have time to worry about her feelings. "Go back to your den," he growled.

Without waiting to see her reaction, he turned and charged out of the camp.

He raced through Tallpines and weaved quickly through the undergrowth that backed on to Twolegplace. As he scrambled on to the fence that bordered his old home, the familiar smell of the garden filled his nostrils. Memories flooded his mind, making him dizzy for a moment. He thought of sunny afternoons playing in the garden with the toys his Twolegs held for him. He almost expected to hear them rattling his dinner and calling his kittypet name. Then he thought of Bluestar, fighting against greencough.

Fireheart leaped down into the garden and bounded across the lawn to the place where he remembered the catnip had grown. He inhaled deeply, his mouth open, and breathed out with relief. The enticing scent was still here somewhere.

Fireheart padded along the row of plants, sniffing the air. He couldn't see the catnip, and all the time he was getting nearer and nearer to his old Twoleg nest. Fireheart's steps grew slower. Scents of his kithood mingled with the catnip now, confusing him.

Fireheart shook his head to clear it, and concentrated on the catnip scent. He pushed his way under a large bush, still dripping from the overnight rain, and found a large patch of the soft, fragrant herb. The recent frost had killed some of the leaves, but the sheltering bush had protected enough for Yellowfang to use. Fireheart bit off as many leaves as he could carry. Their flavour seeped deliciously into his mouth, but he was careful not to chew, much as he wanted to. Bluestar would need every drop of their precious juice.

With his jaws full, he turned and raced back up the garden. He leaped over the fence and pelted back through the forest, ignoring the brambles that dragged at his coat. He felt as if his lungs would burst – with his jaws closed to hold the herbs, he could breathe only through his nose.

Yellowfang was waiting for him in the gorse tunnel. Fireheart dropped the catnip at her paws and took a long gulp of air, his sides heaving. With a grateful look, Yellowfang picked up the leaves and rushed away towards Bluestar's den.

As he sat gasping for air, Fireheart realised he could smell Cinderpaw's excited scent in the gorse tunnel. He sniffed the ground around him. Had Cinderpaw left the camp even after he'd warned her about the ShadowClan warriors?

Fireheart dashed to the apprentices' den and stuck his head inside. Brackenpaw was alone, sleeping.

"Where's Cinderpaw?" Fireheart meowed.

Brackenpaw lifted his head sleepily. "Uh, what?"

"Cinderpaw! Where is she?"

"Don't know," answered Brackenpaw, confused.

Fireheart withdrew his head and looked around the clearing. Frostfur was pacing outside Bluestar's den, her coat ruffled with agitation.

Fireheart wondered what to do. He didn't have time to find Cinderpaw himself and he didn't want to tell the other warriors that she was missing. *Greystripe!* he thought suddenly. Greystripe could look for her while he went to find Tigerclaw. Fireheart hurried to the warriors' den and slipped inside.

Greystripe's nest was empty. A flash of anger shot through Fireheart. Where was his friend when he needed him? As if he couldn't guess! Fireheart snorted crossly. Cinderpaw would have to fend for herself until he had found Tigerclaw and told him Bluestar was sick.

Fireheart raced back through the gorse tunnel and began the journey to the Thunderpath. As he followed the trail up the side of the ravine and into the woods, he was aware that Cinderpaw's scent hung in the air. She must have come this way. Of course! She had gone to meet Tigerclaw herself! The fur on Fireheart's spine prickled with worry and frustration. How could she be so foolish?

As he skirted Snakerocks, Fireheart began to smell the Thunderpath and hear the roar of its monsters.

Suddenly a shrill, high-pitched squeal sounded from the edge of the trees. Fireheart felt the blood run cold in his veins. It was the same cry he had heard in his dream.

He raced out of the trees and skidded to a halt on the grass border beside the Thunderpath. He looked desperately up and down the verge and spotted an ash tree, charred by lightning. That must be the place where

Dustpaw had said Tigerclaw wanted to meet Bluestar. But the deputy was still some way in the distance, padding calmly towards the ash.

Fireheart broke into a run. The verge was very narrow here, with scarcely room for a rabbit, but Fireheart kept going. He called out to Tigerclaw as he ran.

"Did you hear that cry?" But the roar of an approaching monster drowned out his words.

Fireheart shuddered as it passed, waiting for the noise to die away so he could call out again to Tigerclaw. Then he noticed something beneath the ash, a dark shape on the thin strip of grass. With a sickening jolt, he recognised the small body lying motionless beside the Thunderpath. It was Cinderpaw.

CHAPTER 17

FIREHEART STARED IN horror. Ahead of him, Tigerclaw had reached the limp body and stood looking down at it, his massive shoulders rigid with shock. Fireheart forced himself nearer. Tentatively he stretched his head forwards and sniffed Cinderpaw's flank. She smelled of Thunderpath. One of her hind legs was twisted and glistening with blood. Fireheart was trembling so much he could hardly stand. Then he saw her side moving. She was still breathing! Speechless with relief, he looked up at Tigerclaw.

"She's alive," the deputy growled. He fixed his amber stare on Fireheart. "What was she doing here?"

"She came to find you," Fireheart whispered.

"You mean you sent her here?"

Fireheart's eyes widened with surprise. Did Tigerclaw

think he would be so stupid? "I told her to stay in camp!" he protested. "She came by herself." *Because I couldn't make her listen to me!* he realised with dismay.

Tigerclaw snorted. "We must get her home." He bent down with his mouth open, reaching for the small, crumpled body, but Fireheart dipped his head and picked up the apprentice by the scruff of her neck before Tigerclaw could touch her. He began to drag Cinderpaw into the woods as gently as he could, her body hanging limply between his front paws.

Darkstripe came bounding up to them. "I've checked Snakerocks again, Tigerclaw. There's no sign of Shadow—" He broke off when he saw Cinderpaw dangling from Fireheart's mouth. "What's happened?"

Fireheart didn't wait to hear Tigerclaw's answer. He stumbled away through the trees with his precious burden. He could have prevented this accident! If only he'd made Cinderpaw listen to him – if only he'd been a better mentor. Now her body was damaged and bleeding and she made no sound as she dangled from his jaws. Her hind paws scored a shallow trail through the leaves as, carefully, Fireheart carried her home.

Yellowfang was not in her clearing. The two kits with whitecough were curled together in their shelter, fast asleep. Fireheart laid Cinderpaw on the cold ground, then made a nest for her in the bracken by circling around and around.

When he had finished, he grasped Cinderpaw's scruff and gently pulled her inside.

"Fireheart?" Yellowfang meowed from the clearing. Tigerclaw must have told her about Cinderpaw. Fireheart hopped out of the nest. "She's in here," he croaked, feeling weak with relief at seeing the medicine cat.

"Let me look," Yellowfang ordered. She brushed past Fireheart and climbed into the bracken to examine Cinderpaw. Fireheart sat down and waited.

At last Yellowfang jumped out. "She's hurt very badly," she meowed, her eyes dark with concern. "But I think I might be able to save her."

It was a tiny hope, like a single sparkling dewdrop clinging to his pelt. Fireheart felt it glisten for a moment before Yellowfang went on: "I can't promise anything." She looked deep into Fireheart's eyes and murmured, "Bluestar is very sick and I can do no more for her. StarClan must decide her fate now."

Fireheart felt his eyes cloud with emotion; he could hardly see Yellowfang's face, but he heard her speak to him again, her voice gentle. "Go and sit with Bluestar," she meowed. "She was asking for you earlier. I will take care of Cinderpaw."

Fireheart nodded blindly and turned away. Bluestar had been his mentor, and more than that, there had been a bond between them since their first meeting. But he felt torn. He should be with Cinderpaw, too.

A shadow loomed at the far end of the fern tunnel. Tigerclaw was sitting at the entrance to Yellowfang's den, his head held high as usual. Fireheart's shoulders stiffened with anger. Why couldn't the great warrior show some sign of sorrow? After all, Cinderpaw had come looking for him. And for what? There hadn't been any evidence of ShadowClan fresh-kill that Fireheart had noticed! He walked past Tigerclaw without a word and headed across the clearing towards Bluestar's den.

Longtail was sitting on guard outside. He glanced sideways but didn't try to stop Fireheart as the young warrior pushed through the lichen.

Goldenflower, one of the queens, was inside. Fireheart could see her eyes shining in the gloom, and the pale fur of Bluestar lying curled in her nest. Goldenflower leaned forwards and gently licked Bluestar's head to cool it, like a mother nursing her kit. Fireheart's heart ached as he thought of Cinderpaw. Would Frostfur be at her daughter's side by now?

"Yellowfang has given her catnip and feverfew," Goldenflower murmured to Fireheart. "We can only watch and wait now." She got to her paws and touched Fireheart's nose with her muzzle. "Will you be OK to sit with her?" she asked gently. Fireheart nodded and Goldenflower padded softly out of the den.

Fireheart lowered himself on to his belly, stretching his forepaws in front of him so that they just touched his leader's face. He lay very still, his eyes fixed on Bluestar's limp body. She didn't even have the strength to cough now. Fireheart could hear her breathing in the darkness, shallow and rasping, and he listened to the faltering rhythm as the night slowly passed.

Her breathing stopped just before dawn. Fireheart had almost dozed off when he realised the cave was silent. There was no noise from the camp outside either, just a deathly hush, as if the whole Clan were holding its breath.

Bluestar was completely still. Fireheart knew she was with StarClan, preparing for her remaining life. He had watched Bluestar lose a life before. He felt his fur prickle at the eerie peace that seemed to enfold her body, but there was nothing he could do, so he waited.

Suddenly Bluestar gasped. "Fireheart, is that you?" she meowed in a croaky voice.

"Yes, Bluestar," Fireheart murmured. "I'm here."

"I have lost another life." Bluestar's voice was weak, but the relief made Fireheart want to reach forwards and lick her between the ears, as Goldenflower had done. "When I lose this one, I will not be able to return."

Fireheart swallowed hard. The thought of the Clan losing its great leader pained him, but the thought of losing his mentor and friend hurt even more. "How do you feel? Shall I fetch Yellowfang?"

Bluestar shook her head slowly. "The fever has gone. I am well enough. I just need to rest."

"Very well," meowed Fireheart. Light was beginning to filter through the lichen, and his head swam from his wakeful night.

"You must be tired," meowed Bluestar. "Go and get some sleep."

"Yes." Fireheart heaved himself up. His legs felt stiff from lying so long. "Is there anything you need?"

"No. Just tell Yellowfang what has happened," answered Bluestar. "Thank you for sitting with me."

Fireheart tried to purr but it caught in his throat. There would be time for more words later. He pushed his way out through the lichen.

Outside a harsh brightness made him blink. It had snowed in the night. Fireheart stared in amazement. He had never seen snow before – his Twoleg owners had kept him shut inside when he was a very young kit whenever it was cold. But he'd heard the Clan elders talk of it. He nodded to Darkstripe, who had replaced Longtail guarding Bluestar's den, and stepped into the strange powder. It felt wet and cold, crunching loudly under his paws.

Tigerclaw was standing in the clearing. It was still snowing and the flakes settled on the tabby's thick fur without melting. Fireheart could hear him giving orders for the nursery wall to be padded with leaves to keep out the cold. "Then I want a hole to be scraped out where we can store prey," the ThunderClan deputy instructed. "Use snow to line it and cover it with more snow once it has been filled.

We may as well make use of the snow while it's here."

Warriors raced around Tigerclaw, following his orders. "Mousefur, Longtail! Organise some hunting parties. We need as much fresh-kill as we can get before the prey take to their burrows for good!" Tigerclaw spotted Fireheart padding across the clearing. "Fireheart, wait," he called. "Oh, I suppose you'll have to rest. I can't imagine you'll be any use on a hunting party this morning."

Fireheart stared at the dark warrior, hostility rising like bile in his throat. "I'm going to see Cinderpaw first," he growled.

Tigerclaw held his gaze for a moment. "How's Bluestar?"

Mistrust ruffled Fireheart's fur like a cold breeze. He'd heard Bluestar lie to Tigerclaw once before about how many lives she had left. "I'm no medicine cat," he answered. "I can't say."

Tigerclaw snorted impatiently, then turned away and went back to giving orders. Fireheart walked over to Yellowfang's den, relieved to escape the frenetic bustle of the camp. His heart began to pound as he wondered what state he would find Cinderpaw in. "Yellowfang," he called.

"Hush!" Yellowfang sprang from Cinderpaw's bracken nest. "She's sleeping at last. She's had a hard night. I couldn't give her poppy seeds to ease the pain until she'd recovered from the shock."

"But she's going to live?" Fireheart's legs felt wobbly with relief.

"I can't be for sure for a few days. She's hurt inside, and one of her hind legs is badly broken."

"But it'll mend, won't it?" Fireheart pleaded desperately. "She'll be training again by newleaf?"

Yellowfang shook her head, her orange eyes sympathetic. "Fireheart, whatever happens, Cinderpaw will never be a warrior now."

Fireheart's head spun. He was dizzy with lack of sleep, and this devastating news sapped the last of his energy. Cinderpaw had been entrusted to him for her warrior training. Memories of the naming ceremony pricked like cruel thorns – Cinderpaw's excitement, Frostfur's motherly pride..."Does Frostfur know?" he meowed, feeling hollow.

"Yes, she was here till dawn. She's back in the nursery now; there are other kits to tend to. I'll ask one of the elders to sit with Cinderpaw. She needs to be kept warm."

"I can do that." Fireheart padded over to the nest where Cinderpaw was sleeping and looked inside. She squirmed, and her blood-smeared sides heaved, as though she were fighting a battle as she slept.

Yellowfang gently nudged Fireheart with her nose. "You need to get some sleep," she rasped. "Leave Cinderpaw to me."

Fireheart stayed where he was. "Bluestar lost another life," he burst out. Yellowfang blinked for a moment, then lifted her head to StarClan. She didn't utter a word, but Fireheart could see the anguish in her orange eyes. "You know, don't you?" he murmured.

Yellowfang lowered her chin and gazed into Fireheart's eyes. "That this is Bluestar's final life? Yes, I know. A medicine cat can tell these things."

"Will the rest of the Clan be able to tell as well?" Fireheart asked, thinking of Tigerclaw.

Yellowfang narrowed her eyes. "No. She will be no weaker in this life than she was in any of her others."

Fireheart blinked gratefully at her.

"Now," Yellowfang ordered, "do you want some poppy seeds to help you sleep?"

Fireheart shook his head. Part of him longed for the deep, easy sleep they would bring. But if Tigerclaw was right and ShadowClan really was about to attack ThunderClan's borders, he did not want to dull his senses. He might be needed to defend the camp.

Greystripe was back in the warriors' den. Fireheart did not speak to him; his rage at finding him missing the night before lingered like a dull bruise. He padded silently to his nest, circled once, and settled down to wash.

Greystripe looked up. "You're back, then." He sounded edgy, as if he wanted to say more.

Fireheart stopped licking his forepaw and stared at Greystripe.

"You tried to warn Silverstream off," Greystripe hissed furiously. Willowpelt, who was dozing on the other side of the den, opened one eye, then closed it again.

Greystripe lowered his voice. "Stay out of it, will you?" he spat. "I'm going to keep on seeing her, whatever you do or say."

Fireheart snorted and flashed a resentful glance at his friend. His talk with Silverstream seemed so long ago, he'd almost forgotten it. But he hadn't forgotten that Greystripe had been missing when he'd needed help finding Cinderpaw. He laid his head angrily on his muddy forepaws and closed his eyes. Cinderpaw was battling against her injuries and Bluestar was on her ninth life. As far as Fireheart was concerned, Greystripe could do what he liked.

CHAPTER 18

Greystripe had already left his nest when Fireheart awoke the next day. He could tell it was sunhigh by the light that glowed through the branches. He rose, his body still weary with grief, and pushed his head out of the den. Snow must have been falling all morning, for it lay thick on the ground and had drifted against the den. Fireheart found himself gazing out over a white wall that was as high as his shoulder.

The usual bustle of the camp seemed muted. Fireheart could see Willowpelt and Halftail whispering on the far side of the clearing. Mousefur was picking her way laboriously towards the store of fresh-kill, a rabbit dangling from her jaws. She stopped and sneezed, then carried on.

Fireheart lifted one paw and rested it on top of the snow. It felt hard at first, but when he pressed down, the thin covering of ice cracked and he gasped as his leg plunged into the drift. Fireheart snorted as he found himself up to his muzzle in snow. Shaking his head and lifting his chin, he leaped forwards, only to sink into more deep snow. He struggled on, alarm rising in his chest. He felt as if he were drowning in snow! Then, all of a sudden, there was solid ground under his paws. He had reached the edge of the clearing. The snow here was only a mouse-length deep, and Fireheart sat down with a soft crunch, relieved.

He tensed when he saw Greystripe plowing through the snow towards him. The grey warrior seemed unbothered by it, protected from its damp chill by his thick pelt. His face was shadowed with sorrow. "Have you heard about Bluestar?" he asked as he neared. "She lost a life to greencough."

Fireheart flicked his ears impatiently. He could have told his friend that last night. "I know," he snapped. "I was with her."

"Why didn't you tell me?" mewed Greystripe, shocked.

"You weren't exactly in a friendly mood last night, if you remember. Anyway, if you weren't always off breaking the warrior code, you might know what was going on in your own Clan," he snarled.

Greystripe's ears twitched uncomfortably. "I've just seen Cinderpaw," he meowed. "I'm sorry she's so sick."

"How is she?"

"She looked bad, but Yellowfang said she's pulling

through," replied Greystripe.

Fireheart stared anxiously across the clearing and stood up. He wanted to see his apprentice for himself.

Greystripe meowed, "She's asleep now. Frostfur's with her, and Yellowfang doesn't want anyone else disturbing her."

Fireheart flinched involuntarily. How was he going to tell Frostfur that it was his fault that Cinderpaw went to the Thunderpath? Instinctively, Fireheart turned to Greystripe, seeking reassurance. But Greystripe was trudging across the snowy clearing towards the nursery. *Off to see Silverstream*, Fireheart guessed resentfully, sheathing and unsheathing his claws as he watched his friend disappear from sight.

Fireheart noticed Speckletail, the oldest queen from the nursery and the mother of the kit with whitecough, only when she stopped right in front of him. "Is Tigerclaw inside?" she asked, pointing with her nose to the warriors' den.

Fireheart shook his head.

Speckletail mewed, "There's greencough in the nursery. Two of Brindleface's kits are sick."

"Greencough!" Fireheart gasped, shaken from his anger. "Will they die?"

"They might. But leaf-bare always brings greencough," Speckletail pointed out gently.

"Surely there's something we can do!" Fireheart

protested.

"Yellowfang will do what she can," answered Speckletail. "But in the end, it's up to StarClan."

A new flash of fury flared in Fireheart's belly as Speckletail turned away and padded back to the nursery. How could the Clan tolerate these tragedies? He felt overwhelmed by the need to leave the camp, to escape the gloomy air that the rest of the Clan seemed content to breathe.

He jumped up and raced blindly across the snowy clearing, through the gorse tunnel and out into the forest. He was startled to find himself heading instinctively for the training hollow. The thought that he should be there, teaching Cinderpaw, was more than he could bear. As he veered to avoid it, he heard the voices of Whitestorm and Brackenpaw. The white-furred warrior must have taken Brackenpaw for training while Fireheart had been sleeping. Had no cat stopped to grieve for Bluestar's lost life? Fireheart's throat tightened as he fought back his rage and ran on, desperate to put as much distance as possible between himself and the camp.

He finally stopped beneath Tallpines, his sides heaving with the effort of running through the snow. There was stillness here that calmed him. Even the birds had stopped singing. Fireheart felt as if he were the only creature in the world.

He didn't know where he was going; he just padded on, letting the woods soothe him. As he walked, his mind cleared. He could do nothing for Cinderpaw, and Greystripe was out of reach, but he might be able to help Yellowfang fight the greencough. He would fetch some more catnip.

Fireheart turned his steps towards his old kittypet home, weaving through the brambles in the oak woods that backed on to Twolegplace. He leaped to the top of the fence at the end of his old garden, nudging a ridge of snow into the flowerbed below. It fell with a soft clump. Fireheart peered down into the garden. He could see tracks, smaller than a cat's. A squirrel had been out hunting for its store of nuts.

It didn't take Fireheart long to pluck a generous mouthful of leaves from the catnip bush. He wanted to take as much as he could. Its soft leaves might not survive this weather; this could be his last chance to gather it.

With his mouth crammed, Fireheart stared towards the swinging flap he had used as a kit. He wondered if his Twoleg housefolk still lived there. They'd been kind to him. He had spent his first leaf-bare cosseted in their nest, warm and safe from the cruelties of Thunderpaths and greencough.

The scent of this catnip must be going to my head, he thought sharply. He bounded up the garden and on to the fence with a single leap. He was unnerved by how much the thought of his Twoleg home had stirred him. Did he really want the safety and predictability of a kittypet's life? *Of course not!* Fireheart shook the thought away. But the idea of returning to camp didn't appeal to him just yet.

Suddenly he thought of Princess.

Fireheart raced along the edge of the woods to the part of Twolegplace where his sister's garden lay. When her fence was in sight, he dug down through the snow and buried the catnip beneath a layer of dead leaves to protect it from the cold. He was still panting from his run when he leaped on to the fence and called out to Princess. Then he scrambled back down into the woods to wait for her.

The snow made his paws ache with cold as he paced restlessly under an oak tree. *Perhaps she is kitting*, he told himself, *or shut inside*. He had just persuaded himself he wasn't going to see her today when he heard her familiar mew. He looked up to see her standing on top of her fence. Fireheart felt a shiver of anticipation. Her belly was no longer swollen. Princess must have kitted.

He breathed in her scent as she approached and felt it warm him. "You've kitted!" he meowed.

Princess gently touched his nose with hers. "Yes," she mewed softly.

"Did it go OK? Are the kits all right?"

Princess purred. "It was fine. I have five healthy kits," she meowed, her eyes glowing with pleasure. Fireheart licked her head and she mewed, "I didn't expect to see you out in this weather."

"I came to find some catnip," Fireheart told her. "There's greencough in the camp."

Princess's eyes clouded with worry. "Are many of your

Clan ill?"

"Three so far." Fireheart hesitated for a moment, then meowed sadly, "Our leader lost another life last night."

"Another life?" echoed Princess. "What do you mean? I thought it was only an old she-cat's tale that cats have nine lives."

"Bluestar was granted nine lives by StarClan because she's leader of our Clan," Fireheart explained.

Princess looked at him in awe. "Then it's true!"

"Only for Clan leaders. The rest of us have only one life, like you, and like Cinderpaw..." Fireheart's voice trailed away.

"Cinderpaw?" Princess must have detected the grief in his voice.

Fireheart gazed into her eyes, and the thoughts that had been troubling him began to tumble out. "My apprentice," he meowed. "She was hit on the Thunderpath last night." His voice cracked as he remembered finding her broken, bleeding body. "She's badly hurt. She might still die. And even if she survives, she'll never become a warrior."

Princess moved closer and nuzzled him. "You spoke so fondly of her last time you were here," she mewed. "She sounded full of fun and energy."

"The accident shouldn't have happened," Fireheart growled. "I was supposed to meet Tigerclaw. He'd asked for Bluestar, but Bluestar was ill, so I offered to go instead. I had to fetch catnip first and Cinderpaw went in my place."

Princess looked alarmed and Fireheart added quickly, "I told her not to. But perhaps if I'd been a better mentor she'd have listened to me."

"I'm sure you're a good mentor." Princess tried to soothe him, but Fireheart hardly heard her.

"I don't know why Tigerclaw wanted Bluestar to meet him in such a dangerous place!" he spat. "He said there was evidence that ShadowClan had invaded our territory, but when I arrived there was no scent of them at all!"

"Was it a trap?" Princess suggested.

Fireheart looked into his sister's questioning eyes and suddenly began to wonder. "Why would Tigerclaw want to hurt Cinderpaw?"

"It was Bluestar he asked for," Princess pointed out.

Fireheart's fur bristled. Could his sister be right? Tigerclaw *had* summoned Bluestar to the narrowest part of the Thunderpath verge. Surely even Tigerclaw wouldn't deliberately put his Clan leader in danger? Fireheart shook the thought away. "I d-don't know," he stammered. "Everything's so confusing at the moment. Even Greystripe's hardly speaking to me."

"Why?"

Fireheart shrugged. "It's too complicated to explain." Princess nestled next to him in the snow, pressing her soft fur against his. "I just feel like such an outsider at the moment," Fireheart went on gloomily. "It's not easy being different."

"Different?" Princess looked puzzled.

"Being born a kittypet, when the other cats are all Clanborn."

"You seem like a Clanborn cat to me," mewed Princess. Fireheart blinked gratefully at her. She went on, "But if you're not happy in the Clan, you can always come home with me. My housefolk would look after you, I'm sure."

Fireheart pictured himself living his old kittypet life: warm, cosy and safe. But he couldn't forget how he'd watched the woods from his Twoleg garden and dreamed of being out in the forest. A breeze stirred his thick fur and carried the scent of a mouse to his nose. Fireheart shook his head firmly. "Thank you, Princess," he meowed. "But I belong with my Clan now. I could never be happy in a Twoleg nest. I would miss the scents of the forest and sleeping beneath Silverpelt, hunting my own food and sharing it with my Clan."

His sister's eyes gleamed. "It sounds like a good life," she purred. She looked down shyly at her paws. "Sometimes even I stare into the forest and wonder what it feels like to live out there."

Fireheart purred and stood up. "Then you understand?"

Princess nodded. "Are you going back now?"

"Yes. I must take the catnip to Yellowfang while it's fresh."

Princess stretched her head forwards to press her muzzle into his side. "Perhaps my kits will be strong enough to meet you next time you come," she mewed.

Excitement tingled in Fireheart's belly. "I hope so!" he meowed.

As he turned to leave, Princess called: "Take care, brother. I don't want to lose you again."

"You won't," Fireheart promised.

"Good thinking, Fireheart," purred Whitestorm. He had seen Fireheart pad back into camp with his jaws crammed with catnip.

Fireheart's mouth had been watering all the way home, although he was beginning to think he'd be happy never to see another catnip bush again. But he was happier than when he'd left the camp. His sister had safely kitted and his head felt clearer.

He was heading towards Yellowfang's den when Tigerclaw appeared at his side.

"More catnip?" observed the great tabby, his eyes suspicious. "I wondered where you'd gone. Brackenpaw can take that to Yellowfang."

Brackenpaw was helping to clear away snow nearby.

"Come and take this catnip to Yellowfang," Tigerclaw ordered the apprentice.

Brackenpaw nodded and bounded over at once.

Fireheart dropped the bunch of leaves on to the ground. "I wanted to visit Cinderpaw," he meowed to Tigerclaw.

"Later," growled the deputy. He waited while

Brackenpaw picked up the catnip and carried it off to Yellowfang's den. Then he turned back to Fireheart. "I want to know where Greystripe has been going."

Fireheart felt the heat rising under his fur. "I don't know," he replied, holding Tigerclaw's gaze.

Tigerclaw stared back at him, his eyes cold and hostile. "When you see him," he hissed, "you can tell him he's confined to the fallen oak."

"Yellowfang's old den?" Fireheart glanced at the tangled branches where the medicine cat had lived when she first came into the ThunderClan camp, when she was still considered a ShadowClan outcast. Swiftpaw was there, lying beside Speckletail's dark tabby kit.

"Cats with whitecough are confined there until they are well again."

"But Greystripe only has a cold," Fireheart protested.

"A cold is bad enough. He'll stay at the fallen oak!" Tigerclaw repeated. "Cats with greencough are to nest with Yellowfang. We must stop this sickness from spreading." The deputy's eyes flashed unsympathetically. Fireheart wondered if he thought of illness as a sign of weakness. "It is for the good of the Clan," Tigerclaw added.

"Yes, Tigerclaw. I'll tell Greystripe."

"And keep away from Bluestar," the deputy warned.

"But the greencough has left her," Fireheart objected.

"I am aware of that, but her den still reeks of the sickness. I can't afford to have any of my warriors falling ill.

Whitestorm tells me that RiverClan warriors have been scented even closer to the camp. He also told me he had to train Brackenpaw today. I expect you to take charge of Brackenpaw's training tomorrow."

Fireheart nodded. "May I go and see Cinderpaw now?"

Tigerclaw looked at him.

"I doubt if Yellowfang has put her anywhere near the cats with greencough," Fireheart added with a flash of irritation. "I won't get infected."

"Very well," Tigerclaw agreed, and stalked away.

Fireheart met Brackenpaw in the middle of the clearing. "Yellowfang was very grateful for the catnip," Brackenpaw mewed.

"Good," answered Fireheart. "By the way, I'm teaching you how to catch birds tomorrow. I hope you're ready for a bit of tree climbing."

Brackenpaw's whiskers twitched excitedly. "Definitely. I'll meet you at the training hollow."

Fireheart nodded and carried on to Yellowfang's den. He spotted Brindleface's poor kits straightaway. They lay quietly in a bracken nest, coughing, their noses and eyes streaming.

Yellowfang greeted him. "Thanks for the catnip; we're going to need it. Patchpelt has greencough now." She gestured with her nose towards another nest in the bracken. Inside, Fireheart could see the old tom's matted fur.

"How's Cinderpaw?" he asked, looking back at the

medicine cat.

Yellowfang sighed. "She was awake earlier, but not for long. She has an infection in her leg. StarClan knows, I've tried everything, but she must fight this one herself."

Fireheart peered into Cinderpaw's nest. The little grey cat was twitching in her sleep, her injured leg twisted awkwardly to one side. Fireheart shuddered, suddenly afraid she might yet lose this struggle. He turned back to Yellowfang, looking for words of encouragement, but the medicine cat sat with her head low. She looked exhausted.

"Do you think Spottedleaf would have been able to save these cats?" she meowed unexpectedly, raising her head to meet his gaze.

Fireheart shivered. He could still sense Spottedleaf's presence here in the clearing. He remembered how efficiently she'd tended to Ravenpaw's shoulder wound after the battle with RiverClan, and how carefully she'd advised him about caring for Yellowfang when the old she-cat had first come to the ThunderClan camp. Then he looked at Yellowfang, her shoulders weighed down with experience. "I'm sure there's nothing Spottedleaf would have done differently," he told her.

One of the kits cried out and Yellowfang sprang up. As she passed, Fireheart leaned forwards and gently stroked the old cat's side with his muzzle. She twitched her shoulder gratefully at him. Then, filled with sadness, he turned and padded towards the fern tunnel.

The white pelt of Frostfur appeared at the other end. She must be coming to see Cinderpaw. As he approached the queen, Fireheart lifted his head and looked into her blue eyes. The sorrow in them made his heart twist with pain. "Frostfur?" he began.

The queen stopped.

"I... I'm sorry." Fireheart trembled as he spoke.

Frostfur looked confused. "What for?"

"I should have been able to stop Cinderpaw from going to the Thunderpath."

Frostfur gazed at him, but her expression gave away nothing except her sadness. "I don't blame you, Fireheart," she murmured. Then she lowered her head and carried on towards her kit.

Greystripe was back, munching a vole beside the nettle clump. Fireheart padded over to him. "Tigerclaw says you've got to move to the fallen oak, with the whitecough cats," he meowed. With a prickle of resentment, he remembered how the deputy had questioned him about his friend.

"That won't be necessary," replied Greystripe cheerfully. "I'm better now. Yellowfang gave me the all-clear this morning."

Fireheart looked closely at Greystripe. His eyes were certainly bright again and his runny nose had dried to an unappealing crust. At any other time Fireheart would have teased him about how much he looked like Runningnose, the ShadowClan medicine cat. Now he spat crossly, "Tigerclaw has noticed your disappearances. You should be more careful. Why can't you stay away from Silverstream, at least for now?"

Greystripe stopped chewing and stared angrily back at Fireheart. "And why can't you mind your own business?"

Fireheart closed his eyes and snorted with frustration. Would he ever get through to his friend? Then he wondered if he even cared any more. After all, Greystripe hadn't asked about Cinderpaw.

Fireheart's stomach growled to tell him he was hungry. He might as well eat. He took a sparrow from the pile of fresh-kill and carried it away to a deserted corner of the camp to eat alone. As he settled down, he thought of Princess, far away in Twolegplace, with her newborn kits. Lonely and anxious, Fireheart stared across the camp and longed to see her again.

CHAPTER 19

IN THE FOLLOWING days, Fireheart struggled against the urge to visit his sister. His yearning to be with his kittypet kin was beginning to make him feel uncomfortable. He kept himself busy hunting in the snowy forests, replenishing the camp store.

He had had a successful hunt this afternoon, returning to camp with two mice and a chaffinch as the sun dipped behind the trees. He buried the mice in the snow store and took the chaffinch for his own supper.

As he finished his meal, he noticed Whitestorm padding towards him. "I want you to take Sandpaw out on the dawn patrol," the great white warrior meowed. "ShadowClan has been scented as close as the Owl Tree."

"ShadowClan?" Fireheart echoed in alarm. Perhaps Tigerclaw really had found evidence of an invasion after all.

"I was planning to take Brackenpaw out again tomorrow."

"Isn't Greystripe better now?" asked Whitestorm. "He can take Brackenpaw."

Of course! thought Fireheart. And perhaps training his apprentice would keep Greystripe away from Silverstream for once. But that meant he would have to go on patrol with Sandpaw. And Fireheart couldn't help thinking of the furious look Sandpaw had given him when he'd interrupted her fight with the RiverClan warrior beside the gorge. "Just me and Sandpaw?" he asked.

Whitestorm looked at him in surprise. "Sandpaw's almost a warrior, and you can take care of yourself," he replied.

Whitestorm had misunderstood Fireheart's concern. He wasn't afraid of being attacked by enemy cats; he was afraid that Sandpaw hated him as much as Dustpaw did. But Fireheart didn't correct him. "Does Sandpaw know?"

"You can tell her," meowed Whitestorm.

Fireheart's ear twitched. He didn't think Sandpaw would be too thrilled by the idea of patrolling with him, but he didn't argue.

Whitestorm nodded briefly and bounded away towards the warriors' den. Fireheart sighed and padded over to where Sandpaw was sitting with the other apprentices.

"Sandpaw." Fireheart shifted uneasily. "Whitestorm wants you to patrol with me at dawn tomorrow."

He waited for a resentful hiss, but Sandpaw merely

looked up at him and meowed, "Fine." Even Dustpaw looked surprised.

"O-OK," echoed Fireheart, taken aback. "Meet you at sunrise then."

"Sunrise," agreed Sandpaw.

Fireheart decided to share the good news about Sandpaw's lack of hostility with Greystripe. It might be a chance for them to start talking to each other again. Greystripe was sharing tongues with Runningwind by the clump of nettles.

"Hi, Fireheart," Runningwind meowed as Fireheart approached.

"Hi." Fireheart looked expectantly at Greystripe. But Greystripe had turned his head away and was staring at the boundary wall. Fireheart's heart sank. He dropped his head and turned back towards his nest. He couldn't wait to be out on patrol tomorrow and away from the camp.

The sky glowed palest pink above Fireheart's head as he pushed his way out of the den the next morning.

Sandpaw was waiting for him outside the gorse tunnel.

"Er, hi," Fireheart meowed, feeling a bit awkward.

"Hi," Sandpaw answered quietly.

Fireheart sat down. "Let's wait for the night patrol to get back," he suggested.

They sat in silence until they heard the familiar rustle of bushes heralding the return of Whitestorm, Longtail and Mousefur.

"Any sign of ShadowClan?" Fireheart asked.

"We definitely picked up some ShadowClan scents," answered Whitestorm grimly.

"It's strange," meowed Mousefur, frowning. "It's always the same group of scents. ShadowClan must be sending the same warriors each time."

"You two had better check out the RiverClan border," suggested Whitestorm. "We didn't get a chance to patrol there. Be careful, and remember, you don't want to start a fight. You're just looking for signs they've been hunting on our land again."

"Yes, Whitestorm," meowed Fireheart. Sandpaw nodded respectfully.

Fireheart led the way. "We'll start at Fourtrees and work our way along the border to Tallpines," he meowed as they climbed out of the camp ravine.

"Sounds good," replied Sandpaw. "I've never seen Fourtrees in the snow." Fireheart listened for sarcasm in her voice, but she seemed to be sincere.

They reached the top of the ravine. "Which way now?" Fireheart decided to test her.

"Do you think I don't know the way to Fourtrees?" Sandpaw protested. Fireheart began to regret acting like a mentor until he noticed a good-humoured gleam in her eyes. She charged away through the woods without another word, and Fireheart pelted after her.

It felt good to be running through the woods with

another cat again. He had to admit Sandpaw was fast. She was still two fox lengths ahead when she leaped over the trunk of a fallen tree and disappeared.

Fireheart followed, taking the tree in a single bound. As he landed on the other side, something hit him from behind. He skidded in the snow, rolled over, and sprang to his paws.

Sandpaw faced him, her whiskers twitching. "Surprise!"

Fireheart hissed playfully and leaped on top of her. He was impressed by Sandpaw's strength, but he had the advantage of size. When he finally held her down in the snow, she protested: "Get off, you great lump!"

"OK, OK," meowed Fireheart, letting go of her. "But you asked for it!"

Sandpaw sat up, her orange coat dusted with snow. "You look like you've been caught in a snowstorm!" she mewed.

"So do you." They both shook the flakes from their fur. "Come on," Fireheart meowed. "We'd better get a move on."

They raced side by side, as far as Fourtrees. By the time they reached the top of the slope that overlooked the valley, the sky was milky blue. Pale sunlight lit up the snowy hollow. The four bare oaks stood below them, glittering with frost.

Sandpaw stared down, her eyes wide. Fireheart waited, touched by her enthusiasm, until she turned to leave.

"I didn't know the snow would make everything look so different," she mewed as they began to follow the RiverClan border towards the river. Fireheart nodded in agreement.

Their pace was slower as they travelled in silence along the line of scent markers, alert for any fresh smells of RiverClan this side of the border. Fireheart paused every few trees to leave a new ThunderClan scent mark.

Suddenly Sandpaw stopped dead. "Fancy a little fresh-kill?" she whispered. Fireheart nodded. The apprentice dropped into a hunting crouch and pulled herself forwards through the snow, one slow pawstep after another. Fireheart followed her gaze and saw a young rabbit hopping underneath some brambles. With a quick hiss, Sandpaw pounced, diving into the brambles and pinning the rabbit down with a strong forepaw. In one smooth movement she pulled it towards her to finish it off.

Fireheart bounded over. "Great catch, Sandpaw!"

Sandpaw looked pleased. She dropped the warm fresh-kill to the ground. "Share?"

"Thanks!"

"That's one of the best things about patrols," remarked Sandpaw between mouthfuls.

"What?" Fireheart asked.

"You can eat what you catch instead of having to take it back to the Clan," Sandpaw replied. "I don't know how many hunting missions I've nearly starved on!"

Fireheart purred with amusement.

They set off again, skirting Sunningrocks to follow the trail into the woods again, close to the RiverClan border. As they reached the top of the bracken-covered slope above the river, Fireheart sent a silent prayer to StarClan that they wouldn't find Greystripe here.

"Look!" meowed Sandpaw suddenly. Her body stiffened with excitement. "The river – it's frozen."

Fireheart's heart lurched as he remembered Cinderpaw saying the same words before Greystripe's accident. "We're not going down to look!" he meowed firmly.

"We don't have to. You can see from here. Let's get back and tell the Clan."

"Why?" Fireheart couldn't understand Sandpaw's excitement.

"A patrol of our warriors could cross the river now!" Sandpaw meowed. "We can invade RiverClan's territory and steal back some of the prey they've taken from us."

Fireheart felt a cold chill ripple the fur on his spine. What would Greystripe think about that? And could Fireheart bring himself to go into battle against the starving RiverClan?

Sandpaw circled him impatiently. "Are you coming?"

"Yes," replied Fireheart heavily. He leaped after Sandpaw as she raced off into the woods, back to camp.

Sandpaw tore through the gorse tunnel just ahead of Fireheart. Tigerclaw glanced up as they skidded to a halt in the clearing.

Fireheart heard a noise behind him. Greystripe was padding through the camp entrance with Brackenpaw.

A call sounded from below the Highrock. "Fireheart, Sandpaw, how was your patrol?"

Fireheart felt a flood of relief when he saw Bluestar looking her normal self, sitting with her chin high and her tail tucked over her front paws.

Sandpaw bounded over to the Highrock. "The river's frozen," she burst out. "We could cross it easily right now!"

Bluestar gazed thoughtfully at the apprentice. Fireheart flinched when he saw the ThunderClan leader's eyes gleam. "Thank you, Sandpaw," she meowed.

Fireheart leaned over and murmured into Sandpaw's ear: "Come on, let's tell the others." He guessed that Bluestar would want to discuss the frozen river with her senior warriors.

Sandpaw glanced at him, understanding, and followed him back to the centre of the clearing. "This has been such a great day!" she meowed. Fireheart just nodded and glanced anxiously at Greystripe.

"You two look like you had fun!" Dustpaw had emerged from the apprentices' den. "Drowned another RiverClan cat?" he sneered at Fireheart.

Dustpaw looked at Sandpaw expectantly. Fireheart guessed he was waiting for her to agree with him, like she used to, but Sandpaw wasn't listening. Fireheart felt a small prickle of satisfaction at the irritated look on Dustpaw's face as she meowed breathlessly: "We found out that the river's frozen. I think Bluestar's planning a raid on RiverClan!"

At that moment their leader's call sounded from the Highrock, and the Clan began to gather in the clearing. The sun had reached its high point, which in leaf-bare meant that it was barely above the treetops.

"Sandpaw and Fireheart have brought good news. The river is frozen over," Bluestar announced. "We will take this opportunity to make a raid on RiverClan's hunting grounds to send the message that they must stop stealing our prey. Our warriors will track down one of their patrols and give them a warning that they'll remember for a long time!"

Fireheart winced as he remembered what Silverstream had told him about her starving Clan. Around him, the other cats raised their voices in eager yowls. Fireheart had not heard the Clan this excited for many moons.

"Tigerclaw!" Bluestar called above the din. "Are our warriors fit enough for a raid on RiverClan?"

Tigerclaw nodded.

"Excellent." Bluestar lifted her tail. "Then we shall leave at sunset." The Clan yowled with delight. Fireheart's paws prickled. Was Bluestar going too? Surely she wouldn't risk her last life on a border raid?

Fireheart looked over his shoulder at Greystripe. He was staring up at the Highrock, the tip of his tail twitching nervously. As the yowls died away, Greystripe called out: "It feels warmer today. A thaw would make the ice too dangerous to cross."

Fireheart held his breath as the other cats turned to look

curiously at Greystripe.

Tigerclaw stared down at Greystripe, his amber eyes puzzled. "You're not usually reluctant to fight," the dark warrior meowed slowly.

Darkstripe craned his neck and added, "Yes, Greystripe – you're not afraid of those RiverClan fleabags, are you?"

Greystripe fidgeted uncomfortably as the Clan waited for an answer.

"Looks like he's scared!" hissed Dustpaw from Sandpaw's side.

Fireheart's tail flicked angrily, but he managed to keep his voice light as he called, "Yes, of getting his paws wet! Greystripe's fallen through the ice once this leaf-bare; he's not keen to do it again."

The tension in the Clan dissolved into amused purrs. Greystripe looked down at the ground, his ears flat. Only Tigerclaw kept his suspicious frown.

Bluestar waited until the murmurings had died away. "I must discuss the raid with my senior warriors." She leaped down from the Highrock, landing so lightly that it was hard to believe that she had been fighting for her lives just days ago. Tigerclaw, Whitestorm and Willowpelt followed her to her den, and the rest of the Clan broke away into groups to discuss the proposed attack.

"I suppose you expect me to thank you for embarrassing me!" Fireheart heard Greystripe's angry hiss in his ear.

"Not at all," he snapped. "But you could at least be

grateful I'm still covering up for you!" He bounded away to the edge of the clearing, his fur bristling with fury.

Sandpaw ran over to join him. "It's about time we showed those RiverClan cats that they can't hunt in our territory whenever they like," she meowed, her eyes shining.

"Yes, I suppose so," Fireheart answered absently. He couldn't take his eyes off Greystripe. Was he imagining it, or was the grey warrior edging further and further towards the nursery? Was Greystripe planning on slipping away to warn Silverstream?

Fireheart began to pad towards the nursery. Greystripe glared at Fireheart as he approached, but before either warrior could speak, Bluestar's call sounded once more from the Highrock. Fireheart stopped where he was but didn't take his eyes off Greystripe.

"Willowpelt agrees with young Greystripe," Bluestar declared. "A thaw is on the way." Greystripe lifted his chin and flashed a defiant look at Fireheart, but Fireheart didn't care. Bluestar was going to call off the raid! Now Greystripe wouldn't have to choose between his Clan and Silverstream, and Fireheart wouldn't have to join a raiding party against a Clan he knew was already suffering.

But Bluestar hadn't finished. "So we will attack at once!"

Fireheart glanced sideways – Greystripe's look of triumph had turned to one of sheer horror.

Bluestar continued, "We will leave a patrol of warriors here to guard the camp. We have to remember the possible threat from ShadowClan. Five warriors will make the raid. I will remain here."

Good, thought Fireheart. She wasn't planning to risk her final life after all. "Tigerclaw will lead the raiding party. Darkstripe, Willowpelt and Longtail will go with him. That leaves one more place."

"Can I go?" Fireheart burst out. Even though his heart felt heavy at the thought of attacking hungry RiverClan cats, it meant that Greystripe wouldn't have to make a choice.

"Thank you, Fireheart. You may join the patrol." Bluestar was clearly pleased by her former apprentice's eagerness. Tigerclaw didn't look so happy. He narrowed his eyes at Fireheart, gazing at him with undisguised suspicion. "There's no time to lose," Bluestar yowled. "I can smell the warm winds myself. Tigerclaw will brief you as you travel. Go now!"

Darkstripe, Longtail and Willowpelt sped after Tigerclaw. Fireheart followed them as they thundered through the gorse tunnel and headed up the ravine, towards RiverClan territory.

They charged past Sunningrocks and reached the enemy border as the low leaf-bare sun began to dip towards the forest. Fireheart sniffed the air – Greystripe and Willowpelt had been right; he could smell warmer winds, and rain clouds were already pushing in over the treetops.

As they raced down the slope towards the river,

Fireheart felt a deep sense of disquiet. Silverstream's desperate story rang in his ears and he fought to push away his feelings of sympathy.

The ThunderClan warriors emerged from the bracken and skidded to a stop at the edge of the river. The sight that greeted them made Fireheart weak with relief. The shining sheet of ice that Fireheart had seen earlier with Sandpaw had broken up into a rushing flow of cold, black water.

CHAPTER 20

TIGERCLAW TURNED TO his warriors, his pale eyes flashing with frustration. "We'll have to wait," he snarled.

The patrol turned and began to trudge home. Fireheart sent up a wordless prayer of thanks to StarClan, but there was a bitter taste in his throat. Now he would never know if he could have gone through with the raid. It wasn't only Greystripe he didn't trust; he didn't even trust himself.

Fireheart kept silent all the way home. Every now and then he saw Tigerclaw flash a glance at him over his massive brown shoulder. It was a slow journey. The light of the short leaf-bare day was fading when they finally reached the top of the ravine. Fireheart waited for the other warriors to pick their way down first. By the time he padded through the gorse tunnel, Tigerclaw was already explaining to the disappointed Clan that the river had thawed.

Fireheart skirted the edge of the clearing, looking for Greystripe. He needed to know if his friend had slipped out of the camp. Instinctively he headed for the nursery. As he approached the tangled mass of brambles, he heard a familiar meow. "Fireheart!"

Fireheart felt a glimmer of hope. Perhaps Greystripe was actually grateful he had offered to take the final place in the raiding party? He followed his friend's voice into the shadows behind the nursery.

Fireheart mewed quietly into the gloom, but he couldn't see Greystripe anywhere. Suddenly something crashed into his side with a mighty thump. Fireheart spun around, all his senses alert. He saw Greystripe with his hackles raised, silhouetted in the dimness.

Greystripe lunged again. Fireheart ducked just in time as Greystripe swung a wide grey paw at his ear.

"What are you doing?" Fireheart spluttered.

Greystripe flattened his ears and hissed, "You didn't trust me! You thought I would betray ThunderClan!" He aimed another swipe. This one caught the tip of Fireheart's ear.

Pain and fury shot through him. "I just wanted to save you from having to make a choice!" he spat. "Although it's true that I'm not sure where your loyalties lie right now."

Greystripe flew at him and knocked him backwards. The two cats tussled, claws unsheathed. "I make my own choices," Greystripe snarled.

Fireheart struggled free and leaped on to Greystripe's back. "I was trying to protect you."

"I don't need protecting!"

Blinded by anger, Fireheart dug his claws into Greystripe's pelt, but Greystripe flipped Fireheart over and together they rolled out from behind the nursery.

The cats in the clearing sprang out of the way as the two young warriors bundled into them. Fireheart yowled with rage as Greystripe bit his foreleg. He thrust upwards with a claw and raked Greystripe above his eye. Greystripe retaliated by lunging downward and sinking his teeth into Fireheart's hind leg.

"Stop this at once!" Bluestar's stern yowl made Fireheart and Greystripe freeze. Fireheart released his grip on Greystripe and shuffled painfully sideways. Greystripe backed away, his fur bristling. Out of the corner of his eye, Fireheart saw Tigerclaw sneering with barely suppressed delight, curling his lip back to reveal his teeth.

"Fireheart, I want to see you in my den – now!" Bluestar growled, her blue eyes flashing fire. "Greystripe, go to your nest and stay there!"

The rest of the Clan melted away into the shadows. Fireheart limped after Bluestar to her den. He kept his eyes fixed on the ground, feeling worn out and confused.

Bluestar sat down on the sandy floor and stared at Fireheart in disbelief for a moment. Then she meowed angrily: "What was that all about?"

Fireheart shook his head. As furious as he was, he could not reveal his friend's secret.

Bluestar closed her eyes and took a deep breath. "I realise feelings are running high in the camp right now, but I never expected to see you and Greystripe fighting. Are you hurt?"

Fireheart could feel his ear and hind leg stinging, but he shrugged and murmured, "No."

"Are you going to tell me what this is about?"

Fireheart met her gaze as steadily as she could. "Bluestar, I'm sorry. I can't explain." *At least that much is true*, he thought.

"Very well," meowed Bluestar at last. "You two can sort it out on your own. The Clan is facing a difficult time and I won't tolerate this sort of infighting. Do you understand?"

"Yes, Bluestar," Fireheart answered. "May I go?"

Bluestar nodded and Fireheart turned and slunk out of her den. He knew he had let his old mentor down. But there was no way he could confide in her. Last time he'd done that, about Ravenpaw's accusation against Tigerclaw, she hadn't believed him. And if she believed him this time, he would be betraying his best friend.

Feeling sick with worry, Fireheart crept across the clearing and slipped inside the warriors' den. He settled into his nest beside Greystripe and curled himself into a tight ball. He lay there, unmoving, aware of Greystripe's tense body beside his, until sleep finally overcame him.

*

Fireheart awoke early the next morning. The sun hadn't yet risen and the clearing was empty as he padded across to Yellowfang's den. He wanted to see Cinderpaw.

Yellowfang was asleep, curled up beside Brindleface's sick kits. They squirmed quietly in their nest, their eyes closed. Yellowfang was snoring loudly. Fireheart didn't want to wake her, so he crept over to Cinderpaw's nest and peered in.

The little grey cat was asleep too. The blood had been washed from her fur. Fireheart wondered whether she had cleaned it herself or whether Yellowfang had washed it off. Fireheart crouched beside Cinderpaw and watched her breathe. There was something calming about the way her sides rose and fell. She seemed much more peaceful than when he last visited.

He stayed with her until the dawn light filtered through the ferns and he heard the Clan begin to stir. Fireheart got to his paws. He leaned into Cinderpaw's nest and touched her side softly with his nose.

As he turned to leave, Yellowfang stretched and opened her eyes. "Fireheart?"

"I came to see Cinderpaw," he whispered.

"She's doing well," meowed Yellowfang, pushing herself up.

Fireheart's eyes clouded with relief. "Thank you, Yellowfang."

When he reached the clearing, Tigerclaw was addressing a group of warriors and apprentices. He spotted Fireheart straightaway. "Nice of you to show up," he growled.

"Greystripe's just joined us, too. He's been having a word with Bluestar." Fireheart glanced at his friend, but Greystripe was staring at the ground. The other warriors watched in silence as Fireheart hurried over and sat down beside Sandpaw.

"During this thaw, the woods will be alive with prey," Tigerclaw meowed. "They'll be hungry after sheltering in their burrows. This will be a good chance to catch as much as we can."

"But there's still fresh-kill in the snow store," Dustpaw mewed.

"It'll be crowfood soon," Tigerclaw told him. "We need to take every opportunity to hunt. As leaf-bare goes on, the prey will start to disappear, and what stays around will be too thin." The warriors nodded in agreement.

"Longtail" – Tigerclaw turned his eyes on the pale tabby warrior – "I want you to organise the hunting parties." Longtail nodded and Tigerclaw got up and padded towards Bluestar's den. As Fireheart watched him disappear through the lichen, he couldn't help wondering if the leader and deputy would discuss his fight with Greystripe.

Longtail's voice summoned him away from his thoughts. "Fireheart! You and Sandpaw can join Mousefur. Greystripe can hunt with Whitestorm and Brackenpaw. It's probably best if I don't put you two in the same group."

Amused purrs rippled through the group, but Fireheart narrowed his eyes angrily. He comforted himself by studying the nick he had left in the pale tabby's ear when Longtail had taunted him on his first day in the camp.

"Good fight last night," Mousefur rasped beside him, her eyes gleaming with mischief. "It almost made up for missing out on a battle."

Fireheart scowled as Dustpaw added: "Yeah! Nice moves, Fireheart – for a kittypet." Fireheart gritted his teeth and looked at the ground, sheathing and unsheathing his claws.

The two groups left the camp together. As the hunters filed up the trail out of the ravine, Fireheart looked at the sky. The rain clouds he had seen rolling in last night had covered the sun, and the snow underpaw was turning to slush.

Mousefur led Sandpaw and Fireheart through Tallpines. "I'll take Sandpaw with me," the brown warrior told Fireheart. "You can hunt alone. Meet us back at camp at sunhigh."

Fireheart couldn't help feeling relieved at the thought of being alone. He stalked away through the trees, still hardly able to believe that he and Greystripe had fought so bitterly. Fireheart felt lost and alone without his old friend, though he barely recognised him any more. He wondered if they could ever be friends again.

It wasn't until he felt the softness of leaves beneath his paws that Fireheart realised he'd wandered all the way to the oak woods that backed on to the Twolegplace. Instantly he thought of Princess, and wondered if his paws had carried him to her Twoleg nest for a reason.

Fireheart made straight for her fence and called softly down into the garden. Then he jumped back into the woods and waited in the undergrowth for his sister to come looking.

He didn't have to wait long before there was a scrabbling noise on the fence and he smelled her distinctive scent. Fireheart was about to leap out to meet her when he smelled a second, unfamiliar scent.

The bracken rustled, and Princess appeared. In her mouth she carried a tiny white kit. As Fireheart pushed his way out to meet her, she mewed a warm greeting through the bundle of fur in her teeth.

The kit was very small; Fireheart guessed it would not be weaned for another moon. Princess cleared away some slush with her paw and laid it gently down on the leaves. Then she sat down and wrapped her thick tail around it.

Fireheart was overwhelmed with emotion. This was his own kin, kittypet born like he had been! He walked quietly over to Princess, nuzzled a greeting, then bent down and sniffed the kit. It smelled of warmth and milk – strange but somehow familiar. Fireheart gave it a tender lick on the head and it mewled, opening its pink mouth to reveal tiny white teeth.

Princess looked at Fireheart, her eyes shining. "I have brought him for you, Fireheart," she meowed softly. "I want you to take him back with you to your Clan so that he can be your new apprentice."

CHAPTER 21

FIREHEART STARED AT the tiny kit. "I never expected..." he began. He dragged his gaze away and stared wordlessly at his sister.

"My housefolk will choose where the rest will live," Princess went on. "But this is my firstborn and *I* want to decide his future." She raised her chin. "Make him a hero, please. Like you!"

The unsettling sense of loneliness that had been dragging at Fireheart for so long began to ebb away. He pictured the white kit among the Clan, as he showed him the ways of the forest and hunted by his side through the thick ferns. At last, there would be another cat in ThunderClan who shared Fireheart's kittypet roots.

Princess tilted her head. "I know how upset you were about your apprentice. I thought if you had a new apprentice

– one who's your own kin – you wouldn't feel so lonely." She stretched her neck and rested her nose against Fireheart's side. "I don't understand all your Clan ways, but seeing you, and hearing you talk about your life, I know I would be honoured if my son was brought up as a Clan cat."

As the first flare of happiness settled inside him, Fireheart thought of the rest of his Clan, and how desperately they needed fighting cats. Cinderpaw would never be a warrior now. And what if the greencough took more lives than just Bluestar's? ThunderClan might need this kit.

He was suddenly aware of the rain clinging to his fur. The kit needed shelter, and soon. It looked strong, but it was still too small to withstand the cold and wet for long.

"I'll take him," he meowed. "This is a great gift you've given to ThunderClan. And I'll train him to be the finest warrior the Clan has ever seen!" He dipped his head and scooped up the kit by his scruff.

Princess's eyes shone with gratitude and pride. "Thank you, Fireheart," she purred. "Who knows, maybe he'll even become a leader and be given nine lives!"

Fireheart gazed fondly at her trusting, hopeful face. Did his sister really believe this might happen? Then a twinge of doubt pricked him. He was taking this tiny kit back to a camp infected by greencough. What if he didn't even make it to newleaf? But the cozy scent of the kit under his muzzle soothed him. The kit would survive. It was strong, and it shared his blood. Fireheart took a deep breath. He must be quick – the kit was getting cold already. He blinked a farewell at Princess and raced away into the bushes.

The kit was heavier than he'd expected. It dangled from his mouth, bumping against his forelegs with faint protesting squeaks. By the time Fireheart reached the top of the ravine, his neck was aching. He made his way down to the camp, putting one paw carefully in front of the other, wary of slipping on the fast-melting snow.

At the entrance, Fireheart hesitated. For the first time he wondered how he would explain this kit to the Clan – he was going to have to admit to visiting his kittypet sister. But it was too late now. He could feel the kit shivering. Fireheart squared his shoulders and padded through the gorse tunnel. The kit let out a deafening wail as a thorn tugged at its fur. Several pairs of eyes turned to look in amazement as Fireheart emerged into the clearing.

Both hunting parties had returned. Mousefur, Whitestorm, Sandpaw and Brackenpaw were all in the clearing. Only Greystripe was missing. One by one the rest of the Clan were drawn out of their dens by the noise and the unfamiliar scent. None of the cats made a sound. They stared at Fireheart with hostile, puzzled eyes as though he were a stranger.

Fireheart turned slowly in the centre of the clearing, the kit still dangling from his mouth, and looked at the ring of questioning eyes. His mouth began to feel dry. Why had he assumed the Clan would accept a kit that wasn't even forest-born?

He felt a rush of relief when Bluestar emerged from Yellowfang's den. But her eyes widened in surprise as she saw him. "What is this?" she demanded.

A tremor of foreboding ran along Fireheart's spine. He placed the kit between his front paws and wrapped his tail over it to keep it warm. "It's my sister's firstborn," he replied.

"Your *sister*!" Tigerclaw glared at him accusingly.

"You have a sister?" called Speckletail. "Where?"

"The same place as Fireheart was born, of course," Longtail hissed with disgust. "Twolegplace!"

"Is that true?" Bluestar asked, her eyes widening further.

"Yes," Fireheart admitted. "My sister gave it to me to bring to the Clan."

"And why would she do that?" Bluestar asked with menacing calm.

Fireheart stammered nervously. "I told her about Clan life – how great it was..." His voice trailed away under Bluestar's incredulous gaze.

"How long have you been visiting Twolegplace?"

"Not long, just since leaf-bare began. But only to see my sister. My loyalty still lies with ThunderClan."

"Loyalty?" Darkstripe's yowl rang out across the clearing. "And yet you bring a kittypet here?"

"Isn't having one kittypet in the Clan enough?" croaked one of the elders.

"Trust a kittypet to find another kittypet!" snarled Dustpaw, ruffling his fur indignantly. He turned to Sandpaw and nudged her with his nose. Sandpaw glanced uncomfortably at Fireheart and then looked down at her paws.

"Why have you brought it here?" Tigerclaw growled.

"We need warriors..." The tiny kit squirmed beneath his belly as he spoke, and Fireheart realised how ridiculous he must sound. He bowed his head as yowls of scorn met his words.

When the insults had died away, Runningwind spoke up. "The Clan has enough to worry about already without this."

"It'll be nothing but a burden," Mousefur agreed. "It'll be at least five moons before it's ready to begin training."

Whitestorm nodded his head in agreement. "You shouldn't have brought this kittypet here, Fireheart," he meowed. "It'll be too soft for Clan life."

Fireheart bristled. "I was born a kittypet. Am I soft?" He thought that he'd begun to challenge the Clan's prejudice against kittypets, but he was wrong. He couldn't see one friendly face in the crowd.

A voice sounded from behind Whitestorm. "If it carries Fireheart's blood, it'll make a good Clan cat."

Fireheart felt relief surge through his body. It was Greystripe! A brief flame of hope flared in Fireheart's chest as Whitestorm stood aside and the other cats turned to look at the grey warrior. Greystripe stared around the circle of cats, meeting their gazes one by one with wide, steady eyes.

"Makes a change to see you speak up for your friend, Greystripe. Last night you wanted to shred him!" sneered Longtail.

Greystripe glared at the pale tabby, then whipped around as Darkstripe challenged him. "Yeah, Greystripe! How do you know Fireheart has blood worthy of ThunderClan? Did you taste it last night when you tried to take a chunk out of his leg?"

Bluestar stepped forwards, her blue eyes clouded with worry. "Fireheart, I believe that you meant no disloyalty to the Clan by visiting your sister, but why did you agree to bring her kit here? It is not your place to make decisions like this. What you have done affects the whole Clan."

Fireheart looked at Greystripe, hoping for more support, but Greystripe wouldn't meet his eyes. Fireheart craned his head around and every cat turned their gaze away from him. Fireheart began to panic. Had he endangered his own position in the Clan by bringing Princess's kit here?

Bluestar spoke again. "Tigerclaw, what do you think?"

"What do I think?" meowed Tigerclaw. Fireheart felt his heart sink at the note of arrogant satisfaction in the deputy's voice. "I think he should get rid of it at once."

"Goldenflower?"

"It certainly looks too small to survive until newleaf," the ginger queen remarked.

"It'll have greencough by sunrise!" added Mousefur.

"Or it'll eat our fresh-kill until next snowfall and then die of cold!" spat Runningwind.

Bluestar dipped her head. "That's enough. I must think about this." She padded to her den and disappeared inside. The rest of the Clan slipped away, muttering darkly.

Fireheart picked up the bedraggled kit and carried him to the warriors' den. The kit was shivering and mewling pathetically. Fireheart curled his body around the little scrap and closed his eyes, but hostile faces of the Clan swam around his mind, filling his heart with dread. He thought he had been lonely before, but now it seemed as if the entire Clan had disowned him.

Greystripe pushed his way into the den and settled down into his nest. Fireheart glanced nervously at him. Greystripe had been the only cat to speak in his defence, and Fireheart wanted to thank him. After an uncomfortable pause, in which the kit cried and cried, Fireheart mumbled, "Thanks for sticking up for me."

Greystripe shrugged. "Yeah, well," he meowed, "no one else was going to do it." He twisted his head around and began to wash his tail.

The kit carried on mewling, his cries growing louder. Some of the other warriors padded into the den to escape the rain outside. Willowpelt glanced briefly at Fireheart and the kit, but she didn't speak.

"Can't you shut that thing up?" complained Darkstripe

as he prodded the moss in his nest.

Fireheart licked the kit desperately. It must be very hungry by now. A rustle in the den wall made him lift his head. It was Frostfur. She crept over to Fireheart's nest and looked down at the miserable kit. Suddenly she dipped her head and sniffed the kit's soft fur. "He'd be better off in the nursery," she murmured. "Brindleface has milk to spare. I could ask her to feed it."

Fireheart stared at the queen in surprise.

Frostfur gazed back at him, her eyes warm. "I haven't forgotten that you rescued my kits from ShadowClan."

Fireheart picked up the kit yet again and followed Frostfur out of the warriors' den. The rain was even heavier now. Together they padded quickly to the nursery. Frostfur disappeared through its narrow entrance and Fireheart squeezed in after her. He paused inside the thicket of brambles, blinking until his eyes got used to the dim light.

Inside the dry, dark cocoon, Brindleface was curled around her two healthy kits. She looked suspiciously at Fireheart, then at the kit that dangled from his jaws.

Frostfur whispered to Fireheart, "One of Brindleface's kits died last night." Fireheart remembered the sick kits squirming beside Yellowfang and wondered, with a pang, which one had gone. He put Princess's kit down and turned to Brindleface. "I'm sorry," he murmured.

The queen blinked at him, her grief raw in her eyes.

"Brindleface," Frostfur began. "I can only guess at how

much pain you feel. But this kit is starving and you have milk. Will you feed him?"

Brindleface shook her head and shut her eyes tight as if to deny Fireheart's presence in her den.

Frostfur stretched her head forwards and pressed her muzzle gently against Brindleface's cheek. "I know he won't replace your son," she whispered. "But he needs your warmth and care."

Fireheart waited anxiously. The kit's cries grew louder. It could smell Brindleface's milk and began to squirm blindly towards her soft belly. It nuzzled its way between Brindleface's other two kits. Brindleface looked down as it wriggled forwards, following her milk-scent. She watched, without resisting, as he latched on to her belly and began to suckle. Fireheart ached with relief and gratitude as he saw Brindleface's eyes soften and the white kittypet began to purr, kneading her swollen stomach with tiny paws.

Frostfur nodded. "Thank you, Brindleface. Can I tell Bluestar that you will care for the kit?"

"Yes," replied Brindleface quietly, not taking her eyes off the white kit. She nudged him closer to her belly with one hind paw.

Fireheart purred and bent his head to nose her shoulder. "Thank you. I promise I'll bring you extra fresh-kill every day."

"I'll go and tell Bluestar," meowed Frostfur.

Fireheart looked up at the white queen, stirred by her kindness. "Thank you," he mewed.

"No kit deserves to starve, Clanborn or not." Frostfur turned and pushed her way out of the brambles.

"You can go now," Brindleface murmured to Fireheart. "Your kit will be safe with me."

Fireheart nodded and followed Frostfur out into the rain. He thought about returning to his den, but until he'd heard Bluestar's decision about the kit, he knew he could not settle.

As he paced around the clearing, his fur matting into wet clumps, he saw Frostfur slip out of Bluestar's den and hurry back to the nursery.

Willowpelt was preparing to lead evening patrol out of the camp when Bluestar finally came out of her den. Fireheart stopped, his heart pounding so fast he thought his legs would give way under him. Bluestar leaped on to the Highrock and began the familiar summons. "Let all cats old enough to catch their own prey gather below the Highrock."

The patrol turned away from the camp entrance and padded after Willowpelt, back towards the Highrock. The rest of the Clan began to leave their dry nests, grumbling about the rain. Tigerclaw leaped on to the rock beside Bluestar, his face grim.

They're going to make me take him back, thought Fireheart. His breath began to come in shallow gasps. Darker thoughts pushed their way into Fireheart's mind. *What if Bluestar asks Tigerclaw to abandon him in the forest?*

He'll never survive. Oh, StarClan, what am I going to say to Princess?

When all the cats were settled, Bluestar spoke. "Cats of ThunderClan, no cat can deny that we need warriors. We have lost one cat to greencough already, and there are many moons until newleaf. Cinderpaw has been gravely injured, and she will never be a warrior. As Greystripe rightly pointed out..."

Fireheart heard Dustpaw whispering nearby, "Greystripe's turning into a kittypet himself these days!"

He turned his head sharply, but a warning hiss from one of the elders silenced Dustpaw before Fireheart could say anything.

"As Greystripe pointed out," Bluestar repeated, "this kittypet carries Fireheart's blood. There is every chance the kit will make a fine warrior." Some of the Clan glanced at Fireheart, who had barely heard Bluestar's compliment. Hope was surging in his chest, making him dizzy.

Bluestar paused for a moment to survey the cats in front of her. "I have decided we will take this kit into the Clan," she declared.

No cat made a sound. Fireheart wanted to yowl his thanks to StarClan, but he held his tongue. He took his first deep breath since sunhigh. His own kin was going to be part of ThunderClan!

"Brindleface has offered to nurse it," Bluestar went on, "so Fireheart will take on the duty of providing for her." The

Clan leader met Fireheart's eyes, but he couldn't read her expression. "Finally, the kit should have a name. It shall be known as Cloudkit."

"Will there be a naming ceremony?" Mousefur called from the crowd.

Fireheart looked eagerly up at the Highrock. Would his sister's kit be granted this privilege, as he had been when the Clan had formally accepted him?

Bluestar looked down at Mousefur, her eyes cold. "No," she answered.

CHAPTER 22

THE DAYS LEADING up to the next full moon dragged by slowly for Fireheart. It already seemed ages since the last Gathering. Rain clouds had kept the moon covered the last time and the Clans had stayed away from Fourtrees. Meanwhile patrol after patrol reported scenting RiverClan warriors at Sunningrocks and ShadowClan scent had been discovered again by the Owl Tree.

When he wasn't hunting or patrolling, Fireheart divided his time between Cloudkit, Cinderpaw and Brackenpaw. Even though Greystripe had resumed his role as Brackenpaw's mentor, Fireheart soon began to notice the young apprentice at a loose end from time to time, his mentor nowhere in sight. "Hunting," was all Brackenpaw would say when Fireheart asked where Greystripe had gone.

"Why didn't you go with him?" meowed Fireheart.

"He said I could go tomorrow."

Fireheart felt the usual prickle of anger at Greystripe's stubbornness, but he shrugged it away. He'd given up trying to make Greystripe see sense – they'd hardly spoken since Fireheart had brought Cloudkit into the camp – but he made an effort to take Brackenpaw out whenever Greystripe went missing, just to keep the apprentice out of sight. Fireheart knew that Tigerclaw wouldn't accept Brackenpaw's answers so easily.

Finally the full moon appeared in a cloudless sky. Fireheart came back from hunting early. He passed the fallen oak, deserted now that Swiftpaw and Speckletail's kit had recovered. He dropped his catch on the pile and headed towards Yellowfang's den to visit Cinderpaw. Even the threat of greencough had left the camp – for now. Only Cinderpaw remained with the medicine cat.

As Fireheart padded through the tunnel he could see the small grey she-cat in the clearing ahead. She was helping Yellowfang prepare some herbs. Fireheart winced as he watched Cinderpaw limp heavily towards the split rock with a mouthful of dried leaves.

"Fireheart!" Cinderpaw spat out the herbs and turned to greet him as he emerged from the tunnel. "I could only just scent you through these disgusting things!"

"Those disgusting things helped cure your leg!" growled Yellowfang.

"Well, you should have used more," retorted Cinderpaw, but Fireheart was relieved to see she had a mischievous glint in her eye. "Look at this!" She twitched her twisted hind leg. "I can hardly reach my claws to wash them."

"Perhaps I should give you a few more exercises to loosen it up," meowed Yellowfang.

"No, thanks!" mewed Cinderpaw quickly. "They hurt!"

"They're meant to hurt! It shows they're working." The old medicine cat turned to Fireheart. "Perhaps you'll have more luck persuading her to do them. I'm going into the forest to dig up some comfrey roots."

"I'll try," Fireheart promised as Yellowfang padded past him.

"You'll know if she's doing them right," the medicine cat called over her shoulder, "because she'll complain!"

Cinderpaw limped over to Fireheart and touched her nose to his. "Thanks for coming to see me." She sat down and grimaced as she tucked her bad leg under her.

"I like coming to see you," Fireheart purred. "I miss our training sessions." He regretted his words as soon as he'd uttered them.

A wistful look clouded Cinderpaw's eyes. "Me too," she meowed. "When do you think I'll be able to start again?"

Fireheart stared at her, his heart sinking. Clearly Yellowfang hadn't told her yet that she would never be a warrior. "Perhaps if we try some of your exercises, it'll help," he meowed evasively.

"OK," mewed Cinderpaw. "But just a few."

She lay on her side and stretched out her leg till her face was twisted with pain. Slowly, her teeth clenched, she began to move it backwards and forwards.

"You're doing really well," Fireheart meowed, hiding the sorrow that lay like a rock in his stomach.

Cinderpaw let her leg drop and lay still for a moment; then she pushed herself up. Fireheart watched her quietly as she shook her head. "I'm never going to be a warrior, am I?"

Fireheart couldn't lie to her. "No," he whispered. "I'm so sorry." He stretched his muzzle towards her and licked her head. After a few moments, she gave a long sigh and lay down again.

"I knew it really," she mewed. "It's just that sometimes I dream about being in the forest, hunting with Brackenpaw, and then I wake up and the pain in my leg reminds me I'll never hunt again. It feels too much to bear. I have to pretend that maybe, one day, I'll be able to hunt."

Fireheart couldn't bear to see her in such low spirits. "I'll take you out into the forest again," he promised. "We'll find the oldest, slowest mouse in the woods. It won't stand a chance against you."

Cinderpaw looked at him and purred gratefully.

Fireheart purred back at her, but there was a question that had been nagging at him since the accident. "Cinderpaw," he began, "can you remember what happened when the monster hit you? Was Tigerclaw there?"

Cinderpaw's eyes clouded with confusion. "I d-don't know," she stammered. Fireheart felt a pang of guilt as he saw her flinch away from the memory. "I went straight to the burned ash where Dustpaw said Tigerclaw would be, and then there was the monster and... I don't really remember."

"You wouldn't have realised how thin the verge was there." Fireheart shook his head slowly. "You must have run straight on to the Thunderpath." *Why wasn't Tigerclaw where he said he'd be?* he thought with a flash of rage. *He could have stopped her from running out!* Princess's words rang ominously in his head. *Was it a trap?* He pictured Tigerclaw, crouching downwind, hidden among the trees, staring out at the verge, waiting...

"How's Cloudkit?" Cinderpaw's mew cut short his thoughts. She clearly wanted to change the subject.

Fireheart was happy to oblige, especially if it meant talking about Princess's son. "Getting bigger every day," he meowed proudly.

"I'm dying to meet him. When are you going to bring him to visit me?"

"As soon as Brindleface lets me," Fireheart answered. "She won't let him out of her sight at the moment."

"She likes him, then?"

"She treats him just like her other kits," Fireheart meowed. "Thank StarClan. To be honest, I wasn't sure if she'd take to him. He looks so different from her other kits."

Even Fireheart couldn't deny that Cloudkit's soft, snowy pelt looked out of place beside the other kits, with their forest-coloured coats of short, mottled fur. "At least he gets on well with his nursery mates..." Fireheart's voice trailed away. He stared at the ground, feeling a twinge of anxiety.

"What's the matter?" Cinderpaw prompted gently.

Fireheart shrugged. "I'm just sick of the way some of the other cats look at him, like he's stupid or worthless."

"Does Cloudkit notice these looks?"

Fireheart shook his head.

"Well, don't worry then," Cinderpaw mewed.

"But Cloudkit doesn't even know he was born a kittypet. I think he just assumes he's from a different Clan. But if they keep giving him these dirty looks, he's going to realise there's something wrong with him." Fireheart looked at his paws fretfully.

"Something wrong with him?" echoed Cinderpaw in wonder. "*You* were born a kittypet and there's nothing wrong with you! Look, by the time Cloudkit works out where he comes from, he'll be able to start proving that a kittypet can be as good as any Clanborn warrior. Just like you've done."

"What if someone tells him before he's ready?"

"If he's anything like you, he was *born* ready!"

"When did you get so smart?" Fireheart meowed, rather surprised by his apprentice's sharpness.

Cinderpaw rolled on to her back with a dramatic moan. "Suffering can do that to a cat!" Fireheart prodded her stomach with a paw, and Cinderpaw squeaked before scrambling back on to her side. "No, really," she mewed. "Look who I've been hanging out with lately!"

Fireheart tipped his head on one side questioningly.

"Yellowfang, you dope," Cinderpaw scoffed. "She's one sharp old cat. I'm learning a lot." She sat up. "Yellowfang said there's a Gathering tonight. Are you going?"

"I don't know," Fireheart admitted. "I'm going to ask Bluestar later. I'm not exactly popular with the Clan at the moment."

"They'll get over it," Cinderpaw promised. She nudged his shoulder. "Shouldn't you go and find out if you're going, then? They'll be leaving soon."

"You're right," Fireheart replied. "Will you be OK till Yellowfang gets back? Do you want me to fetch you some fresh-kill?"

"I'll be fine," Cinderpaw assured him. "And Yellowfang'll bring me something. She always does. I'm going to be the fattest cat in the Clan by the time she's finished with me."

Fireheart felt a burst of happiness to see his former apprentice recovering her spirit. He was tempted to stay and keep her company, but she was right – he should find out if he could go to the Gathering. "I'll see you tomorrow, then," he meowed. "There should be plenty of news from the Gathering."

"Yeah, and I want to hear it all," Cinderpaw mewed. "Make sure Bluestar lets you go! Quick!"

"I'm going, I'm going," Fireheart retorted, getting to his paws. "Bye, Cinderpaw."

"Bye!"

Fireheart stopped at the edge of the clearing and looked around for Bluestar. She was talking with Willowpelt outside her den. Fireheart reached them just as Willowpelt stood up to leave. The slender grey warrior nodded to Fireheart as she padded away.

Bluestar gazed at Fireheart with knowing eyes. "You want to go to the Gathering," she meowed. Fireheart opened his mouth to speak, but Bluestar interrupted him. "All the warriors want to go tonight, but I can't take every cat."

Fireheart felt disappointed. "I wanted to see WindClan again," he explained. "To find out how they've been getting on since Greystripe and I brought them home."

Bluestar narrowed her eyes. "I don't need reminding of what you did for WindClan," she meowed sharply, and Fireheart flinched. "But you're right to be concerned," Bluestar went on. "You and Greystripe may come to the Gathering tonight."

"Thank you, Bluestar," Fireheart meowed.

"It'll be an interesting Gathering," Bluestar warned him. "RiverClan and ShadowClan have much to explain."

Fireheart felt his ears twitch nervously, but he couldn't help feeling a thrill of excitement as well. Bluestar clearly meant to challenge Crookedstar and Nightstar about their invasions into ThunderClan territory. He dipped his head respectfully to Bluestar and padded away.

As he collected two voles for Brindleface from the pile of fresh-kill, Fireheart noticed Yellowfang trudging into the camp. Her paws were muddy and her mouth was crammed with fat, knobbly roots. Her search for comfrey had clearly been successful.

Fireheart carried the fresh-kill over to the nursery. Brindleface was curled up inside feeding Cloudkit. The other kits had recently given up their mother's milk, and soon Cloudkit too would have his first taste of fresh-kill.

Brindleface looked up as he entered, her eyes shadowed with concern. "I've just sent for Yellowfang," she mewed.

Fireheart was instantly alarmed. "Is there something wrong with Cloudkit?"

"He's been a little feverish today." Brindleface leaned down and licked the kit's head as he stopped feeding and began squirming restlessly. "It's probably nothing, but I thought I'd see what Yellowfang thought. I... I don't want to take any chances."

Fireheart remembered that the dappled queen had recently lost a kit, and he hoped she was just being overcautious. But Cloudkit did look uncomfortable. "I'll come and see you after the Gathering," he promised.

He ducked out of the nursery and headed back to the pile of fresh-kill to pick out his own food. Brindleface's news had spoiled his appetite, but he knew he should eat something before the journey to Fourtrees tonight.

Longtail and Dustpaw were already standing over the pile. Fireheart sat down and waited for them to leave.

"Haven't seen the Cloudchick today," meowed Longtail. Fireheart felt a familiar ripple of frustration at the snide comment.

"He's probably realised how silly he looks and decided to hide in the nursery!" mewed Dustpaw.

"I'd like to be there when he tries hunting for the first time. The prey'll spot him coming a tree's length away with all that white fluff," Longtail sneered.

"Unless they mistake him for a puffball mushroom!" Dustpaw's whiskers twitched as he threw a sideways glance at Fireheart.

Fireheart flattened his ears and looked away. He watched Yellowfang hurry into the nursery with a mouthful of feverfew. Unfortunately Longtail and Dustpaw noticed too. "Looks like the kittypet's caught a chill. What a surprise," meowed Longtail. "Goldenflower was right – he won't last through leaf-bare!" The tabby warrior turned and stared at Fireheart, waiting for a reaction, but Fireheart ignored him and walked over to the pile of fresh-kill. He chose a thrush and carried it away to eat, feeling drained by the endless spite.

Greystripe was sharing his meal with Runningwind by the nettle clump. "Hi, did you have a good hunt?" Runningwind called as Fireheart passed.

"Yes, thanks," Fireheart replied.

Greystripe didn't look up.

"Bluestar said you could go to the Gathering," Fireheart told Greystripe.

"I know," Greystripe answered, still chewing.

"Are you going?" Fireheart turned to Runningwind.

"You bet! I wouldn't miss this one for anything!"

Fireheart padded on and found a quiet spot at the edge of the clearing. Longtail's words echoed in his head. Would the Clan ever accept the little white kit? Fireheart closed his eyes and began to wash himself.

As he turned to lick his side, his whiskers brushed against something. He opened his eyes to find Sandpaw standing beside him. Her orange pelt glowed silver beneath the rising moon. "Thought you might like some company," she mewed. She sat down and began to wash Fireheart's back with long, soothing strokes.

Through half-closed eyes, Fireheart caught a glimpse of Dustpaw staring from outside the apprentices' den, unable to disguise his envy and amazement. Dustpaw wasn't the only one surprised by Sandpaw's gesture – Fireheart hadn't expected such friendliness from the fiery young she-cat, but her warmth was welcome, and he wasn't going to question it. "Are you going to the Gathering?" he asked.

Sandpaw paused. "Yes. You?"

"Yes. I think Bluestar's going to challenge Crookedstar and Nightstar about their hunting." He waited for Sandpaw to reply, but she was staring up at the darkening sky.

"I wish I were going as a *warrior*," she murmured. Fireheart tensed, but for once there was no hint of jealousy or bitterness in her mew.

Fireheart felt awkward. He knew his training had started after Sandpaw's and he had been a warrior for more than two moons already. "It can't be long till Bluestar gives you your warrior name," he meowed, trying to sound encouraging.

"Why do you think it's taking so long?" Sandpaw asked, turning her pale green eyes on Fireheart.

"I don't know," he admitted. "Bluestar's been ill, and there's RiverClan and ShadowClan causing trouble. I guess she's got other things on her mind."

"You'd think she'd need warriors more than ever!" meowed Sandpaw.

Fireheart felt a stab of sympathy. "I suppose she's just waiting for the... the right time." He knew it didn't sound very helpful, but it was all he could think to say.

"Maybe by newleaf." Sandpaw sighed. "When do you think you'll get a new apprentice?"

"Bluestar hasn't said anything yet."

"Perhaps she'll give you Cloudkit when he's old enough."

"I hope so." Fireheart stared across the clearing at the nursery, wondering if Yellowfang had finished treating Cloudkit. "If he makes it that far."

"Of course he'll make it!" Sandpaw meowed confidently.

"But he has a fever." Fireheart let his shoulders sag with worry.

"All kits get fevers!" Sandpaw retorted. "With his thick fur, he'll recover in no time. That coat's going to be handy in leaf-bare, perfect for hunting in the snow. The prey'll never see him coming, and he'll be able to stay out twice as long as thin-pelts like Longtail!"

Fireheart purred and felt himself relax. Sandpaw had lifted his spirits again. He stood up and gave her a brisk lick on the head. "Come on," he meowed. "Bluestar is calling the cats for the Gathering."

They joined the other cats beside the camp entrance: a silent, purposeful group.

Bluestar signalled to them with a flick of her tail, then led them through the gorse tunnel and out of the ravine. The forest glistened in the cold moonlight as they sprinted towards Fourtrees. Clouds of breath billowed from Fireheart's muzzle, and the forest floor felt frozen beneath his paws.

For the first time since Fireheart had joined the Clan, Bluestar didn't hesitate at the ridge above Fourtrees to prepare herself for the meeting. Instead her cats followed their leader wordlessly as she plunged straight down the slope into the clearing.

CHAPTER 23

RIVERCLAN AND SHADOWCLAN had not yet arrived, but WindClan was already there. Tallstar greeted Bluestar with a respectful nod.

Fireheart spotted Onewhisker and bounded over to meet him. "Hi!" he meowed. It had been over two moons since he'd last seen the small brown tabby warrior who had battled beside him at the gorge. For the first time in ages, Fireheart recalled Whiteclaw's death and felt the familiar bristle of horror as he pictured the RiverClan warrior disappearing beneath the rushing river.

"Where's Greystripe?" Onewhisker asked. "Is he OK?"

Fireheart could see from the concern in his eyes that the WindClan warrior was thinking about Whiteclaw's death too. "He's fine," Fireheart answered. "He's over there with the others." Fireheart remembered the WindClan queen whose kit he'd helped to carry. "How's Morningflower?"

"Happy to be home," replied Onewhisker. "Her kit is growing quickly now." Fireheart purred with pleasure. "The whole Clan is well," Onewhisker added. He glanced at Fireheart with an amused gleam in his eyes. "It's great to eat rabbit again. I hope I never have to taste another rat as long as I live!"

Fireheart detected a fresh scent on the night air. RiverClan was coming. He could smell ShadowClan, too. He scanned the ridge that ran around the edge of the hollow. Sure enough, RiverClan cats were streaming down one side. On the opposite ridge, Fireheart saw ShadowClan cats poised at the top, their coats gleaming in the moonlight. The lean figure of Nightstar stood at the head of the group.

"At last," growled Onewhisker. He'd spotted them as well. "It's too cold to be hanging around tonight."

Fireheart nodded absently. He was searching the crowd of RiverClan cats as they entered the clearing, looking for Silverstream. He recognised the pale grey she-cat easily. She skidded to a halt at the bottom of the slope, then followed her father as he exchanged reserved greetings with the warriors from the other Clans.

Nervously Fireheart scanned the growing throng of cats for Greystripe. Would he dare speak to Silverstream tonight? The grey warrior had his back to Silverstream while he talked with a WindClan warrior.

Fireheart was watching Greystripe so closely that he

didn't hear Deadfoot approach. "Good evening, Fireheart," meowed the WindClan deputy. "How are you?"

Fireheart turned. "Hello," he meowed. "I'm fine, thank you."

Deadfoot nodded. "Good," he meowed, and limped away.

Onewhisker gave Fireheart a friendly nudge. "You're privileged!" Fireheart felt a small glimmer of pride.

Bluestar's yowl sounded from the Great Rock. Fireheart turned and looked up, surprised. The leaders didn't usually call the meeting so soon. Crookedstar and Nightstar were standing close together on the rock. Bluestar waited beside Tallstar for the cats to gather beneath them. It was the first time Fireheart had seen the WindClan leader at a Gathering, he realised with a jolt.

Fireheart and Onewhisker followed the other cats as they settled themselves beneath the rock. Fireheart looked up expectantly, waiting for Bluestar to welcome Tallstar and WindClan back, but the ThunderClan leader was clearly in no mood to waste time on friendly words.

"RiverClan has been hunting at Sunningrocks," she began angrily. "Our patrols have scented your warriors many times, Crookedstar. Sunningrocks belongs to ThunderClan!"

Crookedstar met Bluestar's gaze steadily. "Have you forgotten how recently one of our warriors was killed defending our territory from ThunderClan?"

"You had no need to *defend your territory*," Bluestar answered. "My warriors were not hunting there. They were returning home after finding WindClan. It was a mission we all agreed on! According to the warrior code, they should not have been attacked."

"You speak of the warrior code?" spat Crookedstar. "What about the ThunderClan warrior who has been spying on our territory since then?"

Bluestar was caught off guard. "Warrior?" she echoed. "Have you seen him?"

"Not yet," Crookedstar hissed. "But we find his scent so often, it won't be long before we do."

Fireheart glanced at Greystripe in alarm. He knew only too well which warrior had been detected in Crookedstar's territory. Would any of the RiverClan warriors recognise his scent tonight?

Greystripe sat motionless, not taking his eyes off the leaders on the Great Rock.

Tigerclaw's deep growl sounded from the crowd. "We have scented ShadowClan in our territory as well as RiverClan this past moon. And not just one warrior, but a whole patrol, always the same cats."

The ShadowClan leader's eyes flashed indignantly. "ShadowClan has not been in your territory. Clearly your warriors can't tell the difference in the scents of cats outside their own Clan. You have been smelling the scent of rogue cats. They have been stealing prey from our territory as well!"

Tigerclaw snorted in disbelief and Nightstar glared down at him. "Do you doubt the word of ShadowClan, Tigerclaw?" The crowd murmured uncomfortably as Tigerclaw stared back at Nightpelt with unconcealed distrust.

For the first time, Tallstar spoke, his tail twitching uncertainly. "My warriors have also found strange scents in WindClan territory. They seem to be ShadowClan."

"I knew it!" Tigerclaw snarled. "RiverClan and ShadowClan have united against us!"

"*Us?* What do you mean by *us*!" spat Crookedstar. "I think it's you and WindClan that have formed the alliance! Is that why you were so keen to bring them back? So you can use them to invade the rest of the forest?"

Tallstar's fur bristled. "That's not why we returned and you know it. We have kept to our own hunting grounds these past moons."

"Then why have we found strange warrior scents in our territory?" Crookedstar growled.

"They don't belong to WindClan!" hissed Tallstar. "They must be rogue cats, as Nightstar says."

"But rogue cats would be a convenient excuse for invading our territories, would they not?" Bluestar murmured. She stared dangerously at the RiverClan and ShadowClan leaders.

Crookedstar raised his hackles and Nightstar arched his back. With a flash of alarm, Fireheart saw Tigerclaw stand up and stalk towards the Great Rock, every muscle tensed. Would the leaders really fight at a Gathering?

At that moment a shadow fell over the valley. The cats fell silent as they were plunged into blackness. Fireheart looked up, trembling. A cloud had covered the full moon, completely blocking out its light.

"StarClan has sent the darkness!" Fireheart recognised the meow of Halftail, a ThunderClan elder.

The ShadowClan medicine cat yowled in agreement, "StarClan is angry. These meetings are meant to be held in peace."

"Runningnose is right!" It was Yellowfang. "We shouldn't be fighting among ourselves, especially during leaf-bare. We should be worrying about keeping our Clans safe!" Her voice echoed in the frightened silence. "We must listen to StarClan."

CHAPTER 24

TALLSTAR SPOKE UP, a dim silhouette on top of the Great Rock. "This Gathering is over, by the will of StarClan." The crowd murmured in agreement. The air was thick with the scents of fear and hostility.

"Come, ThunderClan." Fireheart could barely see Bluestar as she leaped down from the Great Rock and headed for the edge of the clearing. He pushed his way through the other cats and hurried after her. He saw the massive outline of Tigerclaw as the deputy fell in step beside his leader, and the pale grey shapes of the other ThunderClan cats as they gathered behind the two great warriors. No cat spoke as they trekked solemnly up the slope towards home. Fireheart glanced over his shoulder. The other Clans were withdrawing too. By the time he reached the top of the slope, Fourtrees was deserted.

The Clan ran silently through the forest, following the familiar scent-lined trail. Fireheart spotted Greystripe at the back and he slowed his pace. Maybe Greystripe would be more prepared to talk about Silverstream, now that it was clear how tense things were between the Clans. His scent had been detected in RiverClan territory! Greystripe was putting himself and the Clan in danger with his secret meetings.

Fireheart searched for the right words but Greystripe hissed first. "I know what you're going to say. And I won't stop seeing her!"

"You're a mouse-brained fool!" Fireheart spat back. "They'll soon work out it's you. Bluestar will guess, or some cat from RiverClan'll recognise your scent. Tigerclaw's probably guessed already!"

Greystripe shot Fireheart an anxious glance. "Do you really think so?"

"I don't know," Fireheart admitted, relieved to hear a note of fear in Greystripe's voice. Greystripe had been acting as if he had no idea what might happen if the Clan found out about his affair. "But once he starts thinking about it..."

"OK, OK!" spat Greystripe. He was silent for a moment. "What if I promise we'll meet only at Fourtrees? That way our scent will be hard to detect, and I won't have to go into RiverClan territory. Will you leave me alone then?"

Fireheart felt his heart sink. Greystripe was not going to give up Silverstream that easily. Then he nodded. This had to be better than creeping into hostile Clan territory to see her.

"Satisfied?" Greystripe's eyes flashed in the gloom, but his voice sounded shaky. Fireheart felt a pang of regret for their lost friendship and a rush of sympathy for the grey warrior. He stretched his head forwards to nuzzle Greystripe's flank, but Greystripe ran on ahead, leaving Fireheart alone at the back of the group.

Even though the cats were tired from the journey, Bluestar called a meeting as soon as they were home. Most of the Clan was still awake anyway. The Gathering had been shorter than usual and the sudden cloud cover had alarmed even the cats left in the camp.

While Bluestar and Tigerclaw settled themselves on the Highrock, Fireheart hurried over to the nursery. He wanted to know how Cloudkit was. He poked his head through the entrance. It was pitch-black and warm inside.

"Hello, Fireheart," Brindleface whispered, a faint shadow shifting in the gloom. "Cloudkit's much better. Yellowfang gave him feverfew. It was just a chill." The queen sounded relieved. "What happened at the Gathering?"

"StarClan sent clouds to cover the moon. Bluestar's called a meeting. Can you come?"

Fireheart listened to Brindleface sniffing her kits. "Yes, I think I can," she answered finally. "My kits will sleep for a while."

Fireheart withdrew his head and together they joined

the cats gathered in the clearing. Fireheart felt fur brush against him and Cinderpaw glanced up at him with wide, worried eyes.

Bluestar had already begun. "The greatest threat seems to be from RiverClan and ShadowClan. We must be prepared for the possibility that these two Clans have united against us."

Shocked meows rippled through the Clan.

"Do you really think they've joined together?" Yellowfang rasped. "RiverClan has the best sources of prey, but I can't imagine they'd want to share with ShadowClan." Fireheart remembered Silverstream's words about RiverClan's hunger after the Twoleg invasion, but he held his tongue, fearful that Bluestar would want to know where he'd heard such a story.

"They didn't deny it," Tigerclaw pointed out.

Bluestar nodded. "Whatever the truth, we must be on full alert. From tonight, each patrol will have four cats, at least three of them warriors. The patrols will be more frequent, two each night, and one during the day, as well as the dawn and dusk patrols. We must put a stop to RiverClan's and ShadowClan's raids on our territory and, since they have chosen to ignore our words, we must be prepared to fight."

The Clan yowled their agreement. Fireheart joined in even though he was worried about what this open hostility might mean for Greystripe. He looked around at the other cats. He could see all their eyes shining – except Greystripe's. The grey warrior sat with his head bowed in the shadows at the edge of the clearing.

When the noise died away, Bluestar spoke again. "The first patrol will leave before dawn." She jumped down from the Highrock. Tigerclaw followed and the rest of the Clan broke up into small groups. Fireheart could hear them murmuring nervously as he padded to the warriors' den.

Fireheart settled into his nest, kneading the moss with his paws to make it comfortable. An owl hooted at the top of the ravine. He knew he would not sleep yet. His mind was racing with the accusations that had flown around the Gathering. He understood RiverClan's anger. They had picked up the scent of ThunderClan cats in their territory and they were hungry now that their prey had been depleted by the Twoleg invasion.

But what about ShadowClan? It was smaller since ThunderClan had helped them to chase out their tyrannical former leader and his band of followers. Brokenstar had even admitted to killing Raggedstar, his own father, to become Clan leader. But the Clan had been left in peace to recover from Brokenstar's bloody rule. And Fireheart couldn't help thinking that, with fewer mouths to feed, ShadowClan had no need to raid ThunderClan's hunting grounds, or anyone else's.

As he puzzled over these thoughts, Whitestorm and Darkstripe pushed their way into the den. Before Whitestorm went to his nest, he stopped beside Fireheart.

"You're to join me with Sandpaw and Mousefur on patrol at sunhigh," he meowed.

"Yes, Whitestorm," Fireheart answered before resting his chin on his paws. He had to get some sleep – his Clan needed him to be fit and ready to fight.

The clouds that had covered the moon had rolled away by the next morning. Fireheart enjoyed the faint warmth of the sun on his back as he washed himself in the clearing. Cloudkit jumped out of the nursery entrance opposite him, looking bright and happy.

Fireheart thanked StarClan that he had recovered so quickly. Sandpaw had been right about the kit's resilience. He looked around to see if Longtail and Dustpaw were there to see it too, but the clearing was empty.

Fireheart crossed over to the nursery. "Hi, Cloudkit," he meowed. "Feeling better?"

"Yep," squeaked Cloudkit. He spun around in a circle, grasping for his tail with his tiny jaws. A small ball of moss that had been sticking to his fur fell off and rolled along the ground. Cloudkit leaped on it and pawed it into the air. It bounced on to the ground beside Fireheart.

Fireheart knocked it back towards the kit and Cloudkit sprang up to catch it in his teeth.

"Well done!" Fireheart was impressed. With one paw he scooped the moss ball high into the air, sending it flying across the clearing.

Cloudkit raced after the moss and grabbed it. He rolled on to his back, threw the ball up with his forepaws and kicked it away with his hind legs. It landed next to the nursery. Cloudkit scrambled up and scooted after it. He crouched a rabbit leap away, his hindquarters bunched in the air.

Fireheart watched as the kit prepared to pounce. Suddenly his fur prickled. A long, dark foreleg was reaching towards the moss ball from behind the nursery.

"Cloudkit," Fireheart called, "wait!" Shadowy images of rogue cats were still fresh in his mind.

Cloudkit sat up and looked around at him, puzzled.

Tigerclaw emerged from behind the kitten, holding the moss ball between his teeth. He carried the ball over to the kit and dropped it by Cloudkit's fluffy white paws. "Be careful," he growled. "You wouldn't want to lose such a precious plaything." As he spoke, the dark warrior stared at Fireheart over Cloudkit's head.

Fireheart shivered. What did Tigerclaw mean by that? He seemed to be talking about the moss ball – but did he really mean that *Cloudkit* was a plaything? An image of Cinderpaw flashed into Fireheart's mind, a wounded huddle beside the Thunderpath. Was that another *plaything* he had lost? A cold feeling of dread seeped into his heart as once more he wondered if the ThunderClan deputy was somehow responsible for his apprentice's accident.

CHAPTER 25

"CLOUDKIT!"

FIREHEART HEARD Brindleface calling from inside the nursery. Tigerclaw turned and padded away. Cloudkit gave the moss ball a final shove and ran over to the nursery entrance. "Bye, Fireheart," he mewed before he disappeared inside.

Fireheart looked up at the sky. It was almost sunhigh: time to join his patrol. He was hungry, but no fresh-kill had been gathered yet. Perhaps he might find something while they were out. He hurried across the clearing and out through the gorse tunnel, frozen leaves crunching beneath his paws.

Sandpaw and Mousefur were already waiting at the foot of the slope. Fireheart raised his tail in greeting, unexpectedly happy to see Sandpaw.

"Hi," meowed Sandpaw.

Whitestorm emerged from the gorse tunnel. "Is the dawn patrol back yet?"

"No sign of them," answered Mousefur. But as she spoke, Fireheart heard the rustle of undergrowth above them. Out of the bushes came Willowpelt, Runningwind, Darkstripe and Dustpaw.

"We've patrolled the entire RiverClan border," Willowpelt reported. "No sign of any hunting parties so far. Bluestar's patrol will check the area again this afternoon."

"Good," replied Whitestorm. "We'll take the ShadowClan border."

"Hopefully they'll have the same good sense as RiverClan and stay away," meowed Darkstripe. "After last night, they must know we'll be looking out for them."

"I hope so," growled Whitestorm. He turned to his patrol. "Are you ready?" Fireheart nodded. Whitestorm flicked the tip of his tail and leaped away into the bracken.

Fireheart followed Mousefur and Whitestorm. They kept up a fast pace as they climbed out of the ravine. Sandpaw was right behind Fireheart; he could feel her warm breath as she scrambled up the boulders.

They had not even reached Snakerocks when Fireheart picked up a sinister, familiar scent. He opened his mouth to warn the others but Mousefur spoke first. "ShadowClan!"

The four cats stopped to pick up the smell for themselves.

"I can't believe they've come back already!" Sandpaw murmured. Fireheart noticed the fur quiver along her spine.

"The scent is recent." Whitestorm's eyes glittered with fury. "I had hoped Nightstar might bring some honour to his Clan. But I suppose the cold winds beyond the Thunderpath blow over every ShadowClan cat's heart."

Fireheart turned away and began pushing his way into a thick patch of bracken. He rubbed his teeth along the fronds to pick up the scent that hung there. It was ShadowClan all right. The smell was familiar. *Very* familiar. Fireheart paused. The scent belonged to a ShadowClan warrior he had encountered before, but which one?

Fireheart pushed onwards, hoping more scent-markings might jog his memory. Now he could smell something else. Fireheart looked down. On the ground, among the bracken stems, lay a pile of rabbit bones. Clan cats normally buried the bones of their prey as a sign of respect for the life they had taken. Suddenly aware of what this might mean, Fireheart picked up a mouthful and wove back through the bracken. He dropped them at Whitestorm's paws.

Whitestorm stared at the bones in fury. "Rabbit bones? The warriors who left these want us to know they've been hunting on our land! Bluestar must know about this immediately."

"Will she send a battle party against ShadowClan?" asked Fireheart. He had never seen Whitestorm so angry.

"She should!" hissed the great white warrior. "And I'll

lead it myself if I can. Nightstar has betrayed our trust and StarClan knows he must be punished."

"Bluestar!" Whitestorm flung the rabbit bones down in the middle of the camp clearing.

"Bluestar has already left on patrol," Tigerclaw told him, stepping out from the shadows.

Halftail and Frostfur came hurrying from their dens to find out what was going on.

Whitestorm stared at Tigerclaw, still furious. "Look at these!" he spat.

Tigerclaw didn't need to be told what they meant; their scent carried the whole story. His eyes began to burn with anger.

Fireheart hung back at the edge of the clearing and watched the two great warriors. The evidence was certainly ominous, but the discovery of the bones had filled his mind with questions, not anger. It was only three moons since ShadowClan had driven out their cruel leader, with the help of ThunderClan. How could that same Clan possibly be ready to risk war with ThunderClan?

Tigerclaw clearly had no such doubts. Already he was calling Darkstripe and Runningwind to him. "Willowpelt and Mousefur will join us too!" he announced. "We'll find a ShadowClan patrol and leave them with some wounds that'll remind them to keep out of our territory in the future."

Whitestorm nodded.

"Can I come?" Sandpaw meowed. She had been pacing excitedly behind the white warrior. Now she stopped and looked at him with glittering eyes.

"Not this time," Whitestorm told her.

Frustration flickered across her face. "But what about Fireheart?" she meowed. "He found the bones."

Tigerclaw narrowed his eyes, his hackles raised. "*Fireheart* can stay here and tell Bluestar when she arrives," he hissed contemptuously.

"You're going to leave before she gets back?" Fireheart asked.

"Of course," Tigerclaw spat. "This needs to be settled now!" He turned to Whitestorm and flicked his tail. Fireheart watched as the two warriors charged out of the camp, Darkstripe, Willowpelt, Runningwind and Mousefur close behind. He could hear their paws pounding the frozen earth as they headed for the side of the ravine.

Fireheart was suddenly aware how empty the camp was. As Frostfur and Halftail came forward and began sniffing the rabbit bones, he meowed, "Who went with Bluestar?"

Frostfur looked up. "Greystripe, Longtail and Swiftpaw."

A cold wind ruffled Fireheart's fur. He hoped that was what made him shiver. He was the only warrior left in camp. "Will you check the apprentices' den to see if Dustpaw's there?" Fireheart asked Sandpaw.

She nodded, bounded across the clearing, and poked

her head into the den. "He's there," she called back, ducking out again. "Asleep, with Brackenpaw."

Yellowfang came padding out of her den and lifted her head. Fireheart relaxed a little at the familiar sight of the old medicine cat. He narrowed his eyes, ready to greet her. But as Yellowfang tasted the air, her eyes clouded with fear. With slow, stiff steps, she approached the rabbit bones and carefully sniffed each one.

Fireheart watched her, wondering why she was so interested in the old bones.

At last she looked up and stared into Fireheart's eyes. "Brokenstar!" she rasped, in a voice choked with horror.

"Brokenstar?" Fireheart echoed. Then it hit him. That was why the scent in the bracken had been so familiar. It was *Brokenstar's* scent. "Are you sure?" he meowed urgently. "Tigerclaw has already left for ShadowClan territory."

"ShadowClan isn't to blame for this!" cried Yellowfang. "This is Brokenstar and his old warrior friends. I was ShadowClan's medicine cat. I was there at their kitting. I know their scents as well as I know my own." She paused. "You must find Tigerclaw and stop him. He will be making a terrible mistake if he attacks them!"

The blood roared in Fireheart's ears, making him dizzy. What should he do? "But I'm the only warrior left!" he meowed breathlessly to Yellowfang. "What if Brokenstar attacks the camp while I'm gone? He's done it before. He might have left the bones as a trap so that our camp was left unguarded."

"You *must* tell Tigerclaw before he—" Yellowfang pleaded, but Fireheart shook his head.

"I can't leave you all alone."

"Then I shall go!" Yellowfang hissed.

"No! I'll go!" meowed Sandpaw.

Fireheart looked from one cat to the other. He couldn't afford to send either – their strength and training were needed here to protect the Clan. But Yellowfang was right; innocent blood couldn't be shed. Brokenstar was the invader here; ThunderClan had no quarrel with ShadowClan. He would have to send another cat. He closed his eyes and thought hard. The answer came in a moment. "Brackenpaw!" Fireheart hissed, opening his eyes wide. He called the apprentice's name out loud.

The young cat pushed his way out of his den and padded across the clearing towards Fireheart. "What is it?" he asked, blinking the sleep from his eyes.

"I have an urgent mission for you," Fireheart told him.

Brackenpaw shook himself and stood taller. "Yes, Fireheart," he mewed.

"You must find Tigerclaw. He's taken a raiding party to attack a ShadowClan patrol. Stop him and tell him that it was Brokenstar who has been invading our territory!" Brackenpaw's eyes widened with alarm, but Fireheart went on. "You might have to cross the Thunderpath. I know you haven't been trained..." Images of Cinderpaw's broken body flashed in Fireheart's mind, but he forced them away. He looked deep into Brackenpaw's eyes. "You must find Tigerclaw," he repeated, "or there will be a war between the Clans for no reason!"

Brackenpaw nodded, his eyes calm and filled with purpose. "I'll find him," the tabby apprentice promised.

"May StarClan go with you," Fireheart murmured, reaching forwards to touch Brackenpaw's flank with his nose.

Brackenpaw turned and sprinted out through the gorse tunnel. Fireheart watched him go, struggling to keep calm. Cinderpaw... the Thunderpath... the images kept flashing back. Fireheart shook his head to clear it. There was no time to worry now. If Brokenstar was in ThunderClan territory, the camp had to prepare for an attack.

"What's happening?" Dustpaw had emerged from the apprentices' den. Fireheart glanced at him, ran to the head of the clearing, and scrambled up on to the Highrock. The clearing seemed a long way below his trembling legs. He swallowed hard and began the customary call. "Let all cats old enough to..." But the words were taking too long! "The camp is in danger. Come here now!" he yowled urgently.

The elders and queens rushed from their dens, followed by their kits. They looked bewildered when they saw Fireheart on top of the Highrock. Cinderpaw limped out of the fern tunnel and looked up at Fireheart with a strong, bright gaze. When Fireheart saw her, the camp suddenly stopped swaying beneath him.

"What's going on?" demanded One-eye, the oldest ThunderClan cat. "What do you think you're doing up there?"

Fireheart didn't hesitate. "Brokenstar is back. He might be in ThunderClan territory right now. All our other warriors are out of the camp. If Brokenstar attacks, we must be ready. Kits and elders stay in the nursery. The rest of you must be ready to fight—"

A menacing yowl from the camp entrance cut short Fireheart's speech. A lean dark brown tabby with matted fur and torn ears strode into the camp. His bristling tail was bent in the middle like a broken branch.

"Brokenstar!" Fireheart gasped, instinctively unsheathing his claws as every hair on his body stood on end.

Four mangy warriors prowled in behind their leader, their eyes glittering with hatred.

"So you're the only warrior left!" Brokenstar hissed, his lips drawn back in a snarl. "This will be easier than I thought!"

CHAPTER 26

YELLOWFANG, DUSTPAW AND Sandpaw rushed forwards in a defensive row, and the queens lined up behind them. Fireheart saw Cinderpaw hobbling to join them, but Dustpaw spat angrily at the small grey cat as she neared and Cinderpaw scrabbled clumsily away, ears flat, back into Yellowfang's den.

The elders grabbed the kits, bundled them into the nursery, and squeezed inside after them. Brindleface picked up Cloudkit in her jaws and pushed him in last. She tugged at the brambles with her paws, ignoring the thorns, and covered the entrance before turning to join the rest of her Clan in the clearing.

Fireheart leaped down from the Highrock and raced to Yellowfang's side. He arched his back and hissed at Brokenstar, "You lost the last time we fought – and you'll lose again!"

"Never!" Brokenstar spat back. "You might have taken my Clan away from me, but you can't kill me – I have more lives than you!"

"One ThunderClan life is worth ten of yours!" Fireheart growled. He gave a warrior's yowl and the clearing exploded into battle.

Fireheart leaped straight for Brokenstar and grasped the dark brown tabby with his claws. Life as an outlaw had treated the former Clan leader harshly – Fireheart could feel the ribs of the flea-bitten tom beneath his fur. But Brokenstar was still strong. He twisted around and sank his teeth into Fireheart's hind leg. Fireheart yowled and hissed with rage, but kept his grip. Brokenstar struggled forwards, scrabbling with his paws on the frozen ground. Fireheart felt his claws raking along Brokenstar's bony flanks as the rogue warrior ripped himself free. Fireheart lunged after him, but other claws were grasping at his hind leg. He looked over his shoulder to see who it was. Clawface crouched there, staring at Fireheart with narrowed, mocking eyes.

Fireheart looked back at him in disbelief. He had never expected to see this cat again. He forgot Brokenstar instantly. It was Clawface who had killed Spottedleaf six moons ago; he had murdered the ThunderClan medicine cat in cold blood so that Brokenstar could steal Frostfur's kits. Rage roared in Fireheart's ears. As he twisted around and threw himself on top of the scrawny brown tom, Fireheart glimpsed a flash of tortoiseshell fur out of the corner of his eye, and the sweet scent of Spottedleaf hit the roof of his mouth. He felt her spirit beside him. She had come to help him avenge her death.

Fireheart hardly noticed the pain in his leg as he tore it free from Clawface's grasp and flew at him. The tom reared up and flailed his wide front paws. Thorn-sharp claws caught Fireheart behind his ear. Pain ripped through him like fire and he staggered. Clawface was on him in an instant, pinning Fireheart to the ground and sinking his teeth into the back of his neck.

Fireheart screeched in agony, "Help me, Spottedleaf! I can't do it!"

Suddenly the weight was wrenched off his back. Fireheart sprang to his paws and spun around. Greystripe! The grey warrior stood motionless, his eyes filled with horror. Clawface's body hung limply from his jaws. Greystripe opened his mouth and Clawface fell to the ground, dead.

Fireheart took a step forwards. "He killed Spottedleaf, Greystripe!" This was no time for remorse. "Is Bluestar with you?" he went on urgently.

Greystripe shook his head. "She sent me back to fetch Tigerclaw," he replied. "We found bones. Bluestar recognised Brokenstar's stench and guessed he must be leading the rogue cats."

A hiss sounded nearby and two cats crashed into Fireheart. He leaped out of the way. It was Frostfur battling with another of the attacking cats. The queen was fighting with all the power of StarClan. These were the cats who had stolen her kits. Hate shone in her eyes as she struggled. Fireheart held himself back – Frostfur didn't need his help. A moment later the rogue warrior was sent screeching away, through the bracken camp wall.

Frostfur chased after him, but Fireheart called her back. "You have given him enough wounds to remember you!" The queen skidded to a halt by the bracken wall and turned, her sides heaving and her white fur stained with her enemy's blood.

Another rogue warrior screeched past Fireheart and headed for the camp wall. Dustpaw chased after him and managed to give the mottled tabby a fierce bite before he let him scrabble out of the camp. *Only Brokenstar and one warrior left*, Fireheart thought.

Sandpaw had the rogue warrior pinned to the ground. The tom was lying motionless beneath her. *Watch out!* thought Fireheart, remembering his favorite trick of letting an enemy think he had won. But Sandpaw was not deceived. When the tom leaped to his paws, she was ready. She sprang off him and then lunged, grasping the warrior with her claws to flip him over and rake his belly with her hind legs. Only when he squealed like a kit did she let go of him. The rogue tore out of the camp entrance, still wailing.

There was an eerie moment of stillness. The ThunderClan cats stood in silence and stared at the blood and fur that was scattered around the clearing. In the middle lay Clawface's body.

Where was Brokenstar? Fireheart spun around in alarm, scanning the camp. Could he have broken into the nursery? He was about to spring towards the bramble den when a wretched howl from Yellowfang's den tore the air. Fireheart tore across to the fern tunnel. Cinderpaw! He raced into the den, expecting the worst, but saw instead Brokenstar lying in a heap on the ground. The old medicine cat stood over him.

Brokenstar's eyes were closed and bloody. Fireheart saw his sides heave once and stop moving. He recognised from the deep stillness in the rogue warrior's body that Brokenstar was losing a life.

Yellowfang's claws were unsheathed and glistened red. Her face was twisted and her eyes glazed.

Suddenly Brokenstar gasped and began to breathe again. Fireheart waited for Yellowfang to lunge at him with another killing bite, but she hesitated. Brokenstar didn't get up.

Fireheart ran to the medicine cat's side. "Is this his last life? Why don't you finish him off?" he urged. "He murdered his father, banished you from your Clan, and tried to kill you."

"It's not his last life," she rasped, "and even if it were, I couldn't kill him."

"Why not? StarClan would honour you for it." Fireheart could not believe her words. The name Brokenstar had always made this old she-cat bristle with rage.

Yellowfang dragged her gaze from Brokenstar and looked at Fireheart. Her eyes clouded with pain and grief as she murmured: "He is my son."

Fireheart felt the ground lurch under his paws. "But medicine cats are forbidden to have kits," he blurted out.

"I know," answered Yellowfang. "I never intended to have kits. But then I fell in love with Raggedstar." Her voice was thick with sorrow. Suddenly Fireheart thought back to the battle when Brokenstar was driven out of the ShadowClan camp. Just before he fled, the cruel leader had told Yellowfang that he had murdered his father. Yellowfang had been devastated, and now Fireheart understood why.

"There were three kits in my litter," Yellowfang went on. "But only Brokenstar survived. I gave him to a ShadowClan queen to bring up as her own. I thought that losing two of my kits was punishment from StarClan for breaking the warrior code. But I was wrong. My punishment wasn't that two of my kits died. It was that *this* one survived!" Yellowfang looked in disgust at Brokenstar's bleeding body. "And now I cannot kill him. I must accept my fate, as StarClan wishes it."

Yellowfang staggered, and Fireheart thought she was going to collapse. He pressed his body against her flank to support her and whispered, "Does he know you're his mother?"

Yellowfang shook her head.

Brokenstar began to wail pitifully. "I can't see!" Fireheart realised with horror that the rogue cat's eyes had been scratched beyond repair.

Fireheart cautiously approached him. Brokenstar lay still. Fireheart poked him with a forepaw and Yellowfang's son moaned again. "Don't kill me," he whined. Fireheart backed away, feeling a shudder of revulsion at the warrior's fear.

Yellowfang took a deep breath. "I will see to him." She walked over to her wounded son, grasped him by the scruff of his neck, and dragged him to the nest that Patchpelt had left.

Fireheart let her go. He wanted to check that Cinderpaw was all right. He caught sight of a dark shape moving inside the split rock where Yellowfang slept. "Cinderpaw?" he called.

Cinderpaw poked her head out.

"Are you OK?" Fireheart asked.

"Have the rogue cats gone?" she whispered.

"Yes, except Brokenstar. He's badly injured. Yellowfang's seeing to him." He waited for Cinderpaw's shocked reaction, but she just shook her head slowly and stared at the ground.

"Are you OK?" Fireheart repeated.

"I should have fought alongside you." Cinderpaw's voice was choked with shame.

"You would have been killed!"

"That's what Dustpaw said. He told me to go and hide with the kits." The small cat's eyes were full of despair. "But I wouldn't have minded being killed. What good am I like this? I'm just a burden on this Clan."

Fireheart felt a thorn-sharp pang of pity. He searched for words to comfort her, but before he could speak, Yellowfang's rasping mew sounded from the bracken.

"Cinderpaw," she called. "Fetch me some cobwebs, quickly!" Cinderpaw turned at once and disappeared inside the rock, returning a moment later with one paw wrapped in a swathe of cobwebs. As quickly as she could, she scrambled awkwardly over to Yellowfang and thrust the cobwebs inside the nest.

"Now get me some of that comfrey root," ordered Yellowfang.

As Cinderpaw limped back to the split rock, Fireheart turned to leave. There was nothing more he could do here. He must find out how the rest of the Clan was.

Hardly any cat had moved in the camp clearing. Fireheart padded straight to Dustpaw and meowed, "Yellowfang is tending to Brokenstar's wounds. Cinderpaw's helping her." He ignored Dustpaw's gasp of disbelief. "Go and guard him." Dustpaw ran to the tunnel and disappeared inside.

Fireheart went over to Greystripe. The grey warrior was still staring at Clawface's body. "You saved my life," Fireheart murmured. "Thank you."

Greystripe lifted his gaze to Fireheart. "I would give my life for you," he answered simply.

Feeling choked, Fireheart watched his friend turn and walk away. Perhaps their friendship was not over after all.

The sound of paws pounding through the gorse tunnel broke into his thoughts. Bluestar came rushing into the camp, followed by Longtail and Swiftpaw. Fireheart felt his shoulders droop with relief at the sight of his Clan leader.

She looked around at the blood-spattered clearing, her eyes wide, until her gaze rested on Clawface's body. "Brokenstar attacked?" she meowed.

Fireheart nodded.

"Is he dead?"

"He's with Yellowfang," Fireheart answered, forcing out the words in spite of his exhaustion. "He's been wounded – his eyes."

"And the other rogue warriors?"

"We chased them off."

"Are any of our Clan badly hurt?" Bluestar demanded, looking once more around the clearing. The cats shook their heads. "Good," she meowed. "Sandpaw, Swiftpaw, take this body out of the camp and bury it. No elders need be present. No rogue deserves to be buried with the honour of StarClan ritual."

Swiftpaw and Sandpaw began to drag Clawface towards the tunnel.

"Are the elders safe?" Bluestar asked.

"They're in the nursery," Fireheart told her. As he spoke a rustling sounded from the bramble den and Halftail appeared, followed by the other kits and elders. Fireheart saw Cloudkit tumble out and scamper excitedly across the clearing to Brindleface. She greeted him with a brisk lick and the kit turned to watch Clawface's body as it disappeared away through the tunnel.

"Is he dead?" Cloudkit asked curiously. "Can I go and see?"

"Hush," whispered Brindleface, tucking her tail around him.

"Where's Tigerclaw?" Bluestar asked.

"He's taken a party to attack a ShadowClan patrol," Fireheart explained. "We found bones on our patrol. They smelled of ShadowClan so Tigerclaw decided to attack. I sent Brackenpaw to stop him when Yellowfang realised it was Brokenstar's scent on them."

"Brackenpaw?" meowed Bluestar, narrowing her eyes. "Even though he might have to cross the Thunderpath?"

"I was the only warrior left in camp. There was no one else I could send."

Bluestar nodded, the concern in her eyes giving way to understanding. "You didn't want to leave the camp unguarded?" she meowed. "You did well, Fireheart. I think Brokenstar hoped to lure all our warriors away from the camp. We found bones, too."

"Greystripe told me." Fireheart looked around for his friend, but Greystripe had disappeared.

"Send Yellowfang to me when she's finished with Brokenstar," Bluestar ordered. She pricked her ears at the noise of more paws in the gorse tunnel. Tigerclaw came racing into the camp, followed by Whitestorm and the rest of the raiding party. Fireheart craned his neck to peer around the warriors until he saw Brackenpaw, right at the back. The young apprentice looked exhausted but unhurt. Fireheart let out a quiet sigh of relief.

"Did Brackenpaw reach you before you found a patrol?" asked Bluestar, walking over to her deputy.

"We hadn't even entered their territory," Tigerclaw answered. "We were just about to cross the Thunderpath." His eyes narrowed. "Was that Clawface they were burying?"

Bluestar nodded.

"Then Brackenpaw was right," meowed the deputy. "Brokenstar was planning to attack the camp. Is he dead too?"

"No. Yellowfang is tending to his wounds."

"Surely not!" Mousefur exclaimed, exchanging a glance with Runningwind beside her.

Tigerclaw's face darkened. "Tending to his wounds?" he snarled. "We should kill him, not waste time making him better!"

"We'll discuss that once I've spoken to Yellowfang," meowed Bluestar calmly.

"You can discuss it with me now, Bluestar." Yellowfang padded into the clearing, her head drooping with exhaustion.

"Have you left Brokenstar alone?" growled Tigerclaw, his amber eyes flashing.

Yellowfang raised her head and looked at the dark warrior. "Dustpaw is guarding him. And I've given him poppy seeds, so he'll sleep for a while. Brokenstar is blind now, Tigerclaw. There's no way he'll try to escape. He'd die of hunger in a week, if a fox or a gang of crows didn't kill him first."

"Well, that makes it easier," Tigerclaw snarled. "We won't have to kill him ourselves. We can let the forest deal with him."

Yellowfang turned to Bluestar. "We cannot let him die," she meowed.

"Why not?"

Fireheart held his breath as he watched the leader's eyes flick from Yellowfang to Tigerclaw and back again. He wondered if Yellowfang was going to tell Bluestar that Brokenstar was her son.

"If we did, we would be no better than he is," replied Yellowfang calmly.

Tigerclaw's tail flicked in anger.

"What do you think, Whitestorm?" Bluestar meowed before Tigerclaw could speak.

"It will be a burden on our Clan to look after him," Whitestorm answered thoughtfully. "But Yellowfang is right – if we send him out into the forest, or kill him in cold blood, StarClan will know we have stooped as low as he."

One-eye stepped forwards. "Bluestar," she meowed in her croaky old voice. "In the past we have sometimes kept prisoners for many moons. We could do it again." Fireheart remembered that Yellowfang herself had been a prisoner when she first came to the camp. He waited for the medicine cat to remind Bluestar of this, but she said nothing.

"So you would really consider keeping this rogue inside our camp?" Tigerclaw's eyes blazed with rage as he challenged his leader. With a pang, Fireheart couldn't help agreeing with the dark warrior's words. The thought of killing Brokenstar appalled him — he knew better than any of these cats what that would mean to Yellowfang — but Brokenstar was a fearsome enemy, even without his sight. Keeping him in the camp would be difficult and dangerous for all the members of the Clan.

"Is he really blind?" Bluestar asked Yellowfang.

"Yes, he is."

"Has he other wounds?"

Fireheart replied this time. "I clawed him pretty badly," he admitted. He looked over to Yellowfang and was relieved when the old she-cat dipped her head just enough for him to know she forgave him for wounding her son.

"How long till they heal?" asked Bluestar.

"About a moon," Yellowfang answered.

"Then you may nurse him till then. After that we will discuss his future again. And from now on, he will be known as Brokentail, not Brokenstar. We cannot take away the lives that StarClan gave him, but this cat is no longer a Clan leader." Bluestar looked questioningly at Tigerclaw. His tail twitched, but he didn't speak.

"It is decided," Bluestar meowed. "He stays."

CHAPTER 27

FIREHEART LIMPED OVER to the clump of nettles and began to lick his wounds. He would go and see Yellowfang later, when she had finished tending to the other cats.

The weak rays of the setting sun threw long shadows across the clearing. Dustpaw had been relieved from his guard duty by Longtail. Tigerclaw had taken the rest of his unscathed raiding party out in search of fresh-kill. Fireheart's stomach growled. He looked up at the sound of pawsteps, but it was only Sandpaw and Swiftpaw returning from their burial duty.

The two cats padded over to Bluestar, who was sitting beneath the Highrock with Whitestorm. Fireheart pushed himself to his paws and walked over to join them. With a flick of his tail he beckoned to Dustpaw, who was licking his own scratches beside the tree stump. Dustpaw flashed him a doubtful look but got up wearily and followed him.

"We've buried Clawface," meowed Sandpaw.

"Thank you," Bluestar replied. The ThunderClan leader looked directly at Swiftpaw. "You may go." The black and white apprentice dipped his head and headed for his den.

Fireheart signalled to Dustpaw again to come closer. The tabby apprentice narrowed his eyes and padded forwards to stand beside Sandpaw.

"Bluestar," Fireheart began hesitantly, "Sandpaw and Dustpaw fought like warriors when Brokentail attacked. We would have been in much more trouble without their strength and courage." Dustpaw's eyes widened and Sandpaw looked at the ground as Fireheart spoke.

A purr rumbled from Whitestorm's throat. "It's not like you to be shy," he meowed to his apprentice.

Sandpaw's ears twitched uncomfortably. "Fireheart's the one who saved the Clan," she burst out. "He was the one who alerted the camp so that we were ready for Brokentail's attack."

It was Fireheart's turn to feel embarrassed. He was relieved when Tigerclaw and the hunting party trotted into the camp at that moment, carrying plenty of fresh-kill.

Bluestar nodded at Tigerclaw and then turned to face Dustpaw and Sandpaw. "It makes me proud to know that ThunderClan has such fine warriors," she meowed. "It's time you both took your warrior names. We shall have the naming ceremony now, while the sun is setting, and then we can eat."

Sandpaw and Dustpaw looked excitedly at each other. Fireheart lifted his chin and purred. Bluestar called to the Clan. Fireheart felt even happier when he saw Greystripe appear from the warriors' den. He hadn't left the camp after all.

The Clan gathered around the edge of the clearing. Elders and queens sat with the apprentices and kits on one side; Fireheart waited with the warriors on the other. He looked at Cloudkit nestled beside Brindleface. The kit's eyes shone with excitement and Fireheart felt a rush of pride that his kin-kit could see him sitting with the Clan warriors. Bluestar stood in the centre with Sandpaw and Dustpaw.

The last arc of sun glowed pink on the horizon. The Clan waited silently as it dipped out of sight, leaving the darkening sky pricked with stars.

Bluestar looked up and fixed her eyes on the brightest star in Silverpelt. "I, Bluestar, leader of ThunderClan, call upon my warrior ancestors to look down on these two apprentices. They have trained hard to understand the ways of your code and I commend them to you as warriors in their turn." She gazed down at the pair of young cats in front of her. "Sandpaw, Dustpaw, do you promise to uphold the warrior code and to protect and defend this Clan, even at the cost of your life?"

Sandpaw stared back, her eyes gleaming. "I do," she replied.

Dustpaw echoed her words, his voice strong and low. "I do."

"Then by the powers of StarClan I give you your warrior names. Sandpaw, from this moment you will be known as Sandstorm. StarClan honours your courage and your spirit and we welcome you as a full warrior of ThunderClan." Bluestar stepped forwards and rested her muzzle on top of Sandstorm's bowed head.

Sandstorm licked Bluestar's shoulder respectfully before she turned and walked towards Whitestorm. Fireheart saw her eyes flash proudly at her mentor as she settled down beside him in her new place with the warriors.

Bluestar turned her eyes to the dark brown tabby. "Dustpaw, from this moment you will be known as Dustpelt. StarClan honours your bravery and your honesty and we welcome you as a full warrior of ThunderClan." She touched his head with her muzzle and he too gave the leader's shoulder a respectful lick before joining the other warriors.

The voices of the Clan rose in tribute, sending clouds of misty breath into the night air. As one they chanted the new warrior names. "Sandstorm! Dustpelt! Sandstorm! Dustpelt!"

"In the tradition of our ancestors," meowed Bluestar, raising her voice, "Sandstorm and Dustpelt must sit in silent vigil until dawn and guard the camp alone while we sleep. But before they begin their vigil, the Clan will share a meal.

It has been a long day and we have reason to be proud of these cats who defended our camp against the rogues. Fireheart, StarClan – thanks you for your courage. You are a great warrior and I'm proud to count you as a member of my Clan."

The cats meowed again. A purr burst from Fireheart's throat as he looked around at his Clan. Only Tigerclaw and Dustpelt eyed him with hostility, but for once he felt untouched by their jealousy. Bluestar had praised him, and that was enough.

One by one the cats stepped forwards to take some of the fresh-kill Tigerclaw's party had brought.

Fireheart walked over to Sandstorm. "We can eat together as warriors tonight," he meowed happily. "If that's OK with you?" he added. Sandstorm purred at him and Fireheart felt a prickle of pleasure.

"Choose something for me," she called as Fireheart dashed away to the pile of fresh-kill. "I'm starving!"

Fireheart picked out a mouse for Sandstorm, temptingly plump for so late in leaf-bare. He took a bluetit for himself and turned to carry his catch back to Sandstorm. Then his heart sank – Dustpelt, Whitestorm, and Darkstripe had joined her. He'd been foolish to expect they would share their meal alone. This was a time for the whole Clan to share together in celebration.

The thought reminded Fireheart of Cinderpaw. He looked around and realised that he hadn't seen her at the naming ceremony. She must still be in Yellowfang's clearing. He bounded over to Sandstorm and dropped the fresh-kill beside her. "I'll be back in five rabbit hops," he meowed. "I want to take something to Cinderpaw."

"Sure." Sandstorm shrugged.

Fireheart quickly collected a vole from the fresh-kill pile and carried it across the clearing. He was surprised to see Yellowfang sitting in her den. She'd been at the naming ceremony, so she must have come straight back afterwards.

"I hope that's not for me," she growled as Fireheart approached. "I've already had my share."

Fireheart dropped the vole on the ground. "I brought it for Cinderpaw," he answered. "I thought she might want something. She wasn't at the naming ceremony."

"I've given her some mouse meat, but you're welcome to give her that as well."

Fireheart looked around the fern-shaded clearing. Brokenstar's brown fur was just visible through the stems of Patchpelt's old nest. The warrior was not moving.

"He's still asleep." Yellowfang's tone was brisk, the voice of a medicine cat rather than a mother. Fireheart couldn't help feeling relieved. He wanted to believe Yellowfang's loyalties still lay with ThunderClan. He picked up the vole and carried it to Cinderpaw's nest. "Hey, Cinderpaw," he meowed softly into the bracken.

The grey cat stirred and pushed herself to a sitting position. "Fireheart."

Fireheart stepped through the fronds and sat in the small space beside her. He dropped the vole at her paws. "Here," he meowed. "Yellowfang's not the only one trying to fatten you up!"

"Thanks," Cinderpaw mewed. But she left the vole lying beside her paw and didn't even bend down to sniff it.

"Are you still thinking about the battle?" Fireheart asked gently.

Cinderpaw shrugged. "I *am* just a burden, aren't I?" She looked up at Fireheart with sad, round eyes.

"Who's a burden?" Yellowfang's growl interrupted them as the old grey medicine cat poked her head into the nest. "Are you upsetting my helper?" she meowed at Fireheart. "I don't know how I would have coped today if it hadn't been for this one." She looked warmly at Cinderpaw, her orange eyes soft. "I even had her mixing herbs this evening!"

Cinderpaw looked down shyly and dipped her head to take a bite of the vole.

"I think I might keep her with me awhile longer," Yellowfang went on. "She's becoming more useful every day. Besides, I'm getting used to her company."

Cinderpaw glanced up at the old medicine cat, a teasing glint in her eyes. "Only because you're deaf enough to put up with my chattering!" Yellowfang pretended to spit crossly at the young cat, and Cinderpaw added to Fireheart, "Well, that's what she keeps telling me, anyway."

Fireheart was surprised to feel a pang of envy at the

close bond these two cats had developed. He'd always thought of himself as Yellowfang's only real friend in the Clan, but now it looked like she had another. But at least Cinderpaw had somewhere to stay – if she couldn't train to be a warrior, she'd feel out of place in the apprentices' den.

Fireheart stood up. It was time he went back to Sandstorm. "Will you be OK here with Brokentail?" he asked.

Yellowfang gave him a disdainful look. "I think we can manage, don't you, Cinderpaw?"

"He wouldn't dare cause trouble," she agreed confidently. "And Longtail's here to help."

Yellowfang ducked her head out of the nest, and Fireheart squeezed out after her. "Bye, Cinderpaw!" he called.

"Bye, and thanks for the food."

"No problem," he meowed. He turned to Yellowfang. "Have you got anything for this bite on my neck?"

Yellowfang looked closely at his wound. "Looks like a nasty one," she growled.

"It's from Brokentail," Fireheart confessed.

Yellowfang nodded. "Wait there." She padded quickly to her den and returned with a bundle of herbs wrapped in leaves. "Can you manage them yourself? Just chew them up and rub the juice into the wounds. It'll sting, but nothing a brave warrior can't handle!"

"Thanks, Yellowfang." Fireheart picked up the bundle in his teeth.

Yellowfang led him to the tunnel entrance. "I appreciate your coming," she meowed, glancing at Cinderpaw's nest. "She was feeling pretty low, I think. She felt bad after the battle, and then the naming ceremony."

Fireheart nodded. He understood. He gave a last wary glance at where Brokentail lay. "You sure you'll be safe?" he asked again through the bundle of herbs.

"He's blind," meowed Yellowfang. She sighed, and then added more brightly, "And I'm not *that* old!"

Fireheart woke the following morning to find dazzling white light streaming through the den wall. He guessed it had snowed again. At least his wounds had stopped aching. Yellowfang had been right – the herb juice *had* stung, but he felt much better after a good night's sleep.

Fireheart wondered how Sandstorm and Dustpelt had managed their vigil. It must have been bitterly cold in the snow. He got to his paws and stretched his forelegs, arching his back and curling his tail up over his head. ThunderClan's two newest warriors were bundled up, fast asleep on the far edge of the den. Whitestorm must have sent them in when he left on the dawn patrol.

Fireheart padded out into the snow-covered clearing. He could just make out Frostfur's white pelt skirting the nursery as she slipped out to stretch her legs. There were two bare spots in the centre of the clearing, where Sandstorm and Dustpelt had spent the night. Fireheart shivered at the thought, but still he envied them as he remembered the thrill of his first night as a warrior. It had filled him with a warmth not even the hardest frost could have chilled.

The sky was thick with snow-heavy clouds. Flakes were still falling, softly and silently. There would be plenty of hunting to do today, Fireheart realised. The Clan would need to stock up if the snow was going to get deeper.

He heard Bluestar call from the Highrock. The Clan cats began to creep from their dens and pick their way through the snow to hear their leader's words. Fireheart settled himself into one of the bare spots. It smelled of Sandstorm. He noticed Greystripe sitting on the other side of the clearing, looking tired. Fireheart wondered if he'd slipped out last night to tell Silverstream about the rogue cats.

Bluestar began to speak. "I wanted to make sure you all know that Brokentail is in the camp." None of the cats uttered a noise. They knew already. The rumour had spread through the camp like a forest fire.

"He is blind, and harmless." A few cats snorted their displeasure, and Bluestar nodded to acknowledge their fears. "I am as concerned as you are for the safety of our Clan. But, StarClan knows, we cannot turn him out to die in the forest. Yellowfang will nurse him until his wounds heal. Once they have, we'll discuss this again."

Bluestar looked around, listening for voices from the crowd, but no cat spoke, so she leaped down from

Highrock. As the cats dispersed Fireheart noticed that the leader was walking towards him.

"Fireheart," she meowed. "One thing concerns me. You still haven't settled things with Greystripe. I've not seen you eat together for days. I told you before, there's no room for fighting within ThunderClan. I want you to hunt together today."

Fireheart nodded. "Yes, Bluestar." That was fine by him. And after yesterday's battle, he felt hopeful that Greystripe would like the idea too. As Bluestar walked away, Fireheart scanned the clearing, hoping that Greystripe hadn't disappeared again. No, there he was, helping to clear the snow from the nursery entrance.

"Hey, Greystripe," Fireheart called. Greystripe carried on with his work. Fireheart bounded over to him. "Do you want to go hunting this morning?"

Greystripe turned to face him, his eyes cold. "Are you making sure I don't disappear again?" he snarled.

Fireheart was startled. "N-no, I just thought... after yesterday... Clawface..."

"I would have done the same for any ThunderClan cat. That's what Clan loyalty is about!" Greystripe's meow was harsh with anger as he went back to pushing snow.

Fireheart's hopes plummeted. Had he lost his friend's trust forever? He turned away, tail down, and began to trudge through the snow towards the camp entrance. He called over his shoulder, "Bluestar told me to go hunting with you this morning, actually, so you can explain to her why you're not coming."

"Oh, I see, you were just trying to please Bluestar, as usual!" Greystripe hissed. Fireheart stopped and whipped around, ready to throw back a retort, but he paused when he saw that Greystripe was crossing the clearing towards him, shaking snowflakes from his wide shoulders.

"Come on, then," Greystripe growled, leading the way through the gorse tunnel.

It was a slow climb out of the ravine, with the boulders covered in snow. When they reached the top, the icebound forest stretched before them. Greystripe charged away at once, his face set with grim determination. Fireheart followed him. As he tracked a mouse around the roots of an oak tree he saw Greystripe racing after a rabbit that had been foolish enough to stray from its burrow. Greystripe pelted furiously after the creature until he finished it off with a well-aimed pounce. Fireheart sat and watched as Greystripe padded back to him and dropped the rabbit at Fireheart's paws.

"That should feed a kit or two." He grunted.

"You don't have to prove anything to me," Fireheart told him.

"No?" Greystripe answered bitterly. His eyes met Fireheart's, cold and angry. "Maybe you should start acting as if you trusted me, then." He turned away before Fireheart could reply.

By sunhigh Greystripe had caught more than Fireheart, but both cats had done well. They returned to the camp, their jaws heavy with fresh-kill. They padded into the clearing and dropped their prey in the usual place. The spot had been empty so far.

Fireheart wondered if they should go out again. The snow was heavier now, and a cold wind was beginning to blow through the ravine. Fireheart was studying the darkening sky when he heard Brindleface's worried meow near the nursery. He bounded over to see what was wrong. "What's the matter?"

"Have you seen Cloudkit?" she demanded.

Fireheart shook his head. "Is he missing?" His paws prickled as Brindleface's rising panic began to infect him.

"Yes. So are my other kits. I only closed my eyes for a moment. I just woke up and I can't find them anywhere! It's too cold for them to be out. They'll freeze to death!" The queen swayed on her paws.

Alarm shot through Fireheart as he pictured the last time a young cat had disappeared from the camp. It had been Cinderpaw.

CHAPTER 28

"I'LL FIND THEM," Fireheart promised. He automatically looked around for Greystripe. The wind was rising and the snow was growing thicker – he didn't want to search alone. Fireheart rushed to the warriors' den and pushed his way inside, but Greystripe wasn't there.

Sandstorm was just waking up. "What's wrong?" she meowed, seeing Fireheart peering around the den.

"Brindleface's kits are missing."

"Cloudkit too?" Sandstorm scrambled to her paws, instantly awake.

"Yes! I was looking for Greystripe so we could look for them together, but he isn't here," Fireheart meowed, his words tumbling out in a rush. He felt a stab of rage that Greystripe was missing yet again – right after accusing Fireheart of not trusting him!

"I'll come with you," Sandstorm offered.

Fireheart blinked. "Thanks," he meowed gratefully. "Come on. We should tell Bluestar before we leave."

"Dustpelt can tell her. Is it still snowing?"

"Yes, and it's getting heavier. We'd better hurry." Fireheart looked at Dustpelt's sleeping form. "You wake him. I'll tell Brindleface we're going and meet you by the entrance." He bounded away, back to the nursery. Brindleface was still sniffing around in search of scents.

"Any sign?" Fireheart asked.

"No, nothing." Brindleface's voice was trembling. "Frostfur's gone to tell Bluestar!"

"Well, don't worry. I'm going out to look for them," he reassured her. "Sandstorm's coming with me. We'll find them."

Brindleface nodded and carried on searching.

Fireheart and Sandstorm arrived at the gorse tunnel together and hurried out into the woods. Outside the camp the wind felt even fiercer. Fireheart narrowed his eyes and hunched his shoulders against the blizzard.

"It's going to be hard picking up a scent through the fresh snow," he warned Sandstorm. "Let's start by checking to see if they've climbed up to the forest."

"OK," meowed Sandstorm.

"You take that side." Fireheart pointed with his nose. "And I'll take the other. Meet you back here. Don't be long."

Sandstorm bounded away and Fireheart leaped over a

fallen tree, heading towards the trail the Clan followed most often. The sides of the ravine were even more thickly coated than they had been that morning, and slippery now where the snow had frozen into ice. Fireheart stopped and lifted his head, his mouth open, but he could find no scent of the kits. He looked in vain for pawsteps – would their trail already be covered by fresh snow?

He trekked along the bottom of the slope but found no sign of any cats, let alone lost kits. The wind blew until Fireheart could hardly feel the tips of his ears. No kits could survive in this weather, and it wouldn't be long before the sun began to set. He had to find them before nightfall.

Fireheart raced back to the camp entrance. Sandstorm was waiting for him, her fur striped with small ridges of snow. She shook them off as she saw him coming.

"Any sign?" Fireheart meowed.

"No, nothing."

"They can't have gone far," Fireheart pointed out. "Come on, let's try this way." He headed towards the training hollow.

Sandstorm battled after him. The snow was getting deeper, and she sank up to her belly with every step.

The training hollow was empty.

"Do you think Bluestar realises how bad the weather is out here?" asked Sandstorm, raising her voice against the wind.

"She'll know," Fireheart called back to her.

"We should go back and get help, join up with another search party," meowed Sandstorm.

Fireheart looked at the shivering warrior. It was not just the kits who might freeze out here. Perhaps Sandstorm was right. "I agree," he meowed. "We can't do this by ourselves."

As they turned towards camp, Fireheart thought he heard a tiny squeal through the wind. "Did you hear that?" he called.

Sandstorm stopped and began sniffing the air furiously. Suddenly she lifted her head. "That way!" she meowed, pointing with her nose to a fallen tree.

Fireheart leaped towards it with Sandstorm right behind him. The squealing grew louder until Fireheart could make out several little voices. He scrambled up on to the log and looked down the other side. Huddled in the snow were two small kits. Fireheart felt a rush of relief until he realised Cloudkit was not with them. "Where's Cloudkit?" he yowled.

"Hunting," squeaked one of the kits. Her voice trembled with cold and fear, but there was a note of defiance in it.

Fireheart lifted his head. "Cloudkit!" he called, peering through the snowflakes.

"Fireheart, look!" Sandstorm was on top of the log. Fireheart spun around. A bedraggled white shape was struggling through the snow towards them. Cloudkit! Every step was a massive leap for the tiny kit – the snow was as high as he was. But he kept coming, and in his mouth he carried a small, snow-encrusted vole.

A surge of relief and fury shot through Fireheart. He left Sandstorm with the others and bounded through the snow to scoop up the kit by the scruff of his neck. Cloudkit grunted in protest but refused to drop the vole that dangled from his mouth.

Fireheart turned to see Sandstorm nudging the others towards him. They stumbled ahead of her, sinking up to their ears in the deep snow, but she kept pushing them on.

Cloudkit squirmed in Fireheart's mouth. Fireheart dropped him back into the snow. Cloudkit looked up at him, proudly holding his catch. Fireheart couldn't help feeling impressed. In spite of the snow and wind, Cloudkit had caught his first prey!

"Wait there," he ordered, and dashed back to help Sandstorm. He picked up a tiny she-kit who was mewling pitifully, and began nosing the other one forwards.

The bedraggled group struggled back to the camp. Brindleface was waiting outside the gorse tunnel. Bluestar stood beside her, her eyes narrowed against the driving snow. As soon as they spotted Fireheart's party, they rushed forwards to help. Bluestar scooped up Cloudkit and Brindleface grabbed the other kit; then they turned and raced into the shelter of the camp with Fireheart and Sandstorm hurrying behind.

Once in the clearing, the three cats dropped their frozen bundles on to the ground. Fireheart shook the snow from his fur and looked down at Cloudkit, who was still stubbornly clinging to his catch.

Bluestar glared at the three kits. "What did you think you were doing out there? You know it's against the warrior code for kits to hunt!"

Brindleface's two kits shrank under their leader's angry gaze, but Cloudkit looked back at her with round blue eyes. He dropped his vole and mewed, "The Clan needed fresh-kill, so we decided to catch some."

Fireheart flinched at his boldness.

"Whose idea was it?" Bluestar demanded.

"Mine," Cloudkit announced, his head still unbowed.

Bluestar fixed her eyes on the defiant little kit and yowled: "You could have frozen to death out there!"

Cloudkit was startled by the anger in her voice and dropped into a crouch. "We did it for the Clan," he mewed defensively.

Fireheart held his breath as he waited to see what Bluestar would do next. Cloudkit had broken the warrior code. Would Bluestar change her mind about letting him stay?

"Your intention," Bluestar meowed slowly, "was good. But it was a foolish thing to do." Fireheart felt a flicker of hope. Then he cringed as Cloudkit piped up again.

"I *caught* something, though."

"I can see that," replied Bluestar coldly. She gazed at all three kits. "I shall leave it to your mother to decide what to do with you. But I don't want to find you doing anything like this again. Do you understand?"

Fireheart relaxed a little as Cloudkit nodded with the others. "Cloudkit, you may add your catch to the fresh-kill pile," Bluestar added. "Then all three of you go straight to the nursery and get yourselves dry and warm." Fireheart felt surprised. Was that a motherly tone he detected in the ThunderClan leader's voice?

Brindleface's kits stumbled towards the nursery, followed by their mother, while Cloudkit picked up his vole and trotted off towards the pile of fresh-kill. The proud tilt of his head made Fireheart's paws prickle with worry, but as Bluestar watched him go, Fireheart thought he detected a glint of admiration in his leader's eyes.

"Well done, you two," she meowed, turning her attention to Sandstorm and Fireheart. "I'll send Longtail out to retrieve the other search party. You should go to your den and try to warm up too!"

"Yes, Bluestar," Fireheart answered. He turned to leave with Sandstorm but Bluestar called him back. "Fireheart," she meowed, "I want to talk to you." Her tone made Fireheart feel apprehensive. Perhaps he'd relaxed too soon.

"Cloudkit showed some fine hunting skills today," Bluestar began. "But all the skill in the world is worthless if he can't learn to obey the warrior code. It may be for his own safety now, but in the future the safety of the whole Clan will depend on it."

Fireheart stared down at the ground. He knew Bluestar was right, but he couldn't help feeling that she was expecting too much of the young kit. Cloudkit was still very young and he'd been with the Clan only a short time. Fireheart swallowed a pang of resentment as he thought of how shamelessly Greystripe, a Clanborn cat, was disobeying the warrior code. He looked up at the Clan leader. "Yes, Bluestar," he meowed. "I'll make sure he learns."

"Good." Bluestar sounded satisfied. She turned away and padded to her den.

Fireheart made his way to the warriors' den even though he no longer felt cold. Bluestar's words had made him burn. He pushed his way inside, settled into his nest, and began to wash. He stayed in his nest all afternoon, brooding about Greystripe and Cloudkit. He knew that Bluestar was right. The pride and defiance he'd seen in the white kit's eyes made Fireheart wonder if he really would be able to adjust to Clan life.

As evening came, hunger drew Fireheart from the den. He picked a thrush from the pile of fresh-kill and settled down by the nettle clump to eat it. It was dark now and the snow had eased. Once his eyes had adjusted to the night, Fireheart could see the camp entrance clearly.

He spotted Greystripe as soon as he appeared, and watched him walk to the pile of fresh-kill. The grey warrior was carrying prey. Perhaps he'd just been hunting after all.

Greystripe dropped most of his catch on to the pile. He

kept a large mouse for himself and took it to a sheltered spot near the camp wall. Fireheart's brief hope faded. The distracted look in Greystripe's eyes told him that his suspicions were right – Greystripe had been with Silverstream.

Fireheart got to his paws and padded into the den. He had no trouble falling into a deep sleep. And as he slept, he dreamed again.

The snowy forest spread out around him, glowing white beneath the cold moon. Fireheart stood on a tall, jagged rock. Beside him stood Cloudkit – a fully grown warrior, his thick white pelt rippling in the wind. Frost sparkled on the stone beneath their paws.

"Watch!" Fireheart hissed to Cloudkit. A wood mouse scuttled around the frozen roots of a tree. Cloudkit followed his gaze and leaped silently from the rock on to the forest floor. Fireheart watched the white tom prowl towards the prey. Suddenly he smelled a scent so warm and familiar, his fur quivered. He felt warm breath on his ear and turned sharply. Spottedleaf was standing beside him.

Her dappled pelt shone in the moonlight as she touched her soft pink nose to his. "Fireheart," she whispered. "I have a warning for you from StarClan." Her tone was sombre and her eyes burned into his. "A battle is coming, Fireheart. Beware a warrior you cannot trust."

The squeal of a mouse made Fireheart jump and look around. Cloudkit must have made his kill. He turned back to Spottedleaf but she had disappeared.

Fireheart woke up with a start and turned to the nest beside him. Greystripe was curled up, fast asleep, his nose tucked under his thick tail. Spottedleaf's words echoed in Fireheart's mind: "Beware a warrior you cannot trust!"

He shivered. The bitter cold of the forest seemed to cling to his fur even here, and the sweet fragrance of Spottedleaf lingered in his nostrils. Greystripe stirred beside him, muttering in his sleep, and Fireheart flinched. He knew he wouldn't go back to sleep again, but he stayed in his nest and watched his friend sleeping until the dawn light began to shine through the walls of the den.

CHAPTER 29

As the den grew lighter, Willowpelt woke up. Fireheart watched as she rose and stretched, then pushed her way out of the den. He gave a last glance at Greystripe's sleeping form, and followed her.

"It's stopped snowing," he meowed, desperate to break the ghostly silence that enfolded the snowbound camp. His voice echoed around the clearing and Willowpelt nodded.

A rustling noise accompanied the scent of Tigerclaw and Runningwind as they emerged from the den. They settled themselves beside Willowpelt to wash. *Ready for the dawn patrol*, Fireheart thought. He wondered if he should offer to join them since he could do with a run through the woods, but part of him wanted to stay behind and keep an eye on Greystripe. Spottedleaf's words still lay heavy in his heart. He couldn't shake off the idea that Greystripe was the warrior he could not trust. Greystripe insisted his relationship with Silverstream didn't change his loyalty to the Clan, but how could it not? He was breaking the warrior code just by seeing her!

Suddenly Tigerclaw lifted his head as though he had smelled something. Fireheart tensed. His ears twitched – he could hear paws crunching through the snow in the distance, moving fast. The breeze carried the scent of WindClan. The pawsteps grew louder. As one, the warriors stiffened – a cat was rushing towards them through the gorse tunnel. Tigerclaw arched his back and hissed as Onewhisker burst into the clearing.

The WindClan warrior skidded to a halt in front of them, his eyes filled with dread. "ShadowClan and RiverClan!" he gasped. "They're attacking our camp! We're outnumbered and fighting for our lives. Tallstar refuses to be driven off this time. You must help or my Clan will be wiped out!"

Bluestar bounded out of her den. All eyes turned from Onewhisker to her. "I heard," she meowed. Without mounting the Highrock, the ThunderClan leader gave the yowl she used to call the Clan together. Onewhisker's fear-scent filled the clearing as he watched the cats emerge into the morning light.

As soon as the Clan had gathered, Bluestar began. "There's no time to waste. It's as we feared – ShadowClan and RiverClan have joined together, and now they're attacking the WindClan camp. We must help them." She paused and looked around at the faces staring back at her in dismay. Onewhisker stood beside her, listening silently with wide, hopeful eyes.

Fireheart was appalled. After the rogue cats had been discovered, he'd thought Nightstar could be trusted. Now it seemed the ShadowClan leader had broken the warrior code after all by uniting with RiverClan to drive WindClan from their home yet again.

"But we are leaf-bare-weak!" protested Patchpelt. "We've taken a risk for WindClan once before. Let them take care of themselves this time." A few murmurs of agreement rose from the elders and queens.

It was Tigerclaw who answered him, stepping forwards to stand beside Bluestar. "You're right to be cautious, Patchpelt. But if ShadowClan and RiverClan have united, it is only a matter of time before they turn on us. It's better we fight now, with WindClan, than later, alone!"

Bluestar looked at Patchpelt, who closed his eyes and lifted his tail, accepting Tigerclaw's words.

Yellowfang pushed her way forwards and spoke quietly to the leader. "I think you should remain behind in camp, Bluestar. The fever from the greencough may have gone, but you'll still be weak." The two cats exchanged a look that Fireheart understood with a jolt. Bluestar was on her ninth and final life. For the sake of the Clan, she could not afford to risk it in battle.

Bluestar nodded briskly. "Tigerclaw, I want you to organise two parties, one to head the attack, one to back it up. We need to get there as fast as we can!"

"Yes, Bluestar." Tigerclaw turned to the warriors. "Whitestorm, you'll head the second party; I'll head the first. I'll take Darkstripe, Mousefur, Longtail, Dustpelt and Fireheart." Fireheart lifted his head as Tigerclaw called his name, feeling a thrill run through him. He was to join the lead party!

"You!" Tigerclaw called to Onewhisker. "What's your name?" The WindClan warrior looked startled by Tigerclaw's tone.

Fireheart answered for him. "Onewhisker," he meowed.

Tigerclaw nodded, barely pausing to look at Fireheart. "Onewhisker, you'll be in my party. The rest of the ThunderClan warriors will join Whitestorm. You too, Brackenpaw."

"Are we all ready?" called Tigerclaw. The warriors raised their heads and let out a battle cry. Tigerclaw charged for the gorse tunnel and they raced after him.

Up the ravine they climbed, into the forest. They were heading for Fourtrees and the uplands beyond. Fireheart glanced over his shoulder as he ran through the trees. Greystripe was near the back, his face grim, his eyes staring blankly ahead. Fireheart wondered if Silverstream would be at the battle. Fireheart felt a pang of sorrow for his friend, but this time he had no doubts about his own readiness to fight. After bringing WindClan home, he couldn't help feeling responsible for them. He would not let any Clan drive them back to those Thunderpath tunnels.

Spottedleaf's fragrance filled his nostrils once more, and Fireheart's fur prickled. "Beware a warrior you cannot trust!" This was going to be a difficult battle in more ways than one. Greystripe would have no choice about proving his loyalty now.

Even though the snow had stopped falling, it was hard work getting through the drifts. An icy crust had formed over the top of the snow, but the warriors were heavy enough to break through and sink into the softer snow underneath.

"Tigerclaw!" Willowpelt's yowl sounded from the rear. The deputy halted and turned.

"We're being followed!" Willowpelt called.

Her words sent a quiver of alarm through Fireheart. Had they run into a trap? Quietly the patrol retraced their pawsteps, alert and suspicious. A snow-laden branch creaked above, making Brackenpaw jump.

"Wait," hissed Tigerclaw.

The cats crouched in the deep snow. Fireheart could hear the noise of pawsteps heading towards them. They sounded light, like small paws stepping delicately over the top of the ice crust. With a sinking heart, Fireheart guessed who it was a heartbeat before Cloudkit and Brindleface's two kits appeared from behind a log.

Tigerclaw reared up at them and the kits squealed in fright. The warrior recognised them instantly and dropped down on to all four paws. "What are you doing here!" he spat.

"We wanted to join the battle," mewed Cloudkit. Fireheart winced.

"Fireheart!" called Tigerclaw. Fireheart hurried forwards, and the dark warrior spat impatiently, "You brought this kit into the Clan; you deal with it."

Fireheart looked into Tigerclaw's blazing eyes. He knew that the deputy was trying to force him to choose: Fireheart could either join the battle party and fight for the Clan or take care of his kittypet kin. The whole patrol waited in silence for Fireheart to speak.

Fireheart knew he would choose to fight for the Clan, but he couldn't sacrifice his sister's kit. Cloudkit and the others must be taken home safely by another cat. But which warrior could the raiding party do without?

"Brackenpaw," Fireheart called to Greystripe's apprentice. "Please take these kits home!" Fireheart waited for Greystripe to object, but the grey warrior remained silent as Fireheart ordered his apprentice back to camp.

Brackenpaw's tail drooped and Fireheart felt a stab of guilt. "There'll be plenty more battles for you to fight," he promised.

"But Fireheart, you said one day we'd fight side by side!" Cloudkit's protest rang through the trees. Tigerclaw shot

Fireheart a mocking look. Fireheart felt his fur prickle uncomfortably as amusement rippled through the patrol at the tiny kit's words. But he refused to show his embarrassment. "One day we will," he meowed. "But not today!"

The white kit's shoulders sagged and Fireheart let out a sigh of relief as he watched Cloudkit reluctantly join the other kits following Brackenpaw back to the camp.

"I'm surprised by your choice, Fireheart," Tigerclaw sneered. "I didn't expect you to be so keen to fight *this* battle."

Fireheart stared at Tigerclaw and felt the blood pulse through him, so that his whole body throbbed with rage. "If only you were keen too!" he retorted. "You'd give the battle cry instead of keeping us here while WindClan warriors die!"

Tigerclaw flashed him a look of loathing, threw back his head and yowled to the sky before charging on towards the WindClan camp. Fireheart and the others raced after him, past Fourtrees to the steep slope that led to the uplands. They bounded up, their paws made noiseless by the snow.

When they reached the top, Fireheart was battered by a howling wind that turned his ears inside out. The WindClan hunting grounds looked more barren than ever, the gorse hidden by a layer of snow.

"Fireheart! You know the way to the WindClan camp!" yowled Tigerclaw above the wind. "Lead us there." He slowed to let Fireheart pass. Fireheart wondered if the deputy didn't trust Onewhisker enough to let the WindClan warrior guide them. He looked back at Greystripe, hoping for some help, but the grey warrior had his head bowed low and his shoulders hunched miserably as the wind buffeted his thick fur. There would be little help there. Fireheart turned his eyes to StarClan and sent up a prayer for guidance.

He was surprised to find that he recognised the shape of the land even beneath the snow. There was the badger set and the rock Greystripe had climbed to get a better view. He followed the contours he remembered from his journey with Greystripe until he reached the dip in the land that marked the WindClan camp.

Fireheart paused at the rim of the hollow. "Down there!" he yowled. For a heartbeat the wind dropped, and from below they heard the sounds of battle – screams and howls as cat furiously fought with cat.

CHAPTER 30

TIGERCLAW ADDRESSED THE warriors in a fierce hiss that carried through the blizzard. "Whitestorm, wait until you hear my battle cry! Onewhisker, you lead us through the camp entrance; we'll take care of the rest."

Onewhisker began to race down the slope towards the snow-covered bushes. Tigerclaw thundered after him, Darkstripe at his heels. Fireheart charged behind the sleek grey tabby, through the narrow tunnel that led into the WindClan camp. The gorse was as dense and sharp as he remembered. Greystripe and the other warriors stayed at the top of the slope, a fresh wave of attack ready to strike after the initial barrage.

Fireheart skidded to a halt, reeling at the sight that greeted him in the camp clearing. Last time he'd been here, in search of the scent trail that would lead them to the missing Clan, the place had been deserted and silent. Now the clearing swarmed with writhing, screeching, fighting cats. Onewhisker had been right – the WindClan cats were hopelessly outnumbered. A fresh party of ShadowClan and RiverClan warriors waited at the edge of the clearing, but WindClan could spare no backup group. The whole Clan was fighting, apprentices and elders, warriors and queens.

Fireheart spotted Morningflower wrestling with a ShadowClan warrior. The WindClan queen looked exhausted and frightened, her fur standing in ragged clumps. Still, she nimbly turned and scratched her attacker, but he was much bigger and knocked her easily to the ground with a heavy blow.

With a howl, Fireheart leaped and landed squarely on the shoulders of the ShadowClan tom. He clung on while the surprised warrior spun and tried to shake him loose. Morningflower raked the tom with her claws as Fireheart dragged him to the ground. The ShadowClan warrior screeched and ripped himself free. He ran into the prickly camp wall and pushed his way through. Morningflower shot a grateful glance at Fireheart and turned back to the battle.

Fireheart looked around, shaking drops of blood from his nose. The fresh patrols of ShadowClan and RiverClan cats had joined the fight now. ThunderClan's arrival had evened the numbers for a while, but now the second party was needed. Fireheart heard Tigerclaw's battle cry ring out and a moment later Whitestorm exploded into the clearing, followed by Greystripe, Runningwind and the rest of the ThunderClan warriors.

Fireheart grabbed a RiverClan warrior, tripping him with one paw and holding him down with another. He rolled the tom over and thrashed at his belly with his hind claws. The RiverClan cat leaped away and crashed into a WindClan warrior. The warrior turned in surprise. Fireheart recognised Onewhisker straightaway and watched as he reared and attacked the RiverClan tom without a moment's pause. Fireheart could see the fire in Onewhisker's eyes. He could leave him to finish this fight.

A familiar hiss caught Fireheart's attention. Greystripe was battling with a grey ShadowClan cat. It was Wetfoot, a warrior who had helped them fight to rid ShadowClan of Brokenstar. The two warriors were well matched. Greystripe thrust Wetfoot away with his back legs and spun around, looking for another cat to attack. Fireheart could see a RiverClan cat right behind Greystripe. Above the din of battle, he heard the blood roar in his ears. Would Greystripe attack one of Silverstream's fellow warriors?

Greystripe leaped and Fireheart held his breath. But instead of jumping on to the RiverClan cat, Greystripe sailed over him and landed instead on the back of another ShadowClan warrior.

Fireheart heard Tigerclaw call his name. He twisted his head and saw the warrior at the other end of the clearing.

The fighting was thick up there, with cats from all Clans battling together.

As he charged through to the ThunderClan deputy, Fireheart felt Leopardfur grasp his hind leg, pulling him down.

"You!" hissed the RiverClan deputy. They had last met at the gorge, where Whiteclaw had died.

Fireheart threw her off and flipped over on to his back. Too late, he realised that he'd exposed his soft belly. Leopardfur didn't waste a moment. She reared up and came down on Fireheart with all her might. Fireheart felt the wind knocked out of him before the thorn-sharp claws dug into his belly. He screamed in agony. As his eyes rolled he saw Tigerclaw at the side of the clearing, watching him with cold, expressionless eyes.

"Tigerclaw," Fireheart howled. "Help me!"

But Tigerclaw didn't move. He just stared as Leopardfur clawed Fireheart again and again.

Sheer rage gave Fireheart the strength he needed. He fought through the pain, drew back his hind legs and pushed up against Leopardfur's belly as hard as he could. Fireheart saw a look of shock on the deputy's face as his kick lifted the warrior and flung her halfway across the clearing. Fireheart struggled to his paws and glared at Tigerclaw, burning with pain and rage. Tigerclaw met his gaze with a look of undisguised hatred and leaped away into the thick of the battle.

A blow on the back of his head knocked Fireheart off balance. He staggered and turned to see Stonefur. The RiverClan warrior was preparing to aim another swipe. Fireheart ducked out of the way and shoved Stonefur straight into Whitestorm. The ThunderClan cat whipped around and grasped Stonefur by the scruff of his neck. Fireheart tried to dart forwards and help the white-furred warrior, but claws held him back, digging into his haunches. He twisted to see who it was and glimpsed grey fur. It was Silverstream.

The she-cat's face was twisted with battle rage as she reared up at him. Blood was dripping into her eyes, and Fireheart could tell that she hadn't recognised him. She drew back a paw and he saw her long claws flash as she prepared to swipe him. As Fireheart screwed up his eyes, bracing himself for the blow, he heard an achingly familiar yowl. "Silverstream! No!"

Greystripe, thought Fireheart.

Silverstream hesitated, shook her head, and recognised Fireheart with a muted gasp. She dropped back down to all four paws, her eyes wide with shock.

Fireheart reacted instinctively, his blood aflame with battle. Without thinking, he leaped on to the back of the RiverClan she-cat and pinned her to the ground. She didn't struggle as he drew back his head and prepared to give her a vicious bite on her shoulder. But as Fireheart raised his head he felt Greystripe's eyes boring into him. The grey warrior was watching in horror from the edge of the battle.

The look of pain and disbelief in his friend's eyes brought Fireheart to his senses. He stopped, sheathed his claws, and loosened his grip on Silverstream. The she-cat slipped away from him and disappeared into the surrounding gorse. Fireheart stared, still in shock, as Greystripe raced after her.

Fireheart felt as if he were still being watched. He looked around and his eyes met Darkstripe's on the other side of the clearing. Fireheart flinched. Greystripe's affair had forced him into disloyalty to ThunderClan after all – he had let an enemy warrior go! How much had Darkstripe seen? Just then Fireheart heard Runningwind yowl for help. The tabby warrior was grappling desperately with Nightstar, ShadowClan's treacherous leader. Fireheart darted through the throng to Runningwind's side.

Without pausing to think, Fireheart leaped, grabbing Nightstar from behind. The black warrior howled in rage as Fireheart pulled him backwards and sank his claws deep into Nightstar's fur. He had fought side by side with this warrior only a few moons ago to help him drive out Brokenstar. Now he sank his teeth into Nightstar's shoulder with the same ferocity he had used against the former ShadowClan leader.

Nightstar squealed and twisted in Fireheart's grip. This tom had not been made leader for nothing, thought Fireheart, struggling to hang on. Nightstar scrabbled free, but Runningwind was ready. He pounced, and together the two warriors rolled across the frozen clearing. Fireheart watched them struggle and twist, timing his moment perfectly so that when he finally leaped, he landed squarely on Nightstar's back. He grasped him more firmly this time, ready for the warrior to wriggle free. But Runningwind also had a grip. Together they scratched and bit the ShadowClan leader till he screeched out loud. Then they released him, springing backwards with their claws still unsheathed.

Nightstar leaped to his paws and spun around, hissing. Fireheart saw the fury in his eyes, but the ShadowClan leader knew he was beaten. He backed away, his eyes darting around the clearing where his warriors were suffering similar treatment from the other ThunderClan warriors. He gave the yowl of retreat. Instantly his warriors stopped fighting and, like their leader, backed into the gorse that surrounded the camp. The RiverClan warriors were left alone to fend off ThunderClan and WindClan.

Fireheart paused to catch his breath, blinking blood from his eyes. Whitestorm was grappling with Leopardfur now, with Mousefur at his side. Sandstorm was battling with a RiverClan warrior almost twice her size. But her opponent was only half her speed. Fireheart watched Sandstorm nip and twist around him until the RiverClan warrior looked overwhelmed.

Dustpelt was fighting a smoky-black tom nearby. Fireheart recognised Blackclaw, the RiverClan warrior he had seen chasing rabbits in the uplands. Dustpelt was stubbornly refusing to be cowed by the blows and bites aimed at him. Each time he was struck, the young warrior turned and gave as good as he got. It looked as if he didn't need any help, and Fireheart guessed Dustpelt would not thank him for interfering in this fight.

Where was Crookedstar? Fireheart searched the clearing for the RiverClan leader. It wasn't hard to find him. Now that ShadowClan had run away, the clearing was less crowded. Fireheart soon spotted the light-coloured tabby with the twisted jaw. He was crouching low, face-to-face with Tigerclaw. The two warriors stared at each other, their tails thrashing menacingly. Fireheart's blood pounded through his veins as he waited for one of them to make a move. It was Crookedstar who leaped first, but Tigerclaw jumped nimbly aside and Crookedstar missed. Tigerclaw was more accurate; he turned and lunged at Crookedstar's back. The ThunderClan warrior grasped the RiverClan leader with his long claws and Crookedstar went limp beneath him. Fireheart watched breathlessly as Tigerclaw bared his teeth, lunged forwards, and sank them deep into Crookedstar's neck.

Fireheart gasped. Had Tigerclaw really killed the RiverClan leader? Crookedstar's pained screech told Fireheart that Tigerclaw had missed the spine. But it was a blow to win the battle. Tigerclaw released his opponent and let him race, yowling, towards the camp entrance. As soon as Crookedstar's tail shot out of sight, his warriors struggled free and pelted after him.

In a heartbeat, the WindClan camp fell silent apart from the howling of the wind above the gorse. Fireheart stared around him. The ThunderClan warriors were tired and battered, but the WindClan cats looked far worse. Every one of them was bleeding, while some lay unmoving on the frozen ground. Barkface, their medicine cat, wasted no time in rushing from one cat to another, attending to their injuries.

Tallstar limped towards Tigerclaw, blood dripping from his cheek. As he watched the WindClan leader, Fireheart remembered his dream from moons ago – Tallstar had been silhouetted against a bright fire, like a warrior sent from StarClan to save them. "Fire will save the Clan," according to Spottedleaf's prophecy. But looking at the WindClan cats, exhausted and beaten, Fireheart wondered if his dream had misled him. How could these cats represent the fire that StarClan promised would save his Clan? Surely it was ThunderClan who had just saved WindClan – again?

Tallstar spoke quietly to Tigerclaw. Fireheart couldn't hear the words they shared, but he could guess by Tallstar's bowed head that the WindClan leader was acknowledging the debt he owed to ThunderClan. Tigerclaw sat up straight and accepted the thanks with his chin held high. Fireheart felt a wave of revulsion at the dark warrior's arrogance. He would never forget that Tigerclaw had stood by and watched while Leopardfur had nearly ripped him to shreds.

"Here." Fireheart was shaken from his thoughts by the soft voice of Willowpelt offering him a mouthful of the medicine cat's herbs. Fireheart purred his thanks as Willowpelt began squeezing juice from the herbs into the bite marks on Fireheart's shoulders. The juice stung, but the smell took him straight back to another time, with Spottedleaf. She had given him the same herb to treat Yellowfang so many moons ago. As the odour of the herbs wafted up, Fireheart remembered his dream from the night before. "Beware a warrior..." Spottedleaf had warned him. Beware a warrior?

The truth washed over Fireheart like a chill wind – it wasn't Greystripe he should have been wary of, but Tigerclaw! How could he have suspected his friend, when he knew what Tigerclaw was capable of? Suddenly Fireheart was sure Ravenpaw had been telling the truth, whatever Bluestar had said. Seeing the dark warrior's performance today, Fireheart realised that Tigerclaw could easily have killed Redtail and walked away without remorse.

"You fought well, Fireheart!" Runningwind interrupted his thoughts. The brown tabby blinked warmly at Fireheart as he promised, "I'll make sure Bluestar hears about it!"

"Yes," agreed Willowpelt. "You're a fine warrior. StarClan will honour you for this." Fireheart looked at them both, his ears twitching with pleasure. It was a relief to feel part of the Clan again.

Suddenly Fireheart's fur prickled. Darkstripe was stalking across the clearing towards Tigerclaw. He sat down behind Tallstar and waited until the WindClan leader walked away; then he leaned forwards and whispered urgently into Tigerclaw's ear. The two warriors kept glancing towards Fireheart.

He saw, thought Fireheart, feeling dizzy with horror. *He saw me let Silverstream go.*

"Are you OK?" asked Willowpelt.

Fireheart realised he'd shivered. "Er, yes, sorry. Just thinking." Tigerclaw was stalking towards him, his eyes shining with spiteful satisfaction.

"Well, if you're sure, I'll go and see to some others," meowed Willowpelt.

"Yes – fine," meowed Fireheart. "Thanks."

Willowpelt picked up her herbs and padded away. Runningwind followed her.

Tigerclaw flattened his ears and drew back his lip in a snarl as he looked down at Fireheart. "Darkstripe says you let a RiverClan she-cat escape!"

Fireheart realised there was nothing he could say. No matter how difficult Greystripe had made things for him, there was no way he was going to betray his friend to this warrior. He longed to yowl back that Tigerclaw had stood and watched while a RiverClan warrior tried to kill him. But who would believe him? Darkstripe padded up to stand beside Tigerclaw. Fireheart longed for the wisdom and fairness of Bluestar, but she was far away, back at the ThunderClan camp.

He took a deep breath, preparing to speak as Tigerclaw stared menacingly down at him. Then it dawned on Fireheart that any disloyalty he had shown on Greystripe's behalf meant nothing to this great warrior. That wasn't the real reason for Tigerclaw's persecution of him. The deputy was still afraid of what Fireheart might have learned from Ravenpaw about Redtail's death all those moons ago. But unlike Ravenpaw, Fireheart wasn't going to give in to fear. His eyes challenged the dark deputy, and he growled. "She escaped, yes, like Crookedstar escaped from you. Why? Did you want me to kill her?"

Tigerclaw's tail lashed the cold ground. "Darkstripe says you didn't even scratch her."

Fireheart shrugged. "Perhaps Darkstripe should chase after the she-cat and ask her if it's true!"

Darkstripe looked ready to spit, but he remained silent as Tigerclaw spoke. "He doesn't need to. Darkstripe tells me your young grey friend chased after her. Perhaps *he'll* be able to tell us how badly she was scratched."

For the first time since they'd entered the battle Fireheart felt the chill of the wind. The gleam in Tigerclaw's eye hinted at a veiled threat. Had the dark warrior guessed about Greystripe's love for Silverstream?

Fireheart was still searching for words when Greystripe appeared, squeezing through the camp entrance.

"Look who's back," sneered Tigerclaw. "Do you want to ask him how the she-cat is? No, wait, I can guess his answer. He'll just tell me he didn't manage to catch up with her." Not bothering to disguise the scorn in his eyes, Tigerclaw stalked away with Darkstripe behind him.

Fireheart looked over at Greystripe. His friend's face was lined with exhaustion and worry. Fireheart padded across the clearing to meet him. Would Greystripe still be resentful of Fireheart's interference? Would he be angry that Fireheart had tried to attack Silverstream, or grateful that he'd let her go?

Greystripe stood silently, his broad head hanging down. Fireheart reached forwards with his nose and gently touched his friend's cold, grey flank. He felt Greystripe's rumbling purr and looked up. Greystripe gazed back at him. His eyes were sad, but there was no trace of the anger that Fireheart had seen in them lately.

"Is she OK?" Fireheart asked under his breath.

"Yes," whispered Greystripe. "And thanks for letting her go."

Fireheart blinked at him. "I'm glad she wasn't hurt," he meowed.

Greystripe held his gaze for a moment, then meowed, "Fireheart, you were right. The battle wasn't easy. It felt like I was fighting Silverstream's Clan mates, not enemy warriors." He lowered his eyes, ashamed. "But I still can't give her up."

The grey warrior's words filled Fireheart with foreboding, but he couldn't help sympathising with his friend. "This is something you have to work out by yourself," he meowed. "It's not my place to judge you." Greystripe looked up as Fireheart went on. "Greystripe, whatever you decide to do, I will always be your friend."

Greystripe stared at him, his eyes clouded with relief and gratitude. Then, without speaking, the two warriors lay down, side to side, in the unfamiliar clearing. For the first time in moons, their fur was pressed together in friendship. Above them, the snow-heavy gorse offered them a brief shelter from the storm that raged over their heads.

WARRIOR CATS

Forest of Secrets

Fireheart sprang to his paws at once. "And who gave you the right to question our loyalty?" he spat.

The warrior cats are hungry, waiting for a thaw in the snow. Tensions run high and friends become enemies overnight. Fireheart is determined to find out about the mysteries that lie at the heart of his adopted Clan. But as he searches for answers, he uncovers an ugly truth– that some cats are willing to kill to get what they want.

"The best series ever!" *****
Amazon website

ISBN 10: 0-00-714004-5
ISBN 13: 978 0-00-714004-6

HarperCollins *Children's Books*